29 Mr 07

Rollback

BOOKS BY ROBERT J. SAWYER

NOVELS

Golden Fleece (Aurora winner) *
End of an Era (Seiun winner) *
The Terminal Experiment
  (Nebula and Aurora winner)
Starplex (Hugo and Nebula
  finalist, Aurora winner)
Frameshift (Hugo finalist, Seiun
  winner) *
Illegal Alien (Seiun winner) *
Factoring Humanity (Hugo
  finalist) *
Flashforward (Aurora winner) *
Calculating God (Hugo
  finalist) *
Mindscan (John W. Campbell
  Memorial Award winner) *
Rollback *

The Neanderthal Parallax
Hominids (Hugo winner) *
Humans (Hugo finalist) *
Hybrids *

The Quintaglio Ascension
Far-Seer *
Fossil Hunter *
Foreigner *

COLLECTIONS

Iterations (introduction by James
  Alan Gardner)
Relativity (introduction by Mike
  Resnick)
Identity Theft (introduction by
  Robert Charles Wilson)

ANTHOLOGIES

Tesseracts 6 (with Carolyn
  Clink)
Crossing the Line (with David
  Skene-Melvin)
Over the Edge (with Peter
  Sellers)
Boarding the Enterprise (with
  David Gerrold)

* published by Tor Books

(Readers' group guides available at www.sfwriter.com)

Rollback

Robert J. Sawyer

TOR®

A Tom Doherty Associates Book
New York

ROLLBACK

This novel was serialized in four parts in *Analog Science Fiction and Fact* magazine, with installments in the October 2006, November 2006, December 2006, and combined January–February 2007 issues.

Edited by David G. Hartwell

A Tor Book
Published by Tom Doherty Associates, LLC
175 Fifth Avenue
New York, NY 10010

www.tor.com

Tor® is a registered trademark of Tom Doherty Associates, LLC.

Library of Congress Cataloging-in-Publication Data

Sawyer, Robert J.
    Rollback / Robert J. Sawyer.—1st ed.
        p.   cm.
    ISBN-13: 978-0-765-31108-5 (acid-free paper)
    ISBN-10: 0-765-31108-9 (acid-free paper)
    1. Rejuvenation—Fiction.   2. Human-alien encounters—
Fiction.   3. Ethics—Fiction.   I. Title.
    PR9199.3.S2533R65   2007
    813'.54—dc22

                                                        2006039280

First Edition: April 2007

Printed in the United States of America

0   9   8   7   6   5   4   3   2   1

For
ROBYN META HERRINGTON
(1961–2004)

Great friend, great writer

✳

No wise man ever wished to be younger.
— JONATHAN SWIFT
(1667–1745)

✳

How old would you be
if you didn't know how old you are?
— LEROY "SATCHEL" PAIGE
(1906–1982)

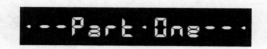

Part One

IT HAD BEEN a good life.

Donald Halifax looked around the living room of the modest house that he and his wife Sarah had shared for sixty years now, and that thought kept coming back to him. Oh, there had been ups and downs, and the downs had seemed excursions into the flames of hell at the time—the lingering death of his mother, Sarah's battle with breast cancer, the rough periods their marriage had gone through—but, on balance, when all was said and done, it had been a good life.

When all was said and done.

Don shook his head, but it wasn't in sadness. He'd always been a realist, a pragmatist, and he knew there was nothing left now but summing up and looking back. At the age of eighty-seven, that's all anyone had.

The living room was narrow. A fireplace was built into the middle of one of the long walls, flanked by autopolarizing windows, but he couldn't remember the last time they'd actually had a fire. It was too much work getting one going and then cleaning up afterward.

The mantel held framed photos, including one of Sarah and Don on their wedding day, back in 1988. She was wearing white, and he was in a tuxedo that had been black in reality but looked gray here, having faded, along with the rest of the photograph. Other photos showed their son Carl as a toddler and again graduating with his M.B.A. from McGill, and there were two pictures of their daughter Emily, one when she was in her twenties, and another, holographic one, from her early forties. And there were several holos of their two grandchildren.

There were also a few trophies: a pair of small ones that Don had won in Scrabble tournaments, and the big one Sarah had been given by the International Astronomical Union. He couldn't remember the wording on that one, so he walked over, taking small steps, and had a look:

> FOR SARAH HALIFAX
> WHO FIGURED IT OUT
> 1 MARCH 2010

He nodded, remembering how proud he'd been that day, even if her fame had briefly turned their lives upside down.

A magphotic flatscreen was mounted above the mantel, and when they weren't watching anything it displayed the time in boxy red numerals a foot high, big enough that Sarah could see them from across the room; as she'd often quipped, it was a good thing that she hadn't been an *optical* astronomer. It was now 3:17 in the afternoon. As Don watched, the remaining segments in the rightmost digit lit up; 3:18. The party was supposed to have begun at 3:00, but no one was here yet, and Sarah was still upstairs getting ready.

Don made a mental vow to try to not be short with the grandchildren. He never meant to snap at them, but somehow, he always did; there was a constant background level of pain at his age, and it frayed his temper.

He heard the front door opening. The house knew the kids' biometrics, and they always let themselves in without ringing the bell. The living room had a short staircase at one end that led down to the entryway and a taller one at the other going up to the bedrooms. Don walked over to the base of the one going up. "Sarah!" he called. "They're here!"

He then made his way to the other end of the room, each foot-fall punctuated by a tiny jab of pain. No one had come up yet—this was Toronto in February, and, global warming be damned, there were still boots and jackets to be removed. Before he reached the top of the stairs, he'd sorted out the mêlée of voices; it was Carl's crew.

He looked at them from his elevated vantage point and felt himself smiling. His son, his daughter-in-law, his grandson, and his granddaughter—part of his immortality. Carl was bent over in a way Don would have found excruciating, pulling off one of his boots. From this angle, Don could clearly see his son's consid-erable bald spot—trivial to correct, had Carl been vain, but nei-ther Don nor his son, who was now fifty-four, could ever be accused of that.

Angela, Carl's blond wife, was ten years younger than her hus-band. She was working to get the boots off little Cassie, who was seated on the one chair in the entryway. Cassie, who took no ac-tive role in this, looked up and saw Don, and a huge grin spread across her little round face. "Grampa!"

He waved at her. Once all the outerwear was removed, every-one came upstairs. Angela kissed him on the cheek as she passed, carrying a rectangular cake box. She went into the kitchen. Twelve-year-old Percy was up next, then came Cassie, pulling on the banister, which she could barely reach, to help her get up the six steps.

Don bent low, feeling twinges in his back as he did so. He wanted to lift Cassie up, but that was impossible. He settled for letting her get her little arms around his neck and giving him a squeeze. Cassie was oblivious to the fact that she was hurting him, and he endured it until she let go. She then scampered through the living room and followed her mother to the kitchen. He turned to watch her and saw Sarah coming down from up-stairs, one painful step at a time, gripping the banister with both hands as she did so.

By the time she reached the bottom step, Don heard the front door opening again, and his daughter Emily—divorced, no kids—coming in. Soon enough, everyone was crowded into the living room. With his cochlear implants, Don's hearing wasn't bad under normal circumstances, but he couldn't really pick out any one thread of conversation from the hubbub that now filled the air. Still, it was his family, all together. He was happy about that, but—

But it might be the last time. They'd gathered just six weeks ago for Christmas at Carl's place, in Ajax. His children and grandchildren wouldn't normally all get together again until next Christmas, but—

But he couldn't count on there being a next Christmas; not at his age . . .

No; that wasn't what he should be dwelling on. Today was a party, a celebration. He should enjoy it, and—

And suddenly there was a champagne flute in his hand. Emily was circling the room, handing them out to the adults, while Carl presented plastic tumblers of juice to the children.

"Dad, go stand by Mom," Carl said. And he did so, making his way across the room to where she was—not standing; she couldn't stand for long. Rather, she was seated in the old La-Z-Boy. Neither of them ever reclined it anymore, although the grandkids loved to operate the mechanism. He stood next to Sarah, looking down on her thinning snow-white hair. She craned her neck as much as she could to look up at him, and a smile crossed her face, one more line in a landscape of creases and folds.

"Everybody, everybody!" shouted Carl. He was the elder of Don and Sarah's kids and always took charge. "Your attention, please!" The conversation and laughter died down quickly, and Don watched as Carl raised his own champagne flute. "I'd like to propose a toast. To Mom and Dad, on their sixtieth wedding anniversary!"

The adults all raised their glasses, and, after a moment, the kids imitated them with their tumblers. "To Don and Sarah!" said Emily, and, "To Grandma and Grandpa," declared Percy.

Don took a sip of the champagne, the first alcohol he'd had since New Year's Eve. He noted his hand was shaking even more than it normally did, not from age but with emotion.

"So, Dad, what do you say?" asked Carl. He was grinning from ear to ear. Emily, for her part, was recording everything with her datacom. "Would you do it all over again?"

Carl had asked the question, but Don's answer was really for Sarah. He set his glass on a little tea table next to the La-Z-Boy, then slowly, painfully, lowered himself onto one knee, so that he was at eye level with his seated wife. He reached over, took her hand, feeling the thin, almost translucent skin sliding over the swollen joints, and looked into her pale blue eyes. "In a heartbeat," he said softly.

Emily let out a long, theatrical, *"Awwww . . ."*

Sarah squeezed his hand, and she smiled at him, the same wry smile he'd fallen for back when they were both in their twenties, and she said, with a steadiness that her voice almost never managed these days, "Me, too."

Carl's exuberance got the better of him. "To another sixty years!" he said, lifting his glass again, and Don found himself laughing at the ridiculousness of the proposition.

"Why not?" he said, slowly rising again, then reaching for his glass. "Why the heck not?"

The phone rang. He knew his kids thought the voice-only phones were quaint, but neither he nor Sarah had any desire to have 2-D picture phones, let alone holophones. His first thought was not to answer; let whoever it was leave a message. But it was probably a well-wisher—maybe even his brother Bill calling from Florida, where he wintered.

The cordless handset was on the other side of the room. Don lifted his eyebrows and nodded at Percy, who looked delighted to be charged with such a task. He raced across the room, and rather than just bringing over the handset, he activated it and very politely said, "Halifax residence."

It was possible that Emily, standing near Percy, could hear the person on the other end of the line, but Don couldn't make out anything. After a moment, he heard Percy say, "Just a sec," and the boy started walking across the room. Don held out his hand to take the handset, but Percy shook his head. "It's for Grandma."

Sarah looked surprised as she took the handset, which, upon recognizing her fingerprints, automatically cranked up its volume. "Hello?" she said.

Don looked on with interest, but Carl was talking to Emily while Angela was making sure her children were being careful with their drinks, and—

"Oh, my God!" exclaimed Sarah.

"What is it?" asked Don.

"Are you sure?" Sarah said, into the mouthpiece. "Are you positive it's not—No, no, of course you'd check. Sorry. But—my God!"

"Sarah," said Don, "what is it?"

"Hang on, Lenore," Sarah said into the phone, then she covered the mouthpiece with a trembling hand. "It's Lenore Darby," she said, looking up at him. He gathered he should know the name, but couldn't place it immediately—the story of his life, these days—and his face must have conveyed that. "You know," said Sarah. "She's doing her master's; you met her at the last astro-department Christmas party."

"Yes?"

"Well," said Sarah, sounding as though she couldn't believe that she was uttering these words, "Lenore says a reply has been received."

"What?" said Carl, now standing on the other side of her chair.

Sarah turned to face her son, but Don knew what she meant

before she spoke again; he knew precisely what she meant, and he staggered a half-pace backward, groping for the edge of a bookcase for support. "A reply has been received," repeated Sarah. "The aliens from Sigma Draconis have responded to the radio message my team sent all those years ago."

Chapter 2

MOST JOKES GET tired with repetition, but some become old friends, causing a smile whenever they come to mind. For Don Halifax, one such was a quip Conan O'Brien had made decades ago. Michael Douglas and Catherine Zeta-Jones had just announced the birth of their baby girl. "Congratulations," O'Brien had said. "And if she's anything like her mother, right now her future husband is in his mid-forties."

There was no such age gap between Don and Sarah. They'd both been born in 1960 and had gone through life in lockstep. They'd both been twenty-seven when they'd gotten married; thirty-two when Carl, their first child, had been born; and forty-eight when—

As Don stood, looking at Sarah, the moment came back to him, and he shook his head in amazement. It had been front-page news, back when there *were* front pages, all over the world. On March first, 2009, a radio message had been received from a planet orbiting the star Sigma Draconis.

The world had puzzled over the message for months, trying to make sense of what the aliens had said. And then, finally, Sarah Halifax herself had figured out what they were getting at, and it was she who had led the team composing the official reply that had been sent on the one-year anniversary of the receipt of the original signal.

The public had initially been hungry for more news, but Sigma Draconis was 18.8 light-years from Earth, meaning the reply wouldn't reach there until 2028, and any response the Dracons might make couldn't have gotten here until October 2047 at the earliest.

And a few TV shows and webcasts had dutifully done little pieces last fall noting that a response could be received "any day now." But none was. Not in October, not in November, not in December, not in January, not . . .

Not until right now.

No sooner had Sarah gotten off the phone with Lenore than it rang again. The call, as she revealed in a stage whisper while holding her hand over the mouthpiece, was from CNN. Don remembered the pandemonium the last time, when she had figured out the purpose of the first message—God, where had the decades gone?

Everyone was now standing or sitting in a semicircle, looking at Sarah. Even the children had recognized that something major was going on, although they had no idea what.

"No," Sarah was saying. "No, I have no comment. No, you can't. It's my anniversary today. I'm not going to let it be ruined by strangers in the house. What? No, no. Look, I really have to go. All right, then. All right, then. Yes, yes. Good-bye." She pushed the button that terminated the call, then looked up at Don, and lifted her frail shoulders a bit. "Sorry for all the bother," she said. "It's—"

The phone rang again, an electronic bleeping that Don disliked at the best of times. Carl, taking command, took the handset from his mother and flicked off the ringer. "They can leave a message if they like."

Sarah frowned. "But what if somebody needs help?"

Carl spread his arms. "Your whole family is here. Who else would call for help? Relax, Mom. Let's enjoy the rest of the party."

Don looked around the room. Carl had been sixteen when his mother had been briefly famous, but Emily had been just ten, and hadn't really understood what had been going on. She was staring at Sarah with astonishment on her narrow face.

Phones in the other rooms were ringing, but they were easy enough to ignore. "So," he said, "did—what was her name? Lenore? Did she say anything about the message's content?"

Sarah shook her head. "No. Just that it was definitely from Sigma Draconis, and seems to begin, at least, with the same symbol set used last time."

Angela said, "Aren't you dying to know what the reply says?"

Sarah reached out her arms in a way that said "help me up." Carl stepped forward and did just that, gently bringing his mother to her feet. "Sure, I'd like to know," she said. "But it's still coming in." She looked at her daughter-in-law. "So let's get started making dinner."

THE KIDS AND grandkids left around 9:00 p.m. Carl, Angela, and Emily had done all the work cleaning up after dinner, and so Don and Sarah simply sat on the living-room couch, enjoying the restored calm. Emily had gone around at one point, shutting off all the other ringers on the phones, and they were still off. But the answering machine's digital display kept changing every few minutes. Don was reminded of another old joke, this one from his teenage years, about the guy who liked to follow Elizabeth Taylor to McDonald's so he could watch the numbers change. Those signs had been stuck at "Over 99 Billion Served" for decades, but he remembered the hoopla when they'd all finally been replaced with new ones that read, "Over 1 Trillion Served."

Sometimes it was better to just stop counting, he thought—especially when it's a counting down instead of a counting up. They'd both made it to eighty-seven, and to sixty years together. But they surely wouldn't be around for a seventieth anniversary; that just wasn't in the cards. In fact . . .

In fact, he was surprised they'd lived this long, but maybe they'd been holding on, striving to reach the diamond milestone.

All his life, he'd read about people who died just days after their eightieth, ninetieth, or hundredth birthdays. They'd clung to life, literally by the force of their wills, until the big day had been reached, and then they'd just let go.

Don had turned eighty-seven three months ago, and Sarah had done so five months before that. That hadn't been what they'd been holding on for. But a sixtieth wedding anniversary! How rare that was!

He would have liked to put his arm around Sarah's shoulders as they sat side by side on the couch, but it pained him to rotate his own shoulder that much, and—

And then it hit him. Maybe she hadn't been hanging on for their anniversary. Maybe what had really kept her going all this time was waiting to see what reply the Dracons would send. He wished contact had been made with a star thirty or forty light-years away, instead of just nineteen. He wanted her to keep holding on. He didn't know what he'd do if she let go, and—

And he'd read *that* news story, too, dozens of times over the years: the husband who dies only days after his wife; the wife who finally seems to give up and let go shortly after hubby passes away.

Don knew a day like today called for some comment, but when he opened his mouth, what came out were just two words, that, he guessed, summarized it all: "Sixty years."

She nodded. "A long time."

He was quiet for a while, then: "Thank you."

She turned her head to look at him. "For what?"

"For—" He lifted his eyebrows and raised his shoulders a bit as he sought an answer. And then, finally, he said, very softly, "Everything."

Next to them, on the little table beside the couch, the counter on the answering machine tallied up another call. "I wonder what the aliens' reply says," Don said. "I hope it's not just one of those damn autoresponders. 'I'm sorry, but I'll be away from the planet for the next million years.'" Sarah laughed, and Don went on. "'If you need immediate assistance, please contact my assistant Zagdorf at . . .'"

"You are a supremely silly man," she said, patting the back of his hand.

EVEN THOUGH THEY only had voice phones, Sarah and Don did have a modern answering machine. "Forty-eight calls were received since you last reviewed your messages," the device's smooth male voice said the next morning as they sat at the dining-room table. "Of those, thirty-nine left messages. All thirty-nine were for Sarah. Thirty-one were from the media. Rather than presenting them in order of receipt, I suggest you let me prioritize them for you, sorting by audience size. Starting with the TV networks, CNN—"

"What about the calls that weren't from the media?" Sarah asked.

"The first was from your hairdresser. The second is from the SETI Institute. The third is from the Department of Astronomy and Astrophysics at the University of Toronto. The fourth—"

"Play the one from U of T."

A squeaky female voice came on. "Good morning, Professor Halifax. This is Lenore again—you know, Lenore Darby. Sorry to be phoning so early, but I thought someone should give you a call. Everyone's been working on interpreting the message as it comes in—here, over in Mountain View, at the Allen, everywhere—and, well, you're not going to believe this, Professor Halifax, but we think the message is"—the voice lowered a bit, as if its owner was embarrassed to go on—"*encrypted*. Not just encoded for transmission, but actually encrypted—you know, scrambled so that it can't be read without a decryption key."

Sarah looked at Don, her face astonished. Lenore went on. "I know sending us an encrypted message doesn't make any sense, but that seems to be what the Dracons have done. The beginning of the message is all math stuff, laid out in that symbol set they used before, and the computer gunks say the math describes a decryption algorithm. And then the rest of the message is total gibberish, presumably because it has indeed been encrypted. Get it? They've told us *how* the message is encrypted, and given us the algorithm to unlock it, but they haven't given us the decryption key to feed into that algorithm to do the actual unlocking. It's the craziest thing, and—"

"Pause," said Sarah. "How long does she go on?"

"Another two minutes, sixteen seconds," said the machine, and then it added, "She's quite chatty."

Sarah shook her head and looked at Don. "Encrypted!" she declared. "That doesn't make any sense. Why in God's name would aliens send us a message we can't read?"

Chapter 3

SARAH FONDLY REMEMBERED *Seinfeld*, although, sadly, it
hadn't aged well. Still, one of Jerry's bits of stand-up seemed as
true today as it had been half a century ago. When it came to TV,
most men were hunters, switching from channel to channel, always on the prowl for something better, while women were
nesters, content to settle in with a single program. But today,
Sarah found herself scanning constantly; the puzzle of the encrypted message from Sigma Draconis was all over the TV and
the web. She caught coverage of oddsmakers paying off winners
who'd correctly guessed the day on which a reply would be received, fundamentalists decrying the new signal as a temptation
from Satan, and crackpots claiming to have already decrypted
the secret transmission.

Of course, she was delighted that there had been a reply, but as
she continued to flip channels on the giant monitor above the
mantel, she reflected that she was also disappointed that in all the
years since they'd detected the first message, no other alien radio
source had been found. As Sarah had once said in an interview
very much like the ones she was looking at today, it was certainly
true that we weren't alone—but we were still pretty lonely.

Her surfing was interrupted each time someone came up to
the front door and rang the bell; an image of whoever it was automatically appeared on the monitor. Mostly it seemed to be re-
porters; there were still a few journalists who did more than send
email, make phone calls, and surf the web.

Those neighbors who had lived here on Betty Ann Drive four decades ago knew Sarah's claim to fame, but most of the houses had changed hands several times since then. She wondered what her newer neighbors made of the succession of news vans that had pulled into her driveway. Ah, well; at least it wasn't something to be embarrassed about, like the cop cars that kept showing up at the Kuchma place across the road, and, so far, Sarah had simply ignored all the people who had rung her doorbell, but—

My God.

But she couldn't ignore *this.*

The face that had suddenly appeared on the monitor was not human.

"Don!" she called, her voice dry. "Don, come here!"

He had gone into the kitchen to make coffee—decaf, of course; it was all Dr. Bonhoff would let either of them have these days. He shuffled into the living room, wearing a teal cardigan over an untucked red shirt. "What?"

She gestured at the monitor. "My . . . goodness," he said softly. "How'd it get here?"

She pointed at the screen. Partially visible behind the strange head was their driveway, which Carl had shoveled before leaving yesterday. An expensive-looking green car was sitting on it. "In that, I guess."

The doorbell rang once more. She doubted the being pushing the button was actually getting impatient. Rather, she suspected, some dispassionate timer told it to try again.

"Do you want me to let it in?" asked Don, still looking at the picture of the round, blue face, with its unblinking eyes.

"Um, sure," Sarah said. "I guess."

She watched as he made his way to the little staircase leading to the entryway, and began the slow pilgrimage down, one painful step at a time. She followed him and stood at the top of the stairs—and noted that one of her grandkids had forgotten a colorful scarf here. By the time Don reached the door, the bell had sounded a third time, which was the maximum number it was programmed to allow. He undid the deadbolt and the chain, and swung the heavy oak door inward, revealing—

It had been weeks since Sarah had seen one in the flesh—not that "in the flesh" was the right phrase.

Standing before them, gleaming in the sunlight, was a robot, one of the very latest models, she guessed; it looked more sophisticated and sleeker than any she'd seen before.

"Hello," the robot said to Don, in a perfectly normal male voice. It was about five-foot-six: tall enough to function well in the world, but not so tall as to be intimidating. "Is Dr. Sarah Halifax in?"

"I'm Sarah Halifax," she said. The robot's head swiveled to look up at her. Sarah suspected it was analyzing both her face and her voice to make sure it was really her.

"Hello, Dr. Halifax," the robot said. "You haven't been answering your household phone, so I've brought you a replacement. Someone would like to talk to you." The robot raised its right hand, and in it Sarah could just make out a clamshell datacom.

"And who might that be?" she asked.

The robot tilted its head slightly, giving the impression that it was listening to someone somewhere else. "Cody McGavin," it said. Sarah felt her heart skip a beat; she wished she'd actually been on the staircase, instead of just above it, so she could have grabbed the banister for support. "Will you take his call?"

Don turned to look at Sarah, his eyes wide, jaw hanging slack.

"Yes," she said.

The word had come out very softly, but the robot apparently had no trouble hearing her. "May I?" it asked.

Don nodded and stepped aside. The robot came into the entryway, and, to Sarah's astonishment, she saw it was wearing simple galoshes, which, in a fluid motion, it bent over and removed, exposing blue metal feet. The machine walked across the vestibule, its heels clicking against the old, much-scuffed hardwood there, and it easily went up the first two steps, which was as far as it had to go to be able to proffer the datacom to Sarah. She took it.

"Flip it open," the robot said helpfully.

She did so, then heard a ringing through the small speaker. She quickly brought the device to her ear.

"Hello, Dr. Halifax," said a crisp female voice. It was a little hard for Sarah to make out; she wished she knew how to adjust the volume. "Please hold for Mr. McGavin."

Sarah looked at her husband. She'd repeatedly told him how much she hated people who made her wait like this. It was almost always some self-important jackass who felt his time was more valuable than anyone else's. But in this case, Sarah supposed, that was actually true. Oh, there might be a few people on Earth who made more per hour than Cody McGavin, but, offhand, she couldn't name any of them.

As Sarah often said, SETI is the Blanche Dubois of scientific undertakings: it has always depended on the kindness of strangers. Whether it was Microsoft co-founder Paul Allen donating 13.5 million dollars in 2004 to fund an array of radio telescopes, or the hundreds of thousands of private computer users who gave up their spare processing cycles to the SETI@home project, the Search for Extraterrestrial Intelligence had managed to struggle on decade after decade through the largesse of those who believed, first, that we might not be alone, and, later, that it actually mattered that we were not alone.

Cody McGavin had made billions by the time he was forty, developing robotic technology. His proprioceptive sensor webs were behind every sophisticated robot on the planet. Born in 1985, he'd been fascinated by astronomy, science fiction, and space travel all his life. His collection of artifacts from the *Apollo* program, an endeavor that had come and gone long before he was born, was the largest in the world. And, after the passing of Paul Allen, he'd become by far SETI's biggest single benefactor.

As soon as Sarah had been put on hold, music started playing. She recognized it as Bach—and got the joke; she was probably one of the few people left alive who would. Years ago, long before the first Draconis signal had been received, during a discussion of what message should be beamed to the stars, Carl Sagan had vetoed the suggestion of Bach, because, he'd said, "That would be bragging."

In the middle of the concerto, the famous voice came on; McGavin spoke with one of those Boston accents that managed to say "Harvard" with no discernible *R* sound. "Hello, Dr. Halifax. Sorry to keep you waiting."

She found her voice cracking in a way that had nothing to do with age. "That's all right."

"Well, they did it, didn't they?" he said, with relish. "They replied."

"It seems so, sir." There weren't many people an eighty-seven-year-old felt inclined to call "sir," but it had come spontaneously to her lips.

"I knew they would," said McGavin. "I just knew it. We've got us a dialogue going here."

She smiled. "And now it's our turn to reply again—once we figure out how to decrypt the message." Don had been moving across the little entryway, and now was climbing the six stairs. When he was all the way up, she held the datacom at an angle to her face so he could hear McGavin, too. The robot, meanwhile, had taken up a position just inside the front door.

"Exactly, exactly," said McGavin. "We've got to keep the conversation going. And that's what I'm calling about, Sarah—you don't mind if I call you Sarah, do you?"

She actually quite liked it when younger people called her by her first name; it made her feel more alive. "Not at all."

"Sarah, I've got a—call it a proposition for you."

Sarah couldn't help herself. "My husband is standing right here."

McGavin chuckled. "A proposal, then."

"Still here," said Don.

"Hee hee," said McGavin. "Let's call it an offer, then. An offer I don't think you'll want to refuse."

Don used to do a good Brando in his youth. He puffed out his cheeks, frowned, and moved his head as if shaking jowls, but said nothing. Sarah laughed silently and swatted his arm affectionately. "Yes?" she said, into the datacom.

"I'd like to discuss it with you face-to-face. You're in Toronto, right?"

"Yes."

"Would you mind coming down here, to Cambridge? I'd have one of my planes bring you down."

"I . . . I wouldn't want to travel without my husband."

"Of course not; of course not. This affects him, too, in a way. Won't you both come down?"

"Um, ah, give us a moment to discuss it."

"Of course," said McGavin.

She covered the mike and looked at Don with raised eyebrows.

"Back in high school," he said, "we had to make a list of twenty things we wanted to do before we die. I came across mine a while ago. One of the ones I haven't checked off yet is 'Take a ride in a private jet.'"

"All right," she said, into the datacom. "Sure. Why not?"

"Terrific, terrific," said McGavin. "We'll have a limo pick you up and take you to Trudeau in the morning, if that's okay."

Trudeau was in Montreal; the Toronto airport was Pearson— but Sarah knew what he meant. "Fine, yes."

"Wonderful. I'll have my assistant come on, and he'll look after all the details. We'll see you in time for lunch tomorrow."

And the Bach started up again.

--- Chapter 4 ---

IT WAS IRONIC, now that Don thought back on it, how often he and Sarah had talked about SETI's failure prior to its success. He'd come home one day, around—let's see; they'd been in their mid-forties, so it must have been something like 2005—to find her sitting in their just-bought La-Z-Boy, listening to her iPod. Don could tell she wasn't playing music; she couldn't resist tapping her fingers or toes whenever she was doing that.

"What are you listening to?" he asked.

"It's a lecture," shouted Sarah.

"Oh, really!" he shouted back, grinning.

She took out the little white earbuds, looking sheepish. "Sorry," she said, in a normal volume. "It's a lecture Jill did for the Long Now Foundation."

SETI, Don often thought, was like Hollywood, with its stars. In Tinsel Town, having to use last names marked you as an outsider, and the same was true in Sarah's circles, where Frank was always Frank Drake, Paul was Paul Shuch, Seth was Seth Shostak, Sarah was indeed Sarah Halifax, and Jill was Jill Tarter.

"The long what?" Don said.

"The Long Now," repeated Sarah. "They're a group that tries to encourage long-term thinking, thinking about *now* as an epoch rather than a point in time. They're building a giant clock—the Clock of The Long Now—that ticks once a year, chimes once a century, and has a cuckoo that comes out every millennium."

"Good work if you can get it," he said. "Say, where are the kids?" Carl had been twelve then; Emily, six.

"Carl's downstairs watching TV. And I sent Emily to her room for drawing on the wall again."

He nodded. "So what's Jill talking about?" He'd never met Jill, although Sarah had.

"Why SETI is, by necessity, a long-term proposition," Sarah said. "Except she's skirting the issue."

"You and she are practically the only SETI researchers who can do that."

"What? Oh."

"I'm here all week."

"Lucky me. Anyway, she doesn't seem to be getting to the point, which is that SETI is something that *must* be a multigenerational activity, like building a great cathedral. It's a trust, something we hand down to our children, and they hand down to their children."

"We don't have a good track record with things like that," he said, perching now on the La-Z-Boy's broad, padded arm. "I mean, you know, the environment is something we hold in trust and pass on to Carl and Emily's generation, too. And look at how little our generation has done to combat global warming."

She sighed. "I know. But Kyoto's a step forward."

"It'll hardly make a dent."

"Yeah, well."

"But, you know," said Don, "we're not cut out for this—what did you call it?—this 'Long Now' sort of thinking. It's anti-Darwinian. We're hardwired against it."

She sounded surprised. "What?"

"We did something about kin selection on *Quirks and Quarks* last month; I spent forever editing the interview." Don was an audio engineer at CBC Radio. "We had Richard Dawkins on again, by satellite through the Beeb. He said that in a competitive situation, you automatically favor your own son over your brother's son, right? Of course: your son has half your DNA, and your brother's son only has a quarter of it. But if things got tough between your brother's son and your cousin, well, you'd favor your brother's son—that is, your nephew—because your cousin only has an eighth of your DNA."

"That's right," Sarah said. She was scratching his back. It felt very nice.

He went on. "And a second cousin only has one-thirty-second of your DNA. And a second cousin once removed has just one-sixty-fourth of your DNA. Well, when was the last time you heard of somebody volunteering a kidney to save a second cousin once removed? Not only do most people have no clue who their second cousins once removed are, but they also, quite bluntly, couldn't give a crap what happens to them. They just don't share enough DNA with them to care."

"I love it when you talk math," she teased. Fractions were about as good as Don's math got.

"And over time," he said, "the DNA share gets cut down, like cheap coke." He grinned, delighted by his simile, although she knew full well that the only coke he had experience with came in silver-and-red cans. "You only have to go six generations to get to your own descendants being as distantly related to you as a second cousin once removed—and six generations is less than two centuries."

"I can name my second cousins once removed. There's Helena, and Dillon, and—"

"But you're special. That's why you *are* interested in SETI. For the rest of the world, they just don't have a vested Darwinian interest. Evolution has shaped us so that we don't care about anything that's not going to manifest soon, because no close relative of ours will be around then. Jill's probably tap-dancing around that, because it's a point she *doesn't* want to make: that, for the general public, SETI doesn't make sense. Hell, didn't Frank"—

whom he'd also never met—"send a signal somewhere thousands of light-years away?"

He looked at Sarah, and saw her nod. "The Arecibo message, sent in 1974. It was aimed at M13, a globular cluster."

"And how far away is M13?"

"Twenty-five thousand light-years," she said.

"So it'll be fifty thousand years before we could get a reply. Who has the patience for something like that? Hell, I got an email today with a PDF attachment, and I thought, geez, I wonder if this thing is going to be worth reading, 'cause, you know, it's going to take, like, *ten whole seconds* for the attachment to download and open. We want instant gratification; we find *any* delay intolerable. How can SETI fit into a world with that mindset? Send a message and wait decades or centuries for a reply?" He shook his head. "Who the hell would want to play that game? Who's got the *time* for it?"

--- Chapter 5 ---

AS THE LUXURY jet landed, Don Halifax mentally checked off that to-do-list item. The few remaining ones, including "sleep with a supermodel" and "meet the Dalai Lama," seemed out of the question at this point, not to mention of no current interest.

It was bitterly cold going down the little metal staircase onto the tarmac. The flight attendant helped Don every step of the way, while the pilot helped Sarah. Downside of a private plane: it didn't use a Jetway. Like so many of the things on Don's list, this one was turning out to be less wonderful than he'd hoped.

A white limo was waiting for them. The robot driver wore one of those caps that limo drivers are supposed to wear, but nothing else. It did an expert job of getting them to McGavin Robotics, all the while providing a running commentary, in a voice loud enough for them to hear clearly, on the sights and history of the area.

The McGavin Robotics corporate campus consisted of seven sprawling buildings separated by wide snow-covered expanses; the company had lots of ties to the artificial-intelligence lab at nearby MIT. The limo was able to go straight into an underground garage, so Don and Sarah didn't have to brave the cold again. The robot driver escorted them as they walked slowly over to an immaculate elevator, which brought them up to the lobby. Human beings took over there, taking their coats, making them welcome, and bringing them up another elevator to the fourth floor of the main building.

Cody McGavin's office was long and narrow, covering one whole side of the building, with windows looking out over the rest of the campus. His desk was made of polished granite, and a matching conference table with a fleet of fancy chairs docked at it was off to the left, while a long, well-stocked bar, with a robot bartender, stretched off in the other direction.

"Sarah Halifax!" said McGavin, rising from his high-backed leather chair.

"Hello, sir," said Sarah.

McGavin quickly closed the distance between them. "This is an honor," he said. "A real honor." He was wearing what Don supposed was the current fashion for executives: a lapel-less dark-green sports jacket and a lighter green shirt with a vertical splash of color down the front taking the place of a tie. No one wore ties anymore.

"And this must be your husband," said McGavin.

"Don Halifax," said Don. He offered his hand—something he disliked doing these days. Too many younger people squeezed too hard, causing him real pain. But McGavin's grip was gentle, and released after only a moment.

"A pleasure to meet you, Don. Please, won't you have a seat?" He gestured back toward his desk and, to Don's astonishment, two luxurious leather-upholstered chairs were rising up through hatches in the carpeted floor. McGavin helped Sarah across the room, offering her his arm, and got her seated. Don shuffled across the carpet and lowered himself into the remaining chair, which seemed solidly anchored now.

"Coffee?" said McGavin. "A drink?"

"Just water," said Sarah. "Please."

"The same," said Don.

The rich man nodded at the robot behind the bar, and the machine set about filling glasses. McGavin perched his bottom on the edge of the granite desk and faced Don and Sarah. He was not a particularly good-looking man, thought Don. He had doughy features and a small, receding chin that made his already large forehead seem even bigger. Still, he'd doubtless had some cosmetic work done. Don knew he was sixty-something, but he didn't look a day over twenty-five.

The robot was suddenly there, handing Don a beautiful crystal tumbler full of water, with two ice cubes bobbing in it. The machine handed a similar glass to Sarah, and one to McGavin, and then silently withdrew to behind the bar.

"Now," said McGavin, "let's talk turkey. I said I've got a"—he paused, and gave the word a special weight, recalling the banter of the day before—"*proposition* for you." He was looking at Sarah exclusively, Don noted. "And I do."

Sarah smiled. "As we used to say about the Very Large Array, I'm all ears."

McGavin nodded. "The first message we got from Sig Drac was a real poser, until *you* figured out its purpose. And this one is even more of a puzzle, it seems. Encrypted! Who'd have guessed?"

"It's baffling," she agreed.

"That it is," said McGavin. "That it is. But I'm sure you can help us crack it."

"I'm no expert in decryption or codes, or things like that," she said. "My expertise, if I have any, is in exactly the opposite: understanding things that were designed to be read by anyone."

"Granted, granted. But you had such insight into what the Dracons were getting at last time. And we know *how* to decrypt the current message. I'm told the aliens made the technique very clear. All we have to do is figure out *what* the decryption key is, and I suspect your skill is going to be valuable there."

"You're very kind," she said, "but—"

"No, really," said McGavin. "You were a crucial part of it then, I'm sure you're going to be a crucial part of it now, and you'll continue to be so well into the future."

She blinked. "The future?"

"Yes, yes, the future. We've got a dialogue going here, and we need *continuity*. I'm sure we'll unlock the current message, and, even if we don't, we'll still send a response. And I want you to be around when the reply to that response arrives."

Don felt his eyes narrowing, but Sarah just laughed. "Don't be silly. I'll be dead long before then."

"Not necessarily," said McGavin.

"It'll be thirty-eight years, minimum, before we get a reply to anything we send today," she said.

"That's right," replied McGavin, his tone even.

"And I'd be—well, um . . ."

"A hundred and twenty-five," McGavin supplied.

Don had had enough. "Mr. McGavin, don't be cruel. My wife and I have only a few years left, at best. We both know that."

Sarah had drained her water glass. The robot silently appeared with a replacement and swapped it for the empty one.

McGavin looked at Don. "The press has had it all wrong, you know, from day one. Most of the SETI community hasn't understood, either. This isn't a case of Earth talking to the second planet of the star Sigma Draconis. Planets don't talk to each other. *People* do. Some specific person on Sigma Draconis II sent the message, and one specific person on this planet—you, Dr. Sarah Halifax—figured out what he'd asked for, and organized our reply. The rest of us—all the humans here, and anyone else on Sigma Draconis who is curious about what's being said—have been reading over your shoulders. You've got a pen pal, Dr. Halifax. It happens that I, not you, pay the postage, but he's *your* pen pal."

Sarah looked at Don, then back at McGavin. She took another sip of her water, perhaps to buy herself a few seconds to think. "That's an . . . *unusual* interpretation," she said. "Because of the long times between sending messages and receiving replies, SETI is something whole civilizations do, not individuals."

"No, no, that's not right at all," said McGavin. "Look, what are the fundamental tenets of SETI? Certainly one of them is this: almost any race we contact will be more advanced than us. Why? Because, as of this year, we've only had radio for a hundred and fifty-three years, which is nothing compared to the fourteen billion years the universe is old. It's a virtual certainty that anyone we make contact with has been around as a radio-using civilization longer than we have."

"Yes," said Sarah, and "So?" added Don.

"So," said McGavin, "short lifespans are something only technologically unsophisticated races will be subject to. How long after a race develops radio do you think it is before they decode DNA, or whatever their genetic material is? How long before they develop blood transfusions and organ transplantation and tissue cloning? How long before they cure cancer and heart disease, or whatever comparable ailments sloppy evolution has left them prey to? A hundred years? Two hundred? Doubtless no more than three or four, right? Right?"

He looked at Sarah, presumably expecting her to nod. She didn't, and, after a moment, he went on anyway. "Just as every race we contact almost certainly must have had radio longer than we have, every race we contact will almost certainly have extended their lifespans way beyond whatever paltry handful of years nature originally dealt them." He spread his arms. "No, it stands to reason: communication between two planets isn't something one generation starts, another continues, and still another picks up after that. Even with the long time frames imposed by the speed of light, interstellar communication is still almost certainly communication between individuals. And you, Dr. Halifax, are *our* individual. You already proved, all those years ago, that you know how they think. Nobody else managed that."

Her voice was soft. "I—I'm happy to be the, um, the public face for our reply to the current message, if you think that's necessary, but after that . . ." She lifted her narrow shoulders slightly as if to say the rest was obvious.

"No," said McGavin. "We need to keep you around for a good long time."

Sarah was nervous; Don could tell, even if McGavin couldn't. She lifted her glass and swirled the contents so that the ice cubes clinked together. "What are you going to do? Have me stuffed and put on display?"

"Goodness, no."

"Then what?" Don demanded.

"Rejuvenation," said McGavin.

"Pardon me?" said Sarah.

"Rejuvenation; a rollback. We'll make you young again. Surely you've heard about the process."

Don had indeed heard about it, and doubtless Sarah had, too. But only a couple of hundred people had undergone the procedure so far, and they'd all been stinking rich.

Sarah reached forward and set her glass down on the granite desktop, next to where McGavin was leaning. Her hand was shaking. "That . . . that costs a fortune," she said.

"I have a fortune," said McGavin simply.

"But . . . but . . . I don't know," said Sarah. "I'm—I mean, does it work?"

"Look at me," said McGavin, spreading his arms again. "I'm sixty-two years old, according to my birth certificate. But my cells, my telomeres, my free-radical levels, and every other indicator say I'm twenty-five. And, if anything, I feel younger even than that."

Don's jaw must have been hanging open in surprise. "You thought I'd had a facelift, or something like that?" McGavin said, looking at him. "Plastic surgery is like a software patch. It's a quick, kludgy fix, and it often creates more problems than it solves. But rejuvenation, well, that's like a code rewrite—it's a *real* fix. You don't just look young again; you *are* young." His thin eyebrows climbed his wide forehead. "And that's what I'm offering you. The full-blown rejuvenation treatment."

Sarah looked shocked, and it was a moment before she spoke. "But . . . but this is ridiculous," she said at last. "Nobody even knows if it really works. I mean, sure, you *look* younger, maybe you even *feel* younger, but the treatment has only been available for a short time. No one who's had it yet has lived appreciably longer than a natural lifespan. There's no proof that this process really extends your life."

McGavin made a dismissive gesture. "There have been lots of rollback tests with lab animals. They all became young again, and then aged forward perfectly normally. We've seen mice and even prosimians live out their entire lengthened lifespans without difficulty. As for humans, well, except for a few oddball indicators like growth rings in my teeth, my physicians tell me that I'm now physiologically twenty-five, and am aging forward naturally from that point." He spread his arms. "Believe me, it works. And I'm offering it to you."

"Mr. McGavin," Don said, "I really don't think that—"

"Not without Don," Sarah said.

"What?" said McGavin and Don simultaneously.

"Not without Don," Sarah repeated. Her voice had a firmness Don hadn't heard for years. "I won't even consider this unless you also offer the same thing to my husband."

McGavin pushed himself forward until he was standing. He walked behind his desk, turning his back on them, and looked out at his sprawling empire. "This is a very expensive procedure, Sarah."

"And you're a very rich man," she replied.

Don looked at McGavin's back, more or less silhouetted against the bright sky. At last, McGavin spoke. "I envy you, Don."

"Why?"

"To have a wife who loves you so much. I understand the two of you have been married for over fifty years."

"Sixty," said Don, "as of two days ago."

"I never . . ." McGavin began, but then he fell silent.

Don had vague recollections of McGavin's high-profile divorce, years ago, and a nasty court case to try to invalidate the pre-nup.

"Sixty years," McGavin continued, at last. "Such a long time . . ."

"It hasn't seemed that way," said Sarah.

Don could hear McGavin make a noisy intake of breath and then let it out. "All right," he said, turning around, his head nodding. "All right, I'll pay for the procedure for both of you." He walked toward them, but remained standing. "So, do we have a deal?"

Sarah opened her mouth to say something, but Don spoke before she could. "We have to talk about this," he said.

"So let's talk," said McGavin.

"Sarah and I. We have to talk about this alone."

McGavin seemed momentarily peeved, as though he felt they were looking a gift horse in the mouth. But then he nodded. "All right, take your time." He paused, and Don thought he was going to say something stupid like, "But not too much time." But instead he said, "I'll have my driver take you over to Pauli's—finest restaurant in Boston. On me, of course. Talk it over. Let me know what you decide."

--- Chapter 6 ---

THE ROBOT CHAUFFEUR drove Sarah and Don to the restaurant. Don got out of the car first and carefully made his way over to Sarah's door, helping her up and out, and holding her arm as they crossed the sidewalk and entered.

"Hello," said the young white woman standing at a small podium inside the door. "You must be Dr. and Mr. Halifax, no? Welcome to Pauli's."

She gave them a hand getting out of their parkas. Fur was back in vogue—the pelts lab-grown, without producing the whole animal—but Sarah and Don were of a generation that had come to frown on fur, and neither could bring themselves to wear any. Their nylon-shelled coats from Mark's Work Wearhouse, his in navy blue, hers beige, looked decidedly out-of-place on the racks in the coat check.

The woman took Don's elbow, and Don took Sarah's, a sideways conga line shuffling slowly to a large booth near a crackling fireplace.

Pauli's turned out to be a seafood restaurant, and even though Don loved John Masefield's poetry, he hated seafood. Ah, well; doubtless the menu would have some chicken or steak.

There were the usual accoutrements of such places: an aquarium of lobsters, fishing nets hanging on the walls, a brass diver's helmet sitting on an old wooden barrel. But the effect was much more upscale than Red Lobster; here everything looked like valuable antiques rather than garage-sale kitsch.

Once they'd managed to get seated, and the young woman had taken their drink order—two decaf coffees—Don settled back against the soft leather upholstery. "So," he said, looking across at his wife, the crags in her face highlighted by the dancing fire-light, "what do you think?"

"It's an incredible offer."

"That it is," he said, frowning. "But . . ."

He trailed off as the waiter appeared, a tall black man of about fifty, dressed in a tuxedo. He handed a menu printed on parchment-like paper bound in leather covers to Sarah, then gave one to Don. He squinted at it. Although this restaurant doubtless had lots of older patrons—they'd passed several on the way to the table—anyone who dined here regularly probably could afford new eyes, and—

"Hey," he said, looking up. "There are no prices."

"Of course not, sir," said the waiter. He had a Haitian accent. "You are Mr. McGavin's guests. Please order whatever you wish."

"Give us a moment," said Don.

"Absolutely, sir," said the waiter, and he disappeared.

"What McGavin's offering is . . . ," started Don, then he trailed off. "It's—I don't know—it's crazy."

"Crazy," repeated Sarah, lobbing the word back at him.

"I mean," he said, "when I was young, I thought I'd live for-ever, but . . ."

"But you'd made your peace with the idea that . . ."

"That I was going to die soon?" he said, lifting his eyebrows. "I'm not afraid of the D-word. And, yes, I guess I had made my peace with that, as much as anyone does. Remember when Ivan Krehmer was in town last fall? My old buddy from back in the day? We had coffee, and, well, we both knew it was the last time we'd ever see or even speak to each other. We talked about our lives, our careers, our kids and grandkids. It was a . . ." He sought a phrase; found it: "A final accounting."

She nodded. "So often, these last few years, I've thought, 'Well, that's the last time I'll visit this place.'" She looked out at the other diners. "It's not even all been sad. There are plenty of times I've thought, 'Thank God I'll never have to do *that* again.' Getting my passport renewed, some of those medical tests they make you have every five years. Stuff like that."

He was about to reply when the waiter reappeared. "Have we decided yet?"

Not by a long shot, Don thought.

"We need more time," Sarah said. The waiter dipped his head respectfully and vanished again.

More time, thought Don. That's what it was all about, suddenly having more time. "So, so he's talking about, what, rejuvenating you thirty-eight years, so you'll still be around when the next reply is received?"

"Rejuvenating *us,*" said Sarah, firmly—or, at least, in what he knew was supposed to be a firm tone; the quaver never quite left her voice these days. "And, really, there's no need to stop at that. That would only take us back to being fifty or so, after all." She paused, took a moment to gather her thoughts. "I remember reading about this. They say they can regress you to any point after your body stopped growing. You can't go back before puberty, and you probably shouldn't go back much earlier than twenty-five, before wisdom teeth have erupted and the bones of the skull have totally fused."

"Twenty-five," said Don, tasting the number, imagining it. "And then you'd age forward again, at the normal rate?"

She nodded. "Which would give us enough time to receive two more replies from . . ." She lowered her voice, perhaps surprised to find herself adopting McGavin's term. "From my pen pal."

He was about to object that Sarah would be over a hundred and sixty by the time two more replies could be received—but, then again, that would only be her chronological age; she'd be just a hundred physically. He shook his head, feeling woozy, disoriented. *Just* a hundred!

"You seem to know a lot about this," he said.

She tipped her head to one side. "I read a few of the articles when the procedure was announced. Idle curiosity."

He narrowed his eyes. "Was that all?"

"Sure. Of course."

"I've never even *thought* about living to be over a hundred," he said.

"Of course not. Why would you? The idea of being *ancient,* withered, worn out, infirm, for years on end—who would fantasize about that? But *this* is different."

He looked at her, studying her face in a way he hadn't for some time. It *was* an old woman's face, just as his face, he knew, was that of an old man, with wrinkles, creases, and folds.

It came to him, with a start, that their very first date all those years ago had ended in a restaurant with a fireplace, after he'd dragged her to see the premiere of *Star Trek IV: The Voyage Home.* He recalled how beautiful her smooth features had looked, how her lustrous brown hair had shone in the dancing light, how he'd wanted to stare at her forever. Age had come up then, too, with Sarah asking how old he was. He'd told her he was twenty-six.

"Hey, me, too!" she'd said, sounding pleased. "When's your birthday?"

"October fifteenth."

"Mine was in May."

"Ah," he'd replied, a mischievous tone in his voice, "an older woman."

That had been so very long ago. And to go back to that age! It was madness. "But . . . but what would you—would *we*—do with all that time?" he asked.

"Travel," said Sarah at once. "Garden. Read great books. Take courses."

"Hmmmph," said Don.

Sarah nodded, apparently conceding that she hadn't enticed him. But then she rummaged in her purse and pulled out her datacom, tapped a couple of keys, and handed him the slim device. The screen was showing a picture of little Cassie, wearing a blue dress, her blond hair in pigtails. "Watch our grandchildren grow up," she said. "Get to play with our great-grandchildren, when they come along."

He blew out air. To get to attend his grandchildren's college graduations, to be at their weddings. That *was* tempting. And to do all that in robust good health, but . . .

"But do you really want to attend the funerals of your own children?" he said. "Because that's what this would mean, you know. Oh, I'm sure the procedure will come down in price eventually, but not in time for Carl or Emily to afford it." He thought about adding, "We might even end up burying our grandchildren," but found he couldn't even give voice to *that* notion.

"Who knows how fast the cost will come down?" Sarah said. "But the idea of having decades more with my kids and grandkids is very appealing . . . no matter what happens in the end."

"Maybe," he said. "Maybe. I—I'm just . . ."

She reached across the dark polished wood of the table and touched his hand. "Scared?"

It wasn't an accusation from Sarah; it was loving concern. "Yeah, I suppose. A bit."

"Me, too," she said. "But we'll be going through it together."

He lifted his eyebrows. "Are you sure you could stand to have me around for another few decades?"

"I wouldn't have it any other way."

To be young again. It was a heady thought, and, yes, it was scary, too. But it was also, he had to admit, intriguing. He'd never liked taking charity, though. If the procedure had been something they could have even remotely afforded, he might have been more enthusiastic. But even if they sold their house, sold every stock and bond they owned, liquidated all their assets, they couldn't begin to pay for the treatment for even one of them, let alone for them both. Hell, even Cody McGavin had had to think twice about spending so much money.

This stuff about Sarah being the one and only person who could communicate with the aliens struck Don as silly. But it wasn't as though the rejuvenation could be taken back; once done, it was done. If it turned out that McGavin was wrong about her being pivotal, they'd still have all those extra decades.

"We'd need money to live on," he said. "I mean, we didn't plan for fifty years of retirement."

"True. I'd ask McGavin to endow a position for me back at U of T, or provide some sort of retainer."

"And what will our kids think? We'll be physically younger than them."

"There is that."

"And we'll be doing them out of their inheritance," he added.

"Which was hardly going to make them rich anyway," replied Sarah, smiling. "I'm sure they'll be delighted for us."

The waiter returned, looking perhaps a bit wary of the possibility that he was going to be rebuffed again. "Have we made up our minds?"

Don looked over at Sarah. She'd always been beautiful to him. She was beautiful now, she'd been beautiful in her fifties, she'd been beautiful in her twenties. And, as her features shifted in the light of the dancing flames, he could see her face as it had been at those ages—all those stages of life they'd spent together.

"Yes," said Sarah, smiling at her husband. "Yes, I think we have."

Don nodded, and turned to the menu. He'd pick something quickly. He did find it disconcerting, though, to see the item descriptions but no accompanying dollar values. *Everything has a price,* he thought, *even if you can't see it.*

Chapter 7

DON AND SARAH had had another discussion about SETI, a year before the original Sigma Draconis signal had been detected. They'd been in their late forties then, and Sarah, depressed about the failure to detect any message, had been worried that she'd devoted her life to something pointless.

"Maybe they *are* out there," Don had said, while they went for a walk one evening. He'd gotten religious about his weight a few years before, and they now did a half-hour walk every evening during the good weather, and he used a treadmill in the basement in winter. "But maybe they're just keeping quiet. You know, so as not to contaminate our culture. The Prime Directive, and all that."

Sarah had shaken her head. "No, no. The aliens have an *obligation* to let us know they're there."

"Why?"

"Because they'd be an existence proof that it's possible to survive technological adolescence—you know, the period during which you have tools that could destroy your entire species but no mechanism in place yet to prevent them from ever being used. We developed radio in 1895, and we developed nuclear weapons just fifty years later, in 1945. Is it possible for a civilization to survive for centuries, or millennia, once you know how to make nuclear weapons? And if those don't kill you, rampaging AI or nanotech or genetically engineered weapons might—unless you find some way to survive all that. Well, any civilization whose signals we pick up is almost certainly going to be much older than we are; receiving a signal would tell us that it's possible to survive."

"I guess," Don said. They'd come to where Betty Ann Drive crossed Senlac Road, and they turned right. Senlac had sidewalks, but Betty Ann didn't.

"For sure," she replied. "It's the ultimate in Marshall McLuhan: the medium *is* the message. Just detecting it, even if we don't understand it, tells us the most important thing ever."

He considered that. "You know, we should have Peter de Jager over sometime soon. I haven't played go in ages; Peter always likes a game."

She sounded irritated. "What's Peter got to do with anything?"

"Well, what's he best remembered for?"

"Y2K," said Sarah.

"Exactly!" he said.

Peter de Jager lived in Brampton, just west of Toronto. He moved in some of the same social circles as the Halifaxes did. Back in 1993, he'd written the seminal article "Doomsday 2000" for *ComputerWorld* magazine, alerting humanity to the possibility of enormous computer problems when the year 2000 rolled around. Peter spent the next seven years sounding the warning call as loudly as he could. Millions of person-hours and billions of dollars were spent correcting the problem, and when the sun rose on Saturday, January 1, 2000, no disasters occurred: airplanes kept flying, money stored electronically in banks didn't suddenly disappear, and so on.

But did Peter de Jager get thanked? No. Instead, he was excoriated. He was a charlatan, said some, including Canada's *National Post,* in a year-end summation of the events of 2000—and their proof was that nothing had gone wrong.

Don and Sarah were passing Willowdale Middle School now, where Carl was just finishing grade eight. "But what's Y2K got to do with the aliens not signaling their existence?" she asked.

"Maybe they understand how *dangerous* it would be for us to know that some races did manage to survive technological adolescence. We got through Y2K because of lots of really hard work by really dedicated people, but once we *were* through it, we assumed that we would have gotten through it *regardless*. Surviving into the year 2000 was taken as—what was your phrase?—'an existence proof' that such survival had been inevitable. Well, detecting alien races who've survived technological adolescence would be taken the same way. Instead of us thinking it was very difficult to survive the stage we're going through, we'd see it as a cakewalk. *They* survived it, so surely we will, too." Don paused. "Say some alien, from a planet around— well, what's a nearby sunlike star?"

"Epsilon Indi," said Sarah.

"Fine, okay. Imagine aliens at Epsilon Indi pick up the television broadcasts from some other nearby star, um . . ."

"Tau Ceti," she offered.

"Great. The people at Epsilon Indi pick up TV from Tau Ceti. Not that Tau Ceti was deliberately signaling Epsilon Indi, you understand; they're just leaking stuff into space. And Epsilon Indi says, hey, these guys have just emerged technologically, and we did that long ago; they must be going through some rough times—maybe the guys on Epsilon Indi can even tell that from the TV signals. And so they say, let's contact them so they'll know it's all going to be okay. And what happens? A few decades later Tau Ceti falls silent. Why?"

"Everybody there got cable?"

"Funny," said Don. "Funny woman. No, they didn't all get cable. They just stopped worrying about somehow surviving having the bomb and all that, and now they're *gone,* because they got careless. You make that mistake once—you tell a race, hey, look, you can survive, 'cause we did—and that race stops trying to solve its problems. I don't think you'd ever make that mistake again."

They'd come to Churchill Avenue, and had turned east, walking by the public school Emily, who was now in grade two, attended. "But they could tell us *how* they survived, show us the answer," said Sarah.

"The answer is obvious," said Don. "You know the least-best-selling diet book of all time? *Losing Weight Slowly by Eating Less and Exercising More.*"

"Yes, Mr. Atkins."

He made his tone one of mock umbrage. "Excuse me! Going for a walk here! Besides, I *am* eating less, and more sensibly, way more sensibly than I was before I started cutting back on carbs. But you want to know what the difference is between me and all the others who lost weight quickly on Atkins, then put it back on as soon as they quit? It's been four years now, and I haven't quit—and I'm never going to. That's the other piece of weight-loss advice no one wants to hear. You can't diet temporarily; you have to make a permanent lifestyle change. I have, and I'm going to live longer for it. There are no quick fixes for anything."

He ceased talking as they crossed Claywood, then began speaking again. "No, the answer is obvious. The way to survive is to stop fighting each other, to learn tolerance, and to put an end to the huge disparity between rich and poor, so that some people don't hate the rest of us so much that they'd do anything, including even killing themselves, to hurt us."

"But we *need* a quick fix," said Sarah. "With terrorists having access to biotech and nuclear weapons, we can't just wait for everyone to get enlightened. You have to solve the problem of high-tech terrorism really quickly—just as soon as it becomes a problem—or no one survives. Those alien races who *have* survived must have found a solution."

"Sure," said Don. "But even if they did tell us their answer, we wouldn't like it."

"Why?"

"Because," he said, "the solution is that time-honored sci-fi cliché, the hive mind. On *Star Trek*, the reason the Borg absorb everyone into the Collective, I think, is that it's the only safe path. You don't have to worry about terrorists, or mad scientists, if you all think with one mind. Of course, if you do that, you might even lose any notion that there could be other individuals out there. It might never occur to you to even try to contact somebody else, because the whole notion of 'somebody else' has become foreign to your way of thinking. That could explain the failure of SETI. And then if you did encounter another form of intelligent life, perhaps by chance, you'd do exactly what the Borg did: absorb it, because that's the only way you can be sure it'll never hurt you."

"Gee, that's almost more depressing than thinking there are no aliens at all."

"There's another solution, too," said Don. "Absolute totalitarianism. Everyone's still got free will, but they're constrained from doing anything with it. Because all it takes is one crazy person and a pile of antimatter, and—kablooie!—the whole stinking planet is gone."

A car coming toward them beeped its horn twice. He looked up and saw Julie Fein driving by and waving. They waved back.

"That's not much better than the Borg scenario," Sarah said. "Even so, it's so depressing not to have detected anything. I mean, when we first started pointing our radio telescopes at the sky, we thought we'd pick up tons of signals from aliens, and, instead, in all that time—almost fifty years now—not a peep."

"Well, fifty years isn't that long," he said, trying now to console her.

Sarah was looking off into the distance. "No, of course not," she said. "Just most of a lifetime."

··· [hapter 8 ···

CARL, THE ELDER of Don and Sarah's two children, was known for his theatrics, so Don was grateful that he didn't spurt coffee all over the table. Still, after swallowing, he managed to exclaim "You're going to do what?" with vigor worthy of a sitcom. His wife Angela was seated next to him. Percy and Cassie—in full, Perseus and Cassiopeia, and, yes, Grandma had suggested the names—had been dispatched to watch a movie in Carl and Angela's basement.

"We're going to be rejuvenated," repeated Sarah, as if it were the most natural thing in the world.

"But that costs—I don't know," said Carl, looking at Angela, as if she should be able to instantly supply the figure. When she didn't, he said, "That costs billions and billions."

Don saw his wife smile. People sometimes thought their son had been named for Carl Sagan, but he wasn't. Rather, he was named for his mother's father.

"Yes, it does," said Sarah. "But we're not paying for it. Cody McGavin is."

"You know Cody McGavin?" said Angela, her tone the same as it would have been if Sarah had claimed to know the Pope.

"Not until last week. But he knew of me. He funds a lot of SETI research." She shrugged a little. "One of his causes."

"And he's willing to pay to have you rejuvenated?" asked Carl, sounding skeptical.

Sarah nodded. "And your father, too." She recounted their

meeting with McGavin. Angela stared in open-mouth wonder; she had mostly only known her mother-in-law as a little old lady, not—as the news-sites kept calling her—"the Grand Old Woman of SETI."

"But, even if it's all paid for," said Carl, "no one knows what the long-term effects of—of—what do they call it?"

"A rollback," said Don.

"Right. No one knows the long-term effects of a rollback."

"That's what everyone says about everything new," said Sarah. "No one knew what the long-term effects of low-carb dieting would be, but look at your father. He's been on a low-carb diet for forty years now, and it's kept his weight, cholesterol, blood pressure, and blood sugar all normal."

Don was embarrassed to have this brought up; he wasn't sure that Angela knew that he used to be fat. He'd started putting on weight during his Ryerson years, and, by the time he was in his early forties, he'd reached 240 pounds—way too much for his narrow-shouldered five-foot-ten frame. But Atkins had taken it off, and kept it off, he had been a trim 175 for decades. While the others had enjoyed garlic mashed potatoes with their roast beef this evening, he'd had a double helping of green beans.

"Besides," continued Sarah, "if I don't do this, nothing else I start today will have any long-term effects—because I won't be around for the long term. Even if twenty or thirty years down the road this gives me cancer or a heart condition, that's still twenty or thirty additional years that I wouldn't have otherwise had."

Don saw a hint of a frown flicker across his son's face. Doubtless he'd been thinking about when his mother had cancer once before, back when he'd been nine. But it was clear he had no comeback for Sarah's argument. "All right," he said at last. He looked at Angela, then back at his mother. "All right." But then he smiled, a smile that Sarah always said looked just like Don's own, although Don himself couldn't see it. "But you'll have to agree to do more babysitting."

AFTER THAT, EVERYTHING happened quickly. Nobody said it out loud, but there was doubtless a feeling that time was of the essence. Left untreated, Sarah—or Don, for that matter, although no one seemed to care about him—might pass away any day now, or end up with a stroke or some other severe neurological damage that the rejuvenation process couldn't repair.

As Don had learned on the web, a company called Rejuvenex held the key patents for rollback technology, and pretty much could set whatever price they felt would give their stockholders the best return. Surprisingly, in the almost two years the procedure had been commercially available, fewer than a third of all rollbacks had been for men and women as old as or older than he and Sarah—and over a dozen had been performed on people in their forties, who had presumably panicked at the sight of their first gray hairs and had had a few spare billion lying around.

Don had read that the very first biotech company devoted to trying to reverse human aging had been Michael West's Geron, founded in 1992. It had been located in Houston, which made sense at the time: its initial venture capital had come from a bunch of rich Texas oilmen eager for the one thing their fortunes couldn't yet buy.

But oil was *so* last millennium. Today's biggest concentration of billionaires was in Chicago, where the nascent cold-fusion industry, spun off from Fermilab, was centered, and so Rejuvenex was based there. Carl had accompanied Don and Sarah on the trip to Chicago. He was still dubious, and wanted to make sure his parents were properly looked after.

Neither Don nor Sarah had ever been to a private hospital before; such things were all but unheard of in Canada. Their country had no private universities, either, for that matter, something Sarah was quite passionate about; both education and health care should be public concerns, she often said. Still, some of their better-off friends had been known to bypass the occasional queues for procedures at Canadian hospitals and had reported back about luxurious facilities that catered to the rich south of the border.

But Rejuvenex's clients were a breed apart. Not even movie stars (Don's usual benchmark for superwealth) could afford their process, and the opulence of the Rejuvenex compound was beyond belief. The public areas put the finest hotels to shame; the labs and medical facilities seemed more high-tech than even what Don had seen in the recent science-fiction films his grandson Percy kept showing him.

The rollback procedure started with a full-body scan, cataloging problems that would have to be corrected: damaged joints, partially clogged arteries, and more. Those that weren't immediately life-threatening would be addressed in a round of surgeries after the rejuvenation was complete; those that required attention right now were dealt with at once.

Sarah needed a new hip and repairs to both knee joints, plus a full-skeletal calcium infusion; all that would wait until after the rejuvenation. Don, meanwhile, really could use a new kidney— one of his was almost nonfunctional—but once he was rejuvenated, they'd clone one for him from his own cells and swap it in. He'd also need new lenses in his eyes, a new prostate, and on and on; it made him think of the kind of shopping list Dr. Frankenstein used to give Igor.

Using a combination of laparoscopic techniques, nanotech robotic drones injected into their bloodstreams, and traditional scalpel work, the urgent structural repairs were done in nineteen hours of surgery for Sarah and sixteen for Don. It was the sort of tune-up that doctors normally didn't recommend for people as old as they were, since the stress of the operations could outweigh the benefits, and, indeed, they were told that there had been a few touch-and-go moments while work was done on one of Sarah's heart valves, but in the end they came through the various surgeries reasonably well.

Just that would have cost a fortune—and Don and Sarah's provincial health plan didn't cover elective procedures performed in the States—but it was nothing compared to the actual gene therapies, which required the DNA in each of their bodies' trillions of somatic cells to be repaired. Lengthening the telomeres was a key part of it, but so much more had to be done: each DNA copy had to be checked for errors that had intruded during previous copying, and when they were found—and there were billions of such errors in an elderly human—they had to be fixed by rewriting the strands nucleotide by nucleotide, a delicate and complex process to perform within living cells. Then free radicals had to be bound up and flushed away, regulatory sequences reset, and on and on, a hundred procedures, each one repairing some form of damage.

When it was done, there was no immediate change in either Don or Sarah's appearance. But it would come, they were told, bit by bit, over the next few months, a strengthening here, a firming there, the erasing of a line, the regrowth of a muscle.

And so Don, Sarah, and Carl returned to Toronto, with Cody McGavin again picking up the tab; the flights to and from Chicago had been the only times in his life that Don had flown Executive Class. Ironically, because of all the little surgeries and petty medical indignities, he felt much more tired and worn-out than he had prior to beginning all this.

He and Sarah would take twice-daily hormonal infusions for the next several months, and a Rejuvenex doctor would fly up once a week—all part of the service—to check on how their rollbacks were progressing. Don had vague childhood memories of his family's doctor making the odd house call in the 1960s, but this was a degree of medical attention that seemed almost sinful to his Canadian sensibilities.

For years, he'd avoided looking at himself in the mirror, except in the most perfunctory way while shaving. He hadn't liked the way he'd looked back when he was fat, and hadn't liked the way he'd looked recently, either: wrinkled, liver-spotted, tired, *old*. But now, each morning, he examined his face minutely in the bathroom mirror, and tugged at his skin, looking for signs of new resiliency. He also examined his bald head, checking for new growth. They'd promised him that his hair would come back, and would be the sandy brown of his youth, not the gray of his fifties or the snow white of the fringe that remained in his eighties.

Don had always had a large nose, and it, and his ears, had grown even larger as he'd gotten older; parts made of cartilage continue to get bigger throughout one's life. Once the rollback was complete, Rejuvenex would trim his nose and ears down to the sizes they'd been when he really had been twenty-five.

Don's sister Susan, dead these fifteen years now, had also been cursed by the Halifax family schnoz, and, when she'd been eighteen, after begging her parents for years, they'd paid for rhinoplasty.

He remembered the big moment at the clinic, the unwrapping of the bandages after weeks of healing, revealing the new, petite, retroussé handiwork of Dr. Jack Carnaby, whom *Toronto Life* had dubbed the finest noseman in the city the year before.

He wished there had been some magical moment like that for this, some *ah hah!* revelation, some sudden return to vim and vigor, some *unveiling*. But there wasn't; the process would take weeks of incremental changes, cells dividing and renewing at an accelerated pace, hormone levels shifting, tissues regenerating, enzymes—

My God, he thought. *My God.* There *was* new hair, an all-but-invisible peach fuzz spreading up from the snowy fringe, conquering the dome, reclaiming territory once thought irretrievably lost.

"Sarah!" shouted Don, and, for the first time in ages, he realized he was shouting without it hurting his throat. "Sarah!" He ran—yes, he veritably *ran*—down the stairs to the living room, where she was seated in the La-Z-Boy, staring at the stone-cold fireplace.

"Sarah!" he said, bending his head low. "Look!"

She came out of whatever reverie she'd been lost in, and although with his head tipped he couldn't see her, he could hear the puzzlement in her voice. "I don't see anything."

"All right," he said, disappointed. "But *feel* it!"

He felt the cool, loose, wrinkly skin of her fingers touching his scalp, the fingertips tracing tiny paths in the new growth. "My goodness," she said.

He tilted his head back to a normal position, and he knew he was grinning from ear to ear. He'd borne it stoically when he'd started to go bald around thirty, but, nonetheless, he found himself feeling inordinately pleased at this almost imperceptible return of hair.

"What about you?" he asked, perching now on the wide arm of the couch near the La-Z-Boy. "Any signs yet?"

Sarah shook her head slowly and, he thought, a little sadly. "No," said his wife. "Nothing yet."

"Ah, well," he said, patting her thin arm reassuringly. "I'm sure you'll see something soon."

··· Chapter 9 ···

SARAH WOULD ALWAYS remember March first, 2009. She had been forty-eight then, a breast-cancer survivor for five years, and a tenured professor at the University of Toronto for ten. She'd been heading down the fourteenth-floor corridor when she heard, just barely, the sound of her office phone ringing. She ran the rest of the way, glad as always to work in a field that never required her to wear heels. Fortunately, she'd already had her key in hand, or she'd never have gotten through the door before the university's voice-mail system grabbed the call. "Sarah Halifax," she said into the beige handset.

"Sarah, it's Don. Have you been listening to the news?"

"Hi, honey. No, I haven't. Why?"

"There's a message from Sigma Draconis."

"What are you talking about?"

"There's a message," Don said again, as if Sarah's difficulty had simply been in hearing the words, "from Sigma Draconis. I'm at work; it's all over the wire services and the Internet."

"There can't be," she said, nonetheless turning on her computer. "I'd have been informed before any public announcement."

"There *is* a message," he repeated. "They want you on *As It Happens* tonight."

"Um, sure. But it's got to be a hoax. *The Declaration of Principles* says—"

"NPR's got Seth Shostak on right now, talking about it. Apparently they picked it up last night, and somebody leaked it."

Sarah's computer was still booting. The handful of musical notes that Windows played on starting up issued from the machine's speakers.

"What does the message say?"

"No one knows. It's a free-for-all, with everybody, everywhere, scrambling to figure it out."

She found herself tapping her fingers rapidly on the edge of her desk and muttering at the computer's slowness. Big icons were filling in on her desktop, and smaller ones were popping up in her system tray.

"Anyway," said Don, "I've got to go. They need me back in the control room. They'll call you for a pre-interview later today. The message is everywhere on the web, including Slashdot. Bye."

"Bye." She put down the phone with her left hand while maneuvering her mouse with her right, and she soon had the message, a vast array of zeros and ones, on screen. Still dubious, she opened three more browser tabs and started searching for information about when and how the message had been received, what was known about it so far, and so on.

There was no mistake. The message was real.

No one was around to hear her speak, but she sagged back in her chair and said the words anyway, words that had been the mantra of SETI researchers since Walter Sullivan had used them as the title of his famous book: *We are not alone . . ."*

"BUT PROFESSOR HALIFAX, isn't it true that we might *never* be able to figure out what the aliens are saying?" the host—a woman named Carol Off—had asked back in 2009, during the *As It Happens* radio interview. "I mean, we share this planet with dolphins, and we can't tell what *they're* saying. How could we possibly understand what someone from another world is trying to say?"

Sarah smiled at Don, who was in the control room on the other side of the window; they'd discussed this before. "First off, there may in fact be no dolphin language, at least not a rich, abstract one like ours. Dolphins have smaller brains relative to their body weight than humans do, and they devote a huge amount of what they do have to echolocation."

"So we might not have figured out their language because there's nothing to figure out?" said the host.

"Exactly. Besides, just because we're from the same planet doesn't necessarily mean we should have more in common with them than with aliens. We actually have very little in common with dolphins. They don't even have hands, but the aliens must."

"Whoa, Professor Halifax. How do you know that?"

"Because they built radio transmitters. They've proven they're a technological species. In fact, they almost certainly live on dry land, again meaning we have more in common with them than with dolphins. You need to be able to harness fire to do metallurgy and all the other things required to make radio. Plus, of course, using radio means understanding mathematics, so they obviously have that in common with us, too."

"Not all of us are good at math," said the host, amiably. "But are you saying that, by necessity, whoever *sent* the message must have a lot in common with the sort of person who was trying to *receive* it?"

Sarah was quiet for a few seconds, thinking about this. "Well, I—um, yes. Yes, I guess that's so."

DR. PETRA JONES was a tall, impeccably dressed black woman who looked to be about thirty—although, with employees of Rejuvenex, one could never be sure, Don supposed. She was strikingly beautiful, with high cheekbones and animated eyes, and hair that she wore in dreadlocks, a style he'd seen come in and out of fashion several times now. She had arrived for her weekly visit to check up on Don and Sarah, as part of a circuit she did visiting Rejuvenex clients in different cities.

Petra sat down in the living room of the house on Betty Ann

Drive and crossed her long legs. Opposite her was a window, one of the two on either side of the fireplace. Outside, the snow had melted; spring was coming. She looked at Sarah, then at Don, then back at Sarah again, and finally, she just said it. "Something has gone wrong."

"What do you mean?" said Don at once.

But Sarah simply nodded, and her voice was full of sadness. "I'm not regressing, am I?"

He felt his heart skip a beat.

Petra shook her head, and beads woven into her dreadlocks made small clacking sounds. "I am so sorry," she said, very softly.

"I knew it," said Sarah. "I—in my bones, I knew it."

"Why not?" Don demanded. "Why the hell not?"

Petra lifted her shoulders slightly. "That's the big question. We've got a team working on this right now, and—"

"Can it be fixed?" he asked. *Please, God, say that it can be fixed.*

"We don't know," said Petra. "We've never encountered anything like this before." She paused, apparently gathering her thoughts. "We did succeed in lengthening your telomeres, Sarah, but for some reason the new endcap sequences are just being ignored when your chromosomes are being reproduced. Instead of continuing to transcribe all the way up to the end of your DNA, the replicator enzyme is stopping short, at where your chromosome arms used to end." She paused. "Several of the other biochemical changes we introduced are being rejected, too, and, again, we don't know why."

Don was on his feet now. "This is bullshit," he said. "Your people said they knew what they were doing."

Petra flinched, but then seemed to find some strength. She had a slight accent to his ears; Georgia, maybe. "Look," she said, "I'm a doctor; I'm not in PR. We *do* know more about senescence and programmed cell death than anybody else. But we've done fewer than two hundred multidecade rejuvenation procedures on humans at this point." She spread her arms a bit. "This is still new territory."

Sarah was looking down at her hands—her swollen-jointed, liver-spotted, translucent-skinned hands, folded in her lap. "I'm going to stay old." It was a statement, not a question.

Petra closed her eyes. "I am *so* sorry, Sarah." But then she made her tone a bit brighter, although it sounded forced to Don. "But some of what we did *was* beneficial, and none of it seems to have been detrimental. Didn't you tell me last time I was here that some of your day-to-day physical discomfort is gone?"

Sarah looked at Don, and she squinted, as if trying to make out someone far, far away. He walked over to her and stood next to where she was seated, placing a hand on her bony shoulder. "You must have some idea what caused this," he said sharply to Petra.

"As I said, we're still working on that, but . . ."

"What?" he said.

"Well, it's just that you had breast cancer, Mrs. Halifax . . ."

Sarah narrowed her eyes. "Yes. So? It was a long time ago."

"When we went over your medical history, prior to commencing our procedures, you told us how it was treated. Some chemotherapy. Radiation. Drugs. A mastectomy."

"Yes."

"Well, one of our people thinks that it might have something to do with that. Not with the successful treatment, which you told us about. But he wanted to know if there were any *unsuccessful* treatments you tried before that."

"Good grief," said Sarah. "I don't remember all the details. It was over forty years ago, and I've tried to put the whole thing out of my mind."

"Of course," said Petra, gently. "Maybe we should speak to the doctors involved."

"Our GP from back then is long dead," Don said. "And the

oncologist treating Sarah was in her sixties. She must be gone by now, too."

Petra nodded. "I don't suppose your old doctors transferred records to your new doctor?"

"Christ, how should we know?" said Don. "When we changed doctors we filled out medical histories, and I'm sure we authorized the handing over of files, but . . ."

Petra nodded again. "But this was in the era of paper medical records, wasn't it? Who knows what's become of them after all these years? Still, the researcher at our facility looking into this uncovered that about that time—early 2000s, right?—there were some interferon-based cancer treatments here in Canada that weren't ever approved by the FDA in the States; that's why we didn't really know about them. They're long off the market; better drugs came along by 2010. But we're trying to find a supply of them somewhere, so that we can run some tests. He thinks that if you had such a treatment, it might be what's caused our process to fail, possibly because it permanently eliminated some crucial commensal viruses."

"Jesus, you should have screened more carefully," Don said. "We could sue you."

Petra rallied a bit and looked up at him defiantly. "Sue us for what? A medical procedure that you didn't pay for that had no adverse effect?"

"Don, please," said Sarah. "I don't want to sue anyone. I don't . . ."

She trailed off, but he knew what she'd been about to say: "I don't want to waste what little time I have left on a lawsuit." He stroked her shoulder reassuringly. "All right," he said. "All right. But can't we try again? Maybe another round of treatments? Another attempt at rolling back?"

"We *have* been trying again," said Petra, "with tissue samples taken from your wife. But nothing is working."

He felt bile climbing his throat. God damn—God damn *everyone*. Cody McGavin, for bringing this crazy idea into their lives. The people at Rejuvenex. The bloody aliens on Sigma Draconis II. They could all go to hell.

"This is ridiculous," said Don, shaking his head back and forth. He lifted his hand from Sarah's shoulder, and then clasped both his hands behind his back and started pacing the length of the narrow living room, the room that had been home to him and his wife, the room his children had first learned to crawl in, the room that held so much history, so many memories—memories that he and Sarah had shared, decade after decade, good times and bad, thick and thin.

He took a deep breath, let it out. "I want you to stop the process for me, then," he said, his back briefly to the two women.

"Dear, no," said Sarah. "Don't do that."

He turned around and started pacing toward them. "It's the only thing that makes sense. I never wanted this in the first place, and I sure as hell don't want it if you're not getting it, too."

"But it's a blessing," said Sarah. "It's everything we talked about: seeing our grandchildren grow up; seeing *their* children. I can't—I *won't*—let you give that up."

He shook his head. "No. I don't want it. Not anymore." He stopped walking, and looked directly at Petra. "Undo it."

Petra's brown eyes were wide. "I can't. We can't."

"What do you mean, you can't?" said Don.

"Your treatment has been *done*," Petra said. "Your telomeres are lengthened, your free radicals are flushed, your DNA has been repaired, and on and on. There's no way to undo it."

"There must be," he said.

Petra lifted her shoulders philosophically. "There hasn't been a lot of research funding for finding ways to shorten the human lifespan."

"But you must be able to arrest the rejuvenation, no? I mean, right, I understand that I can't go back to being eighty-seven physically. Okay, fine. I'm—what?—I suppose I look about seventy now, right? Just stop the rollback here." He pointed his index finger straight down, as if marking a spot. Seventy he could live with; that wouldn't be so bad, wouldn't be an insurmountable gulf. Why, old Ivan Krehmer, he was married to a woman fifteen years younger than himself. Offhand, Don couldn't think of a case in their social circle where the woman was a decade and a half older than the man, but surely these days that was common, too.

"There's no way to stop it early," said Petra. "We hard-coded into the gene therapy how far back the rollback will go. It's inexorable once begun. Each time your cells divide, you'll get physically younger and more robust until the target is reached."

"Do another round of gene therapy, then," Don said. "You know, to countermand—"

"We've tried that with lab animals," Petra said, "just to see what happens."

"And?"

She shrugged her shoulders. "It kills them. Cell division comes to a complete halt. No, you have to let the rollback play out. Oh, we *could* cancel the planned follow-up surgeries—fixing your teeth, your knee joints, getting you that new kidney once you're strong enough to stand going under the knife. But what would be the point of that?"

Don felt his pulse racing. "So I'm still going to end up physically twenty-five?"

Petra nodded. "It'll take a couple of months for the rejuvenation to finish, but when it does, that'll be your biological age, and then you'll start aging forward again from that point, at the normal rate."

"Jesus," he said. *Twenty-five.* With Sarah staying eighty-seven. "Good Jesus Christ."

Petra was looking shell-shocked, and she was slowly, almost imperceptibly, shaking her head back and forth. "What?" demanded Don.

The doctor looked up, and it seemed to take her eyes a moment to focus. "Sorry," she said. "I just—well, I just never thought I'd end up having to apologize for giving someone another sixty or seventy years of life."

Don crouched down next to his seated wife. How excruciating doing that would have been just a short time ago—and yet it gave him no pleasure now to be able to do it with ease. "I am sorry, honey," he said. "I am so sorry."

But Sarah was shaking her head. "Don't be. It's going to be all right. You'll see."

How could it be all right? he wondered. They'd spent their lives in synch, born the same year, growing up with the same events in the background. Both remembered precisely where they were when Neil Armstrong set foot upon the moon during the year they'd each turned nine. Both had been teenagers when Watergate happened; in their twenties when the Berlin Wall fell; in their thirties when the Soviet Union collapsed; in their forties for the first detection of alien life. Even before they'd met, they'd been marching through the stages of life together, jointly aging, and improving, like two bottles of wine of the same vintage.

Don's head was swimming, and so, it seemed, was his vision. Sarah's face appeared blurred, the tears in his eyes doing what Rejuvenex's sorcery couldn't, erasing her wrinkles, smoothing out her features.

Chapter 10

LIKE MOST SETI researchers, Sarah had worked late many nights after that first alien transmission had been received back in 2009. Don had come to see her in her office at the University of Toronto on one of those evenings, after he'd finished his work at the CBC.

"Anybody home?" he'd called out.

Sarah had swung around, smiling, as he came through the door carrying a red-and-white Pizza Hut box. "You're an angel!" she crowed. "Thank you!"

"Oh," he said. "Did you want something, as well?"

"Pig! What did you get?"

"A large Pepperoni Lover's . . .'cause, um, I like pepperoni, and we're lovers . . ."

"*Awww,*" said Sarah. She actually preferred mushrooms, but he couldn't stand them. Coupling that with his dislike for fish had given rise to the little speech she'd listened politely to him give on numerous occasions, a pseudo-justification that he thought was witty for his eating choices: "You should only eat food that's as evolved as you are. Only warm-blooded animals—mammals and birds—and only photosynthesizing plants."

"Thanks for coming by," she said, "but what about the kids?"

"I called Carl, told him to order a pizza for him and Emily. Said he could take some money out of my nightstand."

"When Donald Halifax parties, everybody parties," she said, smiling.

He was looking around for somewhere to set the pizza box. She leapt to her feet and moved a globe of the celestial sphere off the top of a filing cabinet, setting it on the floor. He placed the box where the globe had been and opened its lid. She was pleased to see some steam rising. Not too surprising; the Hut was just up on Bloor Street.

"So, how's it going?" he asked. This wasn't the first time he'd brought food to her office. He kept a plate, knife, and fork in one of the office cupboards, and he got them now. Sarah, meanwhile, pulled out a piece of pizza, severing the cheesy filaments with her fingers.

"It's a race," she said, sitting down in the chair in front of her workstation. "I'm making progress, but who knows how it compares to what everyone else is achieving? I mean, sure, there's a lot of sharing of notes going on online, but I doubt anyone is revealing everything yet."

He found the other office chair—a beat-up folding one—and sat next to her. She was used to the way her husband ate pizza, but couldn't actually say she *liked* it. The crust wasn't part of his diet—of course, the greasy Pizza Hut deep-dish crust probably shouldn't be part of *anyone's* diet, although she found it impossible to resist. He got the toppings off with a fork, swirling it in the molten cheese almost as though he were eating spaghetti. He also ate sandwiches a similar way, digging out the fillings with cutlery while leaving the bread behind.

"Anyway, we'd always expected that math would be the universal language," Sarah continued, "and I guess it is. But the aliens have managed something with it that I wouldn't have thought possible."

"Show me," Don said, moving his chair closer to her workstation.

"First, they establish a pair of symbols that everybody working on this agrees serve as brackets, containing other things. See that sequence there?" She pointed at a series of blocks on her computer screen. "That's the open bracket, and that one there"—

pointing at another place on the screen—"is the closing bracket.
Well, I've been doing a rough-and-ready transliteration of everything as I go along—you know, rendering it in symbols we use.
So, here's what the first part of the message says." She flipped to
another window. It was displaying this:

```
{ } = 0
{ * } = 1
{ * * } = 2
{ * * * } = 3
{ * * * * } = 4
{ * * * * * } = 5
{ * * * * * * } = 6
{ * * * * * * * } = 7
{ * * * * * * * * } = 8
{ * * * * * * * * * } = 9
```

"See how clever they are?" said Sarah. "The brackets let us tell
at a glance that there's nothing in the first set. And see what
they're doing? Establishing digits for the numbers zero through
nine—the aliens are using base ten, which may mean they've got
the same number of fingers we have, or it might just mean that
they've decoded some of our TV, and have seen that that's how
many fingers we've got. Oh, and notice that this chart gives us
their equals sign, too."

He got up and helped himself to another slice; when you
skipped the crust, you went through pizza awfully quickly.

"Anyway," she continued, "they immediately give us the basic
mathematical operators. Again, I've rendered them in familiar
notation." She rotated the wheel on her mouse, and this scrolled
into view:

```
[Question] 2+3
[Answer] 5
```

```
[Question] 2-3
[Answer] -1

[Question] 2*3
[Answer] 6

[Question] 2/3
[Answer] 0.6&
```

"See what they've done here? They've established a symbol for 'question,' and another for 'answer.' And they've also established a symbol for a decimal place, and a symbol for repeating indefi- nitely, which I've shown as that 'and' thingy."

"Ampersand," said Don, helpfully.

She gave him an *I-knew-that* scowl, and went on. "Next up, they give us a symbol for 'the relationship between,' which I've shown as a colon, and that lets us get a bunch of other concepts." She made this appear:

```
[Question] 2/3 : 0.6&
[Answer] =

[Question] 5 : 3
[Answer] >

[Question] 9 : 1
[Answer] >>

[Question] 3 : 5
[Answer] <

[Question] 1 : 9
[Answer] <<
```

```
[Question] 1 : −1
[Answer] [opposite]
```

"See?" she said. "We're getting into judgment calls. Nine is judged to be not just greater than one but *much* greater than one, and one, in turn, is much less than nine. Next they give us their symbols for correct and incorrect." This appeared on screen:

```
[Question] 2+5
[Answer] 7 [correct]

[Question] 3*3
[Answer] 9 [correct]

[Question] 8−3
[Answer] 6 [incorrect]
```

"And then," said Sarah, "things get really exciting."

"I can hardly contain myself," Don said.

She whapped him lightly on the arm, and nibbled at her own piece of pizza before changing the screen. "This came later in the message. Look."

```
[Question] 8/12
[Answer 1] 4/7 [incorrect]
[Answer 2] 4/6 [correct][alpha]
[Answer 3] 2/3 [correct][beta]
```

"See what they're saying there? I've assigned Greek letters to the two new symbols they're establishing. Can you puzzle out what alpha and beta mean?"

To his credit, he stopped shoveling cheese and pepperoni into his mouth and studied the screen carefully.

"Welllll," he said at last, "both answer two and answer three are correct, but, um, well, answer three is *more* correct, right? 'Cause, I mean, they've reduced the fraction."

"Bravo! That's exactly right! Now, think about that: they've just given us a way to express some very powerful concepts." She touched a key, and the terms *alpha* and *beta* were replaced with words:

```
[Question] 8/12
[Answer 1] 4/7 [incorrect]
[Answer 2] 4/6 [correct][bad]
[Answer 3] 2/3 [correct][good]
```

"That is, they've given us a term for distinguishing between an answer that, while technically correct, isn't preferable from one that *is* preferable—distinguishing a bad answer from a good one. And, just to drive home the point that they *are* making that distinction—that these terms should be translated as polar opposites—they give us this."

```
[Question] [bad] : [good]
[Answer] [opposite]
```

Sarah translated. "What is the relationship between 'bad' and 'good'? Why, they're opposites, just like one and negative one, as we saw before. They're saying these terms should be treated as actual opposites, in a way that 'right' and 'more right,' which would have been the other possible way of translating alpha and beta, aren't."

"Fascinating," he said.

She touched her mouse, and a new display appeared. "Now, what about things that aren't clear-cut? Well, try this. What does *gamma* mean?"

```
{3 5 7 11 13 &} = [gamma]
```

"Odd numbers?" he said. "Every other number?"

"Look again. There's no nine."

"Oh, right. Oh, and, um, hey, there's that 'and' thingy again."

"Ampersand," said Sarah, imitating Don's helpful tone from earlier. He grinned. "Right," she said, "but I'll give you a hint— something I gleaned from other examples. When the ampersand is right up against another digit, it means that *digit* is repeated forever. But if there's a space before it—a little gap in the transmission, as there is here—I think it means that this *sequence* goes on forever."

"Three, five, seven, eleven, thirteen . . ."

"I'll give you another hint. The next number in the sequence would be seventeen."

"Um, ah . . ."

"They're primes," she said. "*Gamma* is their symbol for prime numbers."

"Ah. But why start with three?"

She was grinning broadly now. "You'll see. This is the beauty part." She darted her mouse around. "There's a little more set theory, which I won't bore you with, that establishes a symbol for 'belongs to this set,' and then we get this . . ."

```
[Question] 5 [belongs to] [prime numbers]
[Answer] [correct]
```

"Does five belong to the set of prime numbers—or, more col-loquially, the question is 'Is five a prime number?' And the an-swer is yes; indeed, five was one of the sample numbers we used in naming the set 'prime numbers.'"

She made another similar Q&A pair appear:

```
[Question] 4 [belongs to] [prime numbers]

[Answer] [incorrect]
```

"Is four a prime number?" said Sarah, interpreting. "No."
She rotated her mouse's wheel again:

```
[Question] 3 [belongs to] [prime numbers]

[Answer][correct]
```

"Is three prime? Yup, sure is. And what about two? Ah, well,
let's have a look." More mouse movements, and this appeared:

```
[Question] 2 [belongs to] [prime numbers]
[Answer 1] [correct][good]
[Answer 2] [incorrect][good]
[Answer 3] [delta]
```

"Huh?"
"My precise reaction," said Sarah, smiling.
"So what's delta?" Don said.
"See if you can figure it out. Look at answer one and answer
two for a moment."
He frowned. "Hey, wait. They can't both be good answers. I
mean, two *is* a prime number, so saying that it isn't can't be a good
answer."
She smiled cryptically. "They give exactly the same three an-
swers for the number one," she said, scrolling the screen.

```
[Question] 1 [belongs to] [prime numbers]
[Answer 1] [correct][good]
[Answer 2] [incorrect][good]
[Answer 3] [delta]
```

"Again, that's gibberish," he said. "One either is or isn't prime.
And, well, it *is,* isn't it? I mean, a prime is a number that's only
evenly divisible by itself or one, right?"

"Is that what they taught you at Humberside Collegiate? We *used* to define one as a prime; you'll see it called such in some old math books. But these days, we don't. Primes are generally thought of as numbers that have precisely two whole-number factors, themselves and one. One has only one whole-number factor, and so isn't a prime."

"Seems rather arbitrary," said Don.

"You're right. It *is* a debatable point. One is definitely an odd-ball as primes go. And two—well, it's not an *odd*-ball; it's an *even*-ball. That is, it's the only even prime number. You could just as arbitrarily define the set of primes as all *odd* numbers that have precisely two whole-number factors. If you did it that way, then two isn't a prime."

"Ah."

"See? That's what they're conveying. Delta is a symbol that means, I think, 'It's a matter of opinion.' Neither answer is *wrong;* it's just a matter of personal preference, see?"

"That's fascinating."

She nodded. "Now, the next part of the message is really interesting. Elsewhere, they established symbols for 'sender' and 'recipient'—or 'me,' the person sending the message, and 'you,' the person receiving it."

"Okay."

"And with those," said Sarah, "they get down to the nitty gritty. Look at this." Her display changed:

```
[Question] [good] : [bad]
[Answer] [sender] [opinion] [good] >> [bad]
```

"See? The question is, what's the relationship between good and bad. And the response from the sender, who had said previously, when discussing factual matters, that good is the *opposite* of bad, now says something quite a bit more interesting: good is *much greater than* bad—a significant philosophical statement."

"'Does not your sacred book promise that good is stronger than evil?'"

Sarah felt her eyes go wide. "You're quoting the Bible?"

"Um, actually, no. That's *Star Trek*. Second season, 'The Omega Glory.'" He shrugged sheepishly. "'Yes, it is written: good shall always destroy evil.'"

Sarah shook her head in loving despair. "You'll be the death of me yet, Donald Halifax."

Chapter 11

"MCGAVIN ROBOTICS," SAID a crisp, efficient female voice. "Office of the president."

For once, Don wished he did have a picture phone; for all he knew, he was talking to a robot. "I'd like to speak to Cody McGavin, please."

"Mr. McGavin is unavailable. May I ask who's calling?"

"Yes. My name is Donald Halifax."

"May I ask what this is about?"

"I'm the husband of Sarah Halifax."

"Ah, yes. The SETI researcher, no?"

"That's right."

"What can I do for you, Mr. Halifax?"

"I need to talk to Mr. McGavin."

"As you might imagine, Mr. McGavin's schedule is very full. Perhaps there's something I can help you with?"

Don sighed, beginning to get it. "How many layers deep am I?"

"I'm sorry?"

"How many layers between you and McGavin? If I give you a message, and you decide it's worth passing on, it doesn't go to McGavin, does it?"

"Not normally, no. I'm the receptionist for the president's office."

"And your name is?"

"Ms. Hashimoto."

"And who do you report to?"

"Mr. Harse, who is the secretary to Mr. McGavin's secretary."

"So I have to get through you, then the secretary's secretary, then the secretary, before I get to McGavin, is that right?"

"We do have to follow procedures, sir. I'm sure you understand that. But of course things can be escalated quickly, if appropriate. Now, if you'll just tell me what you need . . . ?"

Don took a deep breath, then let it out. "Mr. McGavin paid for my wife and me to undergo rejuvenation treatments—you know, rollbacks. But it hasn't worked for my wife, only for me. The doctor from Rejuvenex says nothing can be done, but maybe if she had a request directly from Mr. McGavin. Money talks. I know that. If he indicated he was dissatisfied, I'm sure—"

"Mr. McGavin has had a full report on this."

"Please," Don said. "Please, my wife . . . my wife is going to die."

Silence. His words were probably more brutally honest than the receptionist to the secretary to the secretary to the president was used to hearing.

"I am sorry," Ms. Hashimoto said with what sounded like genuine regret.

"Please," he said again. "Surely whatever report he's seen came from Rejuvenex, and they've doubtless put a spin on it. I want him to understand what we—what Sarah—is going through."

"I'll let him know you called."

No, you won't, he thought. *You'll just pass it on to the next layer.* "If I could just talk to Mr. McGavin, just for a minute. I just . . ." He hadn't begged for anything for decades—not since . . .

It hit him, just then. It hit him like a sucker punch to the gut.

Forty-five years ago. The oncology ward at Princess Margaret. Dr. Gottlieb talking about experimental therapies, about things that were new and untested.

And Don begging her to try them on Sarah, to try anything that might save her. The details were lost to time, but he did now recall the interferon treatment, not approved for use in the

States. Gottlieb might have agreed to try it because of his begging, his insistent demands that she do everything that might help.

The experimental treatment had failed. But now, four decades on, its lingering effects were blocking another treatment, all—he swallowed hard—because of him.

"Mr. Halifax?" said Ms. Hashimoto. "Are you still there?"

Yes, he thought. *Yes, I'm still here. And I'll* still *be here for years to come, long after Sarah's gone.* "Yes."

"I do understand that you're upset, and, believe me, my heart goes out to you. I'll flag this double-red. That's the best I can do. Hopefully someone will get back to you shortly."

JUST AS HE had all those many years ago, when Sarah had been trying to translate the first Dracon message, Don stopped by from time to time to see how she was faring with decrypting the current one. But instead of working at the university, she was struggling with this one in the study—the upstairs room that had once been Carl's.

The Dracons' original message, the one picked up in 2009, had been divided into two parts: a primer, explaining the symbolic language they were using, and the meat of the message—the MOM, as it rapidly came to be known—which used those symbols in baffling ways. But eventually Sarah had figured out the purpose of the MOM, and a reply had been sent.

This second message from the aliens also had two parts. But in this case, the beginning was the explanation of how to decrypt the rest, assuming the right decryption key could be provided, and the rest, well, that was anybody's guess. Because it *was* encrypted, not even a single symbol that had been established in the original message was visible in the second part of this one.

"Maybe the aliens are responding to one of the unofficial responses," Don said, late one evening, leaning against the study's doorway, hands crossed in front of his chest. "I mean, even before you sent the official reply, didn't thousands of people send their own unofficial responses to the Dracons?"

Sarah looked ancient, almost ghostly, in the glow from her magphotic monitor, her thin white hair backlit from his perspective. "Yes, they did," she said.

"So maybe the decryption key is something that was in one of *those* messages," he said. "I mean, I know you worked very hard on it, but maybe the Dracons weren't interested in the official SETI-team response. Whoever they intended to have read their latest message might already have done so."

Sarah shook her head. "No, no. The current Dracon message *is* a response to our official reply. I'm sure of it."

"That might just be wishful thinking," he said gently.

"No, it's not. We put a special header at the top of the official reply—a long numeric string, to identify that message. That's one of the reasons we didn't post the entire reply we sent on the web. If we had, everyone would have the header, which would have defeated its purpose. The header was like an official letterhead, uniquely identifying the response we sent on behalf of the whole planet. And this reply to our response references that header."

"You mean it quotes it?" he asked. "But, then, doesn't everybody have it now? Any Tom, Dick, or Harry could send a new message to the Dracons and have it look official."

Her wrinkled features shifted in the cold glow as she spoke. "No. The Dracons understood that we were trying to provide a way to distinguish official responses from unofficial ones. They obviously grasped that we didn't want everyone who managed to detect their latest message to know what the header was. So the Dracons quoted every other digit from it, making clear to us that they were responding to the official reply, but without giving away what had distinguished the official reply in the first place."

"Well, there's your answer," Don said, quite pleased with himself. "The decryption key must be the *other* digits from the header, the ones the Dracons didn't echo back."

Sarah smiled. "First thing we tried. It didn't work."

"Oh," he said. "It was just a thought. Are you coming to bed?"

She looked at the clock. "No, I—" She stopped herself, and Don's stomach knotted. Perhaps she'd been about to say *I don't have time to waste on sleeping.* "I'm going to struggle with this some more," she finished. "I'll be along in a bit. You go ahead."

DON CALLED MCGAVIN'S office four more times without any luck, but finally his datacom rang. His ring tone was the five notes from a forgotten film called *Close Encounters of the Third Kind*, the sort of aliens-come-to-Earth story that seemed quaintly passé now. He looked at the caller ID. It said "McGavin, Cody"—not "McGavin Robotics," but the actual man's name.

"Hello?" Don said eagerly, as soon as he'd flipped his datacom open.

"Don!" said McGavin. He was somewhere noisy and was shouting. "Sorry to be so long getting back to you."

"That's all right, Mr. McGavin. I need to talk to you about Sarah."

"Yes," said McGavin, still shouting. "I'm sorry, Don. I've been briefed on all this. It's just awful. How is Sarah holding up?"

"Physically, she's okay. But it's tearing us both apart."

His tone was as gentle as one's could be when shouting. "I'm sure."

"I was hoping you could speak to the people at Rejuvenex."

"I already have, repeatedly and at length. They tell me there's nothing that can be done."

"But there must be. I mean, sure, Rejuvenex has tried all the standard things, but there's got to be a way to make the rollback work for Sarah if you—"

He stopped talking, which was probably just as well. He'd been about to say, "if you just throw enough money at it." But McGavin wasn't listening. Don could hear him saying something to someone else; from the sounds of it, he'd placed a fingertip over his datacom's mike and was talking to a flunky standing beside him. At last McGavin came back on. "They're working on it, Don, and I've told them to spare no expense. But they're totally stumped."

"They thought maybe an experimental cancer drug was the culprit."

"Yes, they told me that. I've authorized them to spend whatever is necessary to try to get hold of a supply of it, or to synthesize it from scratch. But the researchers I've spoken to think the damage is irreversible."

"They've got to keep trying. They can't give up."

"They won't, Don. Believe me, this is a huge problem for them. It's going to affect their stock price, if word gets out, unless they can find a solution."

"If you hear anything," Don said, "please, let me know at once."

"Of course," said McGavin. "But . . ."

But don't have unrealistic hopes; that was the implicit comment. McGavin had probably seen only an executive summary of the longer report Don had now pried out of Rejuvenex, but the bottom line would have been the same: no solution likely in the near future.

"Anyway," continued McGavin, "if there's anything Sarah needs to help with the decryption work, or if there's anything either you or she needs for anything else, just let me know."

"She needs to be rolled back."

"I *am* sorry, Don," McGavin said. "Look, I've got to get on a plane. But we'll keep in touch, okay?"

Chapter 12

BACK IN 2009, those who were part of the formal SETI endeavor had set up a newsgroup to share their progress in figuring out what the various parts of that first, original alien radio message said. It was rumored that the Vatican astronomers were working full-time on trying to translate the message, too, as was, supposedly, a team at the Pentagon. Hundreds of thousands of amateurs were taking a crack at it, as well.

Besides the symbolic-math stuff, parts of the original message turned out to be bitmap diagrams; a researcher in Calcutta was the first to realize that. Someone in Tokyo chimed in shortly thereafter, demonstrating that many of the block-graphic diagrams were actually frames in short animated movies. A new symbol in the last frame of each movie was presumably the word to be used henceforth for the concept that had been illustrated: "growth," "attraction," and so on.

The message also contained a lot about DNA—and, yes, there was no doubt that that was what it was, for its specific chemical formula was given. Apparently it was also the hereditary molecule on Sigma Draconis II—which immediately revived old debates about panspermia, the notion that life on Earth had begun when microorganisms from outer space had chanced to land here. The Dracons, some said, might be our very distant cousins.

The message also contained a discussion of chromosomes, although it took a biologist—in Beijing, as it happened—to recognize that that's what was being talked about, since the chromosomes were shown as rings, rather than long strings. Apparently, Sarah had learned, bacteria had circular chromosomes, and were essentially immortal, being able to divide forever. The innovation of breaking the circle to make shoelace-like chromosomes had led to the development, at least on Earth, of telomeres, the protective endcaps that diminished each time a cell divided, leading to programmed cell death. No one could say whether the senders had ringlike chromosomes themselves, or whether they were just depicting what they guessed to be either the universal ancestral or most-common kind. On Earth, in terms of biomass and number of individual organisms, chromosomal rings outnumbered the shoelace kind by orders of magnitude.

Once that piece of the puzzle was solved, a bunch of people simultaneously posted that the next set of symbols outlined various stages of life: separate gametes, conception, pre-birth growth, birth, post-birth growth, sexual maturity, the end of reproductive capability, old age, and death.

Lots of fascinating stuff, to be sure, but all of it seemed to be prologue, just a language lesson establishing a vocabulary. None of those early bits, except the tantalizing sample phrase that good was much greater than bad, seemed to actually *say* anything of substance.

But there was lots of message left—the MOM, the meat of the message, a mishmash of symbols and concepts that had been established earlier, each one tagged with several numbers. Nobody could make sense of it.

The breakthrough came on a Sunday evening. At *Chez Halifax*, Sunday nights were Scrabble nights, when Don and Sarah sat on opposites sides of the dining-room table, the fancy turntable set that Sarah had bought him many Christmases ago between them.

Sarah didn't like the game nearly as much as Don did, but she played it to make him happy. He, meanwhile, had less fondness for bridge than she did—or, truth be told, for Julie and Howie

Fein, who lived up the street—but he dutifully joined Sarah in a game with them once a week.

They were getting near the end of the Scrabble match; fewer than a dozen tiles were left in the drawstring bag. Don, as always, was winning. He'd already managed a bingo—Scrabble-speak for playing all seven of one's letters in a single turn—making the improbable *wanderous* by building on his previous *de*, one of the many two-letter combos that Scrabble accepted as a word but that Sarah, in all of her forty-eight years, had never seen anyone actually use *as* a word. Don was an expert in what she called Scrabble babble: he'd memorized endless lists of obscure words, without bothering to learn their meanings. She'd given up long ago challenging any string of letters he played. It was always in the *Official Scrabble Players Dictionary*, even if her trusty *Canadian Oxford* didn't have it. Still, it was bad enough when he played something like *muzjik*, as he had just now, with both a Z and a J, but to get it on a triple-word score, and—

And suddenly Sarah was on her feet.

"What?" said Don, indignant. "It's a word!"

"It's not just the symbol, it's where it appears!" She was heading out of the dining room, through the kitchen, and into the living room.

"What?" he said, getting up to follow her.

"In the message! The part that doesn't make sense!" She was speaking as she moved. "The rest of the message defines an . . . an *idea*-space, and the numbers are coordinates for where the symbols go within it. They're relating concepts to each other in some sort of three-dimensional array . . ." She was running down the stairs to the basement, where, back then, the family computer had been kept. He followed. Sixteen-year-old Carl was seated in front of the bulky CRT monitor, headphones on, playing one of those damned first-person-shooter games that Don so disapproved of. Ten-year-old Emily, meanwhile, was watching *Desperate Housewives* on TV.

"Carl, I need the computer—"

"In a bit, Mom. I'm at the tenth level—"

"Now!"

It was so rare for Sarah to yell that her son actually did get up, relinquishing the swivel chair. "How do you get out of this damn thing?" Sarah snapped, sitting down. Carl reached over his mother's shoulder and did something with the mouse. Don, meanwhile, turned down the volume on the TV, earning him a petulant "Hey!" from Emily.

"It's an X-Y-Z grid," Sarah said. She opened Firefox, and accessed one of the countless sites that had the Dracon message online. "I'm sure of it. They're defining the placement of terms."

"On a map?" Don said.

"What? No, no, no. Not on a map—in space! It's like a 3-D page-description language. You know, like Postscript, but for documents that don't just have height and width but depth as well." She was pounding rapidly at the keyboard. "If I can just figure out the parameters of the defined volume, and . . ."

More keystrokes. Don and Carl stood by, watching in rapt attention. "Damn!" said Sarah. "It's not a cube . . . that'd be too easy. A rectangular prism then. But what are the dimensions?"

The mouse pointer was darting about the screen like a rocket piloted by a mad scientist. "Well," she said, clearly just talking to herself now, "if they're not integers, they might be square roots . . ."

"Daddy . . . ?"

He turned around. Emily was looking up at him with wide eyes. "Yes, sweetheart?"

"What's Mommy doing?"

He glanced back. Sarah had a graphing program running; he suspected she was now glad they'd sprung for the high-end video card that Carl had begged for so he could play his games.

"I think," Don said, turning back to his daughter, "that she's making history."

--- Chapter 13 ---

TO BE YOUNG again! So many had wished for it over the years, but Donald Halifax had achieved it—and it felt *wonderful.* He knew his strength and stamina had ebbed these past several decades, but because it'd happened gradually he hadn't been conscious of how much he'd lost. But it had all come rushing back over the last six months, and the contrast was staggering; it was like being on a caffeine jag all the time. The term that came to mind was "vim and vigor"—and, although he'd played "vim" often enough in Scrabble, he realized he didn't actually know precisely what it meant, so he asked his datacom. "Ebullient vitality and energy," it told him.

And that was it! That was precisely it! His energy seemed almost boundless, and he was elated to have it back. "Zest," another word only ever employed on the Scrabble board, came to mind, too. The datacom's synonyms for it—keen relish, hearty enjoyment, gusto—were all applicable, but the cliché "feeling like a million bucks" seemed woefully inadequate; he felt like every one of the billions of dollars that had been spent on him; he felt totally, joyously, happily *alive.* He didn't shuffle anymore; he strode. Just walking along felt like the way he used to feel on those motorized walkways at airports—like he was bionic, moving so fast that it'd all be a blur to onlookers. He could lift heavy boxes, jump over puddles, practically fly up staircases—it wasn't quite leaping tall buildings in a single bound, but it felt damn near as good.

And there was icing on this delicious cake: the constant background of pain that had been with him for so long was *gone*; it was as though he'd been sitting next to a roaring jet engine for years on end, always trying to shut out the sound, to ignore it, and now it had been turned off; the silence was intoxicating. Youth, the old song said, was wasted on the young. So true—because they didn't know what it would feel like once it was gone. But now he had it again!

Dr. Petra Jones confirmed that his rollback was complete. His cell-division rate, she said, had slowed to normal and his telomeres had gone back to shortening with each division, a new set of growth rings was starting to appear in his bones, and so on. And the follow-up work had been completed, too. He had new lenses, a new kidney, and a new prostate, all grown from his own cells; his nose was restored to the merely honker-esque proportions it'd had in his youth; his ears had been reduced; his teeth had been whitened and his two remaining amalgam fillings replaced; and a few nips and tucks had tidied up other things. For all intents and purposes, he was physically twenty-five once more, and aging forward normally from that point.

Don was still getting used to all the wonderful improvements. His hearing was top-notch again, as was his vision. But he'd had to buy a whole new wardrobe. After the recalcification treatments and gene therapies, he'd regained the two inches he'd lost over the years, and his limbs, which had been reduced to not much more than skin and bones, had beefed up nicely. Ah, well; his collection of cardigans and shirts with buttons would have looked silly on a guy apparently in his twenties.

He'd had to stop wearing his wedding ring, too. A decade ago, he'd had it reduced in size, since his fingers had gotten thinner with age; now, it pinched painfully. He'd been waiting until the rollback was over to get it sized back up, and he'd get it done as soon as he found a good jeweler; he didn't want to trust it to just anyone.

Ontario had mandatory driver retesting every two years starting at one's eightieth birthday. Don had failed the last time. He hadn't missed it, and, besides, Sarah was still able to drive when they really needed to go somewhere. Now, though, he probably should take the test again; he had no doubt he'd pass this time.

At some point, he'd also have to get a new passport, with his new face, and new credit cards, also with his new face. Technically, he'd still be entitled to seniors' discounts in restaurants and at movies, but there'd be no way to claim them without convincing incredulous waiters and clerks. Too bad, really. Unlike, he was sure, every other person who had undergone a rollback, he really could use the break.

Despite all the good things, there *were* a few downsides to being young again. Sarah and Don were spending double on groceries now. And Don slept more. For at least ten years, he and Sarah had been doing just fine with six hours' sleep each night, but he found he needed a full eight again. It was a small price to pay: losing two hours a day, but gaining an extra sixty years. And, besides, presumably as he aged the second time, his sleep and food requirements would lessen again.

It was now a little after 11:00 p.m., and Don was getting ready for bed. Usually, he was quick in the bathroom, but he'd gone out today, and it had been hot and muggy. Toronto in August had been unpleasant when he'd been a kid; these days, the heat and humidity were brutal. He knew he wouldn't be able to sleep well if he didn't first have a quick shower. Carl had installed one of those diagonal support bars for them several years ago. Sarah still needed it, but Don now found it got in the way.

He shampooed, quite enjoying the sensation. He now had a full head of inch-long sandy-brown hair, and he just loved the feel of it. His chest hair was no longer white, either, and his other body hair had lost its grayness.

The shower was sensuous, and he luxuriated in it. And, as he cleaned himself down there, he felt his penis growing a little stiff.

As the water ran over him, he idly stroked himself. He was thinking of finishing himself off—that seemed the most expedient course—when Sarah entered the bathroom. He could see her through the translucent shower curtain; she was doing something over by the sink. He rinsed the soap off, his erection fading as he did so. Then he turned off the water, pulled back the shower curtain, and stepped out of the tub. By now, he was used to being able to swing his legs one after the other over the side without it being painful, and without—as he'd been doing in the preceding few years—sitting on the edge of the tub while doing so.

Her back was to him. She was already dressed for bed, wearing, as she always did in summers, a long, loose red T-shirt. He grabbed a towel from the rack and vigorously dried himself off, then headed down the short corridor to the bedroom. He'd always been a pajama man, but he lay naked on top of the green sheets, looking up at the ceiling. After a moment, though, he felt cold—their house had central air conditioning, and an outlet vent was directly above the bed—and so he scurried under the sheets.

A moment later, Sarah entered. She turned off the light as she did so, but there was enough illumination seeping in from outside that he could see her moving slowly to her side of the bed, and he felt the mattress compressing as she climbed in. "Good night, sweetheart," she said.

He rolled over on his side, and touched her shoulder. Sarah seemed surprised by the contact—for the last decade or so, they'd had to plan sex in advance, since Don had needed to take a pill beforehand to kick-start his lower regions—but soon he felt her hand gently on his hip. He moved closer to her and brought his head down to kiss her. She responded after a moment, and they kissed for about ten seconds. When he pulled away, she was lying on her back, and he was looking down at her while leaning on one elbow.

"Hey," she said, her voice soft.

"Hey, yourself," he said, smiling.

He wanted to bounce off the walls, to have wild, athletic sex—but she wouldn't be able to stand that, and so he touched her gently, softly, and—

"Ouch!" she said.

He wasn't sure what he'd done, but he said, "Sorry." He made his touch even lighter, more feathery. He heard her make a sharp intake of breath, but he couldn't tell if it was in pain or pleasure. He shifted positions again, and she moved slightly, and he actually heard her bones creak.

The activity was so slow, and her touch so weak, that he felt himself going soft. While looking into her eyes he vigorously stroked himself, trying to get his erection back. She looked so vulnerable; he didn't want her to think he was rejecting her.

"Tell me if this hurts," he said as he climbed on top of her, making sure that his own arms and legs were bearing almost all his weight; he wasn't the least bit fat, but he was still much heavier than he'd been before the rollback. He maneuvered carefully, gently, looking for a sweet compromise between what his body was now capable of and what hers could endure. But after only a single thrust, one that seemed oh-so-gentle to him, he could see the pain on her face, and he quickly withdrew, rolling onto his back on her side of the bed.

"I'm so sorry," she said, softly.

"No, no," he said. "It's fine." He turned onto his side, facing her, and very gently held her in his arms.

Chapter 14

SARAH HAD LEAPT from her chair in the basement on that fateful night all those years ago, and Don had hugged her, and lifted her up so that her feet weren't touching the ground, and he'd swung her around, and he kissed her hard, right there, in front of the kids.

"My wife the genius!" Don declared, grinning from ear to ear.

"More like your wife the plodding researcher," replied Sarah, but she was laughing as she said it.

"No, no, no," he said. "You figured it out—before anyone else did, you figured out the meat of the message."

"I've got to post something about this," she said. "I mean, it's no damn good if I keep it a secret. Whoever announces this publicly first is the one who . . ."

"Whose name will be in the history books," he said. "I am *so* proud of you."

"Thanks, darling."

"But you're right," he said. "You *should* post something, right now." He let her go, and she started to move back to the computer.

"No, Mom," said Carl. "Let me." Sarah was a hunt-and-peck typist, and not a very fast one. Her father, back in Edmonton, had never understood her wanting to be a scientist, and had encouraged her to take all the typing she could so she'd be ready for a secretarial career. A single typing course had been mandatory. It was the one class in her whole life that Sarah had failed.

She looked at her teenage son, who clearly, in his own way, wanted to share in this moment. "Dictate what you want to say," Carl said. "I'll type it in."

She smiled at him, and began pacing the length of the rec room. "All right, here goes. The meat of the message is . . ."

As she was talking, Don ran upstairs and called an overnight news producer at the CBC. By the time he returned to the basement, Sarah was just finishing dictating her report. He watched as Carl posted it to the SETI Institute newsgroup, then Don said, "Okay, hon, I've got you booked for a TV interview in one hour, and you'll be on both *The Current* and *Sounds Like Canada* in the morning."

She looked at her watch. "God, it's almost midnight. Emily, Carl, you should be in bed. And, Don, I don't want to go downtown this late—"

"You don't have to. A camera crew is on its way here."

"Really? My God!"

"It pays to know the right people," he said with a grin.

"I—um, well, I look a mess . . ."

"You look *gorgeous*."

"Besides, who the hell is watching TV at this hour?"

"Shut-ins, insomniacs, people channel-flipping looking for nudity—"

"Dad!" Emily had her little hands planted on her hips.

"—but they'll keep repeating the report, and it'll be picked up all over the world, I'm sure."

"WE'D BEEN SO *wrong*," Sarah told Shelagh Rogers the next morning. Don wasn't the Toronto sound engineer for *Sounds Like Canada*—Joe Mahoney was doing that these days—but Don stood behind Joe as he operated the board, looking over Joe's shoulder at Sarah.

And, while doing so, he reflected on the irony. Sarah was in

Toronto, but Shelagh was in Vancouver, where Radio One's signature program originated—two people who couldn't see each other, communicating over vast distances by radio. It was *perfect*.

"Wrong in what way?" Shelagh's voice was rich and velvety, yet full of enthusiasm, an intoxicating combination.

"In *every* way," Sarah said. "In everything we'd assumed about SETI. What a ridiculous notion, that beings would send messages across the light-years to talk about *math!*" She shook her head, her brown hair bouncing as she did so. "Math and physics are the same everywhere in the universe. There's no need to contact an alien race to find out if they agree that one plus three equals four, that seven is a prime number, that the value of *pi* is 3.14159, *et cetera*. None of those things are matters of local circumstance, or of opinion. No, the things worth discussing are moral issues—things that are debatable, things that an alien race might have a radically different perspective on."

"And that's what the message from Sigma Draconis is about?" prodded Shelagh.

"Exactly! Ethics, morality—the big questions. And that's the other thing, the other way in which we were totally wrong about what to expect from SETI. Carl Sagan used to talk about us receiving an *Encyclopaedia Galactica*. But no one would bother sending a message across the light-years to *tell* you things. Rather, they'd send a message to *ask* you things."

"And so this message from the stars is . . . what? A questionnaire?"

"Yes, that's right. A series of questions, most of which are multiple choice, laid out like a three-dimensional spreadsheet, with space for a thousand different people to provide their answers to each question. The aliens clearly want a cross section of our views, and they went to great pains to establish a vocabulary for conveying value judgments and dealing with matters of opinion, with sliding scales for precisely quantifying responses."

"How many questions are there?"

"Eighty-four," said Sarah. "And they're all over the map."

"For instance?"

Sarah took a sip from the bottle of water she'd been provided with. " 'Is it acceptable to prevent pregnancy when the population is low?' 'Is it acceptable to terminate pregnancy when the population is high?' 'Is it all right for the state to execute bad people?' "

"Birth control, abortion, capital punishment," said Shelagh, sounding amazed. "I guess those are posers even for extraterrestrials."

"So it seems," said Sarah. "And there are lots more, all in one way or another about ethics and acceptable behavior. 'Should systems be set up to thwart cheaters at all costs?' 'If an identifiable population is disproportionately bad, is it permissible to restrict the entire population?' These are just preliminary translations, of course. I'm sure there'll be a lot of quibbling over the exact meaning of some of them."

"I'm sure there will be," said Shelagh, affably.

"But I wonder if the aliens aren't a bit naïve, at least by our standards," said Sarah. "I mean, basically, we're a race of hypocrites. We believe societal norms should be followed by others, and that there are always good reasons for ourselves to be exempt. So, yeah, asking about our morals is interesting, but if they actually expect our espoused beliefs to have any strong relationship to our actual behavior, they could be in for a big surprise. The fact that we even need a platitude 'practice what you preach' underscores just how natural it is for us to do exactly the opposite."

Shelagh made her trademark throaty laugh. "Do as I say, not as I do."

"Exactly," said Sarah. "Still, it's amazing, really, the sociological concepts the aliens were able to get to from talking about math. For instance, building on some discussion of set theory, several of their questions deal with in-groups and out-groups. William Sumner, who coined the term 'ethnocentrism,' noted that what he called 'primitive peoples' had very different ideas about morality for in-group versus out-group members. The aliens seem to want to know if we've risen above that."

"I'd like to think we have," said Shelagh.

"For sure," agreed Sarah. "One might also expect them to wonder whether we'd outgrown religion." She looked through the glass at Don. "The vocabulary the Dracons established certainly would have made it possible to formulate questions about whether we believed an intelligence existed outside the universe—essentially, whether a God exists. They could have also asked if we believed any information persisted after death—in other words, whether souls exist. But they didn't ask those things. My husband and I were arguing about that on the way down here this morning. He said the reason they didn't ask about religious matters is obvious: no advanced race could still be caught up in such superstitious beliefs. But maybe it's just the opposite. Maybe it's so blindingly obvious to the aliens that God exists that it never even occurred to them to ask us if we'd failed to notice him."

"Fascinating," said Shelagh. "But why, do you think, do the aliens want to know all this?"

Sarah took a deep breath, and let it out slowly—causing Don to briefly cringe at the dead air. But, at last, she spoke. "That's a very good question."

Chapter 15

LIKE MOST ASTRONOMERS, Sarah fondly remembered the movie *Contact,* based on Carl Sagan's novel of the same name. Indeed, she argued it was one of the few cases where the movie was actually better than the overlong book. She hadn't seen it for decades, but a reference to it in one of the news stories about the attempts to decrypt the response from Sigma Draconis had brought it to mind. With pleasant anticipation, she sat down next to Don on the couch to watch it on Wednesday night. Slowly but surely, she was getting used to his newly youthful appearance, but one of the reasons she felt like watching a movie was that she'd be doing something with Don in which they'd be sitting side by side and not really looking at each other.

Jodie Foster did a great job portraying a passionate scientist, but Sarah found herself smiling in amusement when Foster said, "There are four hundred billion stars out there, just in our galaxy alone," which was true. But then she went on to say, "If only one out of a million of those had planets, and if just one out of a million of those had life, and if just one out of a million of those had intelligent life, there would be literally millions of civilizations out there." Nope, a million-million-millionth of four hundred billion is so close to zero as to practically *be* zero.

Sarah looked at Don to see if he'd caught it, but he gave no sign. She knew he didn't like being interrupted by asides during movies—you couldn't memorize trivia the way he did if you weren't able to concentrate—and so she let the screenwriter's minor flub pass. And, besides, despite its inaccuracy, what Foster had said rang true, in a way. For decades, people had been plugging numbers made up out of whole cloth into the Drake equation, which purported to estimate how many intelligent civilizations existed in the galaxy. Foster's wildly inaccurate figure, pulled out of the air, was actually quite typical of these debates.

But Sarah's amusement soon turned to downright cringing. Foster went to see a large corporation to get funding for SETI, and, when it initially turned her down, she went ballistic, exclaiming that contacting an extraterrestrial civilization would be the biggest moment in human history, more significant than anything anyone had ever done or could possibly imagine doing, a species-altering moment that would be worth any cost to attain.

Sarah cringed because she remembered giving such patently ridiculous speeches herself. Granted, the detection of the original signal from Sigma Draconis had been page-one news. But until the second message had been received, it had been over thirty years since a mention of aliens had appeared on the front page or main screen of any newspaper that didn't have the words "National" and "Enquirer" in its title.

It wasn't just SETI researchers who had overhyped the impact of such things. Sarah had forgotten that then-president Bill Clinton appeared in *Contact,* but there he was, talking about how this breakthrough was going to change the world. Unlike the cameos by Jay Leno and Larry King, though, which had been specifically staged for the movie, she immediately recognized the Clinton speech as archival footage—not about the detection of alien radio messages, but about the unveiling of ALH84001, the Martian meteorite that supposedly contained microscopic fossils. But despite the presidential hyperbole, that hunk of rock hadn't changed the world, and, indeed, when it was ultimately discredited several years later, there was almost no press coverage, not because the story was being buried, but rather because no one in the public even really cared. The existence of alien life was a curiosity to most people, nothing more. It didn't change the way they treated their spouses and kids; it didn't make stocks rise or fall; it just didn't matter. Earth went on spinning, unperturbed, and its denizens continued to make love, and war, with the same frequency.

As the film continued, Sarah found herself getting increasingly pissed off. The movie had its extraterrestrials beaming blueprints to Earth so humans could build a ship that could tunnel through hyperspace, taking Jodie Foster off to meet the aliens face-to-face. SETI, the movie hinted, wasn't really about radio communication with the stars. Rather, like every other cheapjack Hollywood space opera, it was just a stepping stone to *actually going to other worlds*. From the beginning with Jodie Foster's cockeyed math, through the middle with the stirring speeches about how this would completely transform humanity, to the end with the totally baseless promise that SETI would lead to ways to travel across the galaxy and maybe even reunite us with dead loved ones, *Contact* portrayed the hype, not the reality. If Frank Capra had made a propaganda series called "Why We Listen," *Contact* could have been the first installment.

As the credits started to roll, Sarah looked at Don. "What did you think?" she asked.

"It's a bit dated," he said. But then he lifted his hands from his lap, as if to forestall an objection. "Not that there's anything wrong with that, but . . ."

But he was right, she thought. Things are of their times; you can't plug something meant for one era into another. "What ever happened to Jodie Foster, anyway?" she asked. "I mean, is she still alive?"

"She might be, I guess. She's about your . . ." He trailed off, but it had been obvious what he was going to say: "She's about your age." Not "about *our* age." Although he still saw her as an eighty-seven-year-old, it seemed he was now in full denial about the chronological facts that applied to himself—and that was driving Sarah up the walls.

"I always liked her," she said. When *Contact* had come out, the American press had said that Ellie Arroway, Jodie Foster's character, was based on Jill Tarter, and the Canadian papers had tried to spin it that Sarah Halifax had been the inspiration. And although it was true enough that Sarah had known Sagan back then, the comparison was a stretch. Why the press refused to believe that characters were just made up was beyond her. She remembered all the theories about who the paleontologists in *Jurassic Park* were based on; every woman who had taken even one paleo course was reputed to be the model for the Laura Dern character.

"You know what movie Jodie Foster is really good in?" Sarah said.

Don looked at her.

"It's um—oh, you know the one. It was one of my favorites."

"I need another clue," he said, a bit sharply.

"Oh, you know! We bought it on VHS, and then DVD, and then downloaded it in HD. Now, why can't I think of the title? It's on the tip of my tongue . . ."

"Yes? Yes?"

Sarah winced. Don was becoming more and more impatient with her as time went on. When he'd been slow, too, he hadn't seemed to mind her slowness as much, but now they were out-of-synch, like the twins in that film she used to show her undergrads about relativity. She thought about snapping that she couldn't help being old, but, then again, *he* couldn't help that he was young. Still, his impatience made her nervous, and that made it even harder for her to dredge up the title she was looking for.

"Um," she said, "it had that guy in it, too . . ."

"Maverick?" snapped Don. *"The Silence of the Lambs?"*

"No, no. You know, the one about the—" Why wasn't the term coming to her?—"the, the . . . the child prodigy."

"Little Man Tate," Don said at once.

"Right," said Sarah, very softly, looking away.

--- Chapter 16 ---

DON MOVED OVER to the La-Z-Boy after Sarah had gone to bed, and sat glumly in it. He knew he'd made her feel bad earlier, when she'd been trying to remember the title of that movie, and he hated himself for it. Why had he been patient when his days were numbered, but impatient now that he had so much time? He'd tried not to snap at Sarah, he really had. But he just couldn't help himself. She was so *old,* and—

The phone rang. He glanced at the call display, and felt his eyebrows going up: "Trenholm, Randell." It was a name he hadn't thought about for thirty years or more, a guy he'd known at the CBC back in the Twenty-Teens. Ever since the rollback had gone bad for Sarah, Don had been avoiding seeing people he knew—and now he was doubly glad they didn't have picture phones.

Randy was a couple of years older than Don was, and, as he picked up the handset, it occurred to him that it might be Randy's wife calling. So often these last few years, calls from old friends were really calls from their surviving spouses with word that the friend had passed on.

"Hello?" said Don.

"Don Halifax, you old son of a gun!"

"Randy Trenholm! How the hell are you?"

"How is anyone when they're eighty-nine?" Randy asked. "I'm alive."

"Glad to hear it," Don said. He wanted to ask about Randy's wife, but couldn't remember her name. "What's up?"

"You're in the news a lot lately," Randy said.

"You mean Sarah is," said Don.

"No, no. Not Sarah. You, at least in the newsgroups I read."

"And, um, what groups are those?"

"Betterhumans. Immortality. I Do Go On."

He knew gossip about what had happened to him had to have spread further than just the block he lived on. But "Yeah, well" was all he said in reply.

"So Don Halifax is rubbing shoulders with the movers and shakers," said Randy. "Cody McGavin. Pretty impressive."

"I only met him once."

"Guy must have written you a pretty big check," Randy said.

Don was feeling more and more uncomfortable. "Nah," he said. "I never saw the bill for the procedure."

"Didn't know you were interested in life prolongation," Randy said.

"I'm not."

"But you got it."

"Randy, look, it's getting late. Is there something I can help you with?"

"It's just that, like I said, you know Cody McGavin—"

"Not really."

"And so I thought maybe you could have a word with him, you know, on my behalf."

"Randy, I don't—"

"I mean, I've got a lot to offer, Don. And a lot of things still to do, but—"

"Randy, honestly, I—"

"Come on, Don. It's not like you're special. But he paid for your rollback."

"It was Sarah he wanted to have rollback, and—"

"Oh, I know, but it didn't work for her, right? That's what they say, anyway. And, look, Don, I'm really sorry about that. I've always liked Sarah."

Randy apparently expected a response, as if having made this obeisance he was now due something in return. But Don remained quiet. After the silence had grown to an uncomfortable length, Randy spoke again. "So, anyway, he did it for you, and—"

"And you think he'll do it for you, too? Randy, I honestly don't know how much all the work I had done cost, but—"

"They estimate eight billion on Betterhumans. Most people on I Do Go On think it's more like ten."

"*But,*" continued Don, firmly, "I didn't ask for it, and I didn't want it, and—"

"And that's pocket change to the likes of Cody McGavin."

"I don't think that's pocket change to *anybody,*" said Don, "but that's beside the point. He can spend his money any way he likes."

"Sure, but now that he's doling it out to let some of those who aren't insanely rich have a rollback, well, I thought, you know, maybe . . ."

"There's nothing I can do for you. I'm sorry, but—"

The voice was getting more desperate. "Please, Don. I've still got a lot to contribute. If I had a rollback, I could . . ."

"What?" asked Don, his tone sharp. "Cure cancer? It's been done. Invent a better mousetrap? Gene-splicers will just make a better mouse."

"No, important things. I'm—you don't know what I've done in the last twenty years, Don. I've—I've done things. But there's a lot more I want to accomplish. I just need more time, is all."

"I'm sorry, Randy. Really, I am—"

"If you'd just *call* McGavin, Don. That's all I'm asking. Just make one phone call."

He thought about snapping that it had taken forever to get through to McGavin the last time, but that was none of Randy's business. "I'm sorry, Randy," he said again.

"Damn it, what did you do to deserve this? You're not that special. You're not that bright, that talented. You just fucking won the lottery, is all, and now you won't even help me buy a ticket."

"For Christ's sake, Randy . . ."

"It's not fair. You said it yourself. You aren't even interested in transhumanism, in life extension. But me, I've spent most of my life pursuing that. 'Live long enough to live forever'—that's what Kurzweil said. Just hold on for a few more decades, and we'll have rejuvenation techniques, we'll have practical immortality. Well, I *did* hold on, and it's here, the techniques are here. But I can't afford them."

"They'll come down—"

"Don't fucking tell me they'll come down in price. I *know* they'll come down in price. But not in time, damn it. I'm eighty-nine! If you'd just call McGavin, just pull a couple of strings. That's all I'm asking—for old times' sake."

"I'm sorry," Don said. "I really am."

"Damn you, Halifax! You've got to do this. I—I'm going to die. I'm going—"

Don slammed the handset down and sat quaking in his chair. He thought about going upstairs to see Sarah, but she couldn't understand what he was going through any more than Randy Trenholm did; he so wished he had someone to talk to. Of course, there were other people who had undergone rollbacks, but they were totally out of his league—the financial gulf separating him from them was so much greater than their shared experience of rejuvenation.

Eventually, he did head upstairs, went through the motions of getting ready for bed, and, at last, he lay down next to Sarah, who had already turned in, and he stared at the ceiling—something he found himself doing more and more these days.

Randy Trenholm was right, in a way. Some people probably should be kept around. The last of the twelve men who had walked on the moon had died in 2028. The greatest thing the human race had ever done had happened in Don's lifetime, but no one who had actually ever set foot upon the lunar surface was still alive. All that was left were photos and videos and rocks and a scant few poetic descriptions, including Aldrin's "magnificent desolation." People kept saying it was inevitable that humans would someday return to the moon. Perhaps, thought Don, he might now live to see that, but, until they did, the actual experience of those small steps, those giant leaps, had passed from living memory.

And, even more tragic, the last survivor of the Nazi death camps—the final witness to those atrocities—had died in 2037; the worst thing humanity had ever done had also passed out of living memory.

Both the moon landing and the Holocaust had their deniers: people who claimed that such wonder, and such horror, never could have happened, that humans were incapable of such technological triumphs, or of such conscienceless evil. And now, every last one of those who could gainsay that from personal experience was gone.

But Donald Halifax lived on, with nothing special to attest to, no important experience to which he alone bore witness, nothing that needed to be shared with future generations. He was just some guy.

Sarah stirred in her sleep next to him, rolling onto her side. He looked over at her in the darkness, at the woman who had done what no one else had ever done: figured out what an alien radio message meant. And, if Cody McGavin was right, she was the best bet to do it again. But she'd be gone all too soon, while he would go on. If the rollback were only going to work for one of them, it should have been *her*, Don knew. She mattered; he didn't.

He shook his head, his hair rustling against the pillow. He knew logically that he hadn't taken the rejuvenation away from

Sarah, that its success with him had nothing to do with its failure for her. And yet the guilt was oppressive, like the weight of six feet of earth pressing down upon him.

"I'm sorry," he whispered into the dark, facing the ceiling again.

"For what?" Sarah's voice startled him. He hadn't realized she was awake, but now that he turned his head to face her, he could see little reflections of the dim outside lights in her open eyes.

He scooched closer to his wife and gently hugged her to him. He thought about letting the words he'd spoken apply only to his having been short with her earlier that evening, but there was more—so much more. "I'm sorry," he said at last, "that the rollback worked on me but not on you."

He felt her expand in his embrace as she took a deep breath, then contract again as she let it out slowly. "If it could only have worked on one of us," said Sarah, "I'm glad it was you."

He hadn't been expecting that at all. "Why?"

"Because," she said, "you're such a good man."

He could think of no reply, and so he just held her. Eventually, her breathing grew regular and noisy. He lay there for hours, listening to it.

Chapter 17

IT WAS TIME, Don knew, that he got a job. Not that he and Sarah were desperate for money; they both had pensions from their employers and the federal government. But he needed to do *something* with all the energy he now had, and, besides, a job would probably help get him out of his deepening funk. Despite the physical wonders of being young again, it was all weighing heavily on him—the difficulty in relating to Sarah, the jealousy of old friends, the endless hours he spent staring into space while wishing things had turned out differently.

And so he walked over to North York Centre station, just a couple of blocks from their house, and got on the subway at the station located beneath the library tower there. It was a hot August day, and he couldn't help noticing the scantily clad young women aboard the train—all of them healthy-looking, tanned, and lovely. Watching them made the trip go quickly, although he was stunned, and a bit embarrassed, to note that a girl who got off at Wellesley had in fact been looking at him with what seemed to be admiration.

When he reached his own stop—Union Station—he got out and walked the short distance to the CBC Broadcast Centre, a giant Borg cube of a building.

He knew this place like—well, not like the back of his hand; he was still getting used to that appendage's new, smooth, liver-spot-free appearance. But he no longer had an employee's pass-card, and so had to wait for someone to come and escort him up from the Front Street security desk. While he waited, he looked at the full-size holograms of current CBC Radio personalities. Back in his day, they'd been a collection of cardboard standees. None of the faces were familiar to him, although he recognized most of the names.

"Donald Halifax?" Don turned and saw a slight Asian man in his mid-thirties, with incongruous peach-colored hair. "I'm Ben Chou."

"Thank you for agreeing to see me," Don said, as Ben got him through the gate.

"Not at all, not at all," said Ben. "You're a bit of a legend around here."

He felt his eyebrows go up. "Really?"

They entered an elevator. "The only audio engineer John Pellatt would work with? Oh, yes indeed."

They left the elevator, and Ben led them into a cramped office. "Anyway," he said, "I'm glad you came down. It's a pleasure to meet you. But I don't get what you're doing applying for a job. I mean, if you can afford a rollback, you hardly need to work here." He looked around the windowless office. It happened that they were on the fifth floor, and so should have been able to see Lake Ontario, but no matter where you were in this building, it felt subterranean.

"I can't afford a rollback," he said, taking the seat Ben was gesturing at.

"Oh, yeah, well, your wife . . ."

He narrowed his eyes. "What about her?"

Ben looked cornered. "Um, isn't she rich? She decoded that first message, after all."

"No, she's not rich, either." Perhaps she could have been, he thought, if she'd struck the right book deal at the right time, or had charged for all the public lectures she'd given in the first few months after the original message had been received. But that was water under the bridge; you don't get a second chance at *everything*.

"Oh, well, I—"

"So I need a job," Don said. Interrupting his potential boss probably wasn't a strategy a career counselor would have approved of, he thought, but he couldn't take this.

"Ah," said Ben. He looked down at the flatsie reader on his desktop. "Well, you did Radio and Television Arts at Ryerson. Good man; so did I." Ben squinted a bit. "Class of 1982." He shook his head. "I was class of 2035."

The point was obvious, so Don tried to deflect it by making light of it. "I wonder if we had any of the same instructors?"

To his credit, Ben snorted a laugh. "And how long did you work here at the CBC?"

"Thirty-six years," said Don. "I was a recording-engineer/producer when I . . ."

He backed away from saying the word, but Ben provided it, underscored by a crisp nod of his head: "Retired."

"But," continued Don, "as you can see, I'm young again, and I want to go back to work."

"And what year did you retire?"

It was right in front of him, Don knew, on his resumé, but the bastard was going to force him to say it aloud. "Twenty Twenty-Two."

Ben shook his head slightly. "Wow. Who was prime minister back then?"

"Anyway," said Don, ignoring the remark, "I need a job, and, well, once the Mother Corp is in your blood . . ."

Ben nodded. "Ever worked on a Mennenga 9600?"

Don shook his head.

"An Evoterra C-49? Those are what we use now."

He shook his head again.

"What about editing?"

"Sure. Thousands of hours"—at least half of which had been cutting physical audio tape with razor blades.

"But on what sort of equipment?"

"Studer. Neve Capricorn. Euphonix." He deliberately left off model numbers, and he also refrained from mentioning Kadosura, which had been out of business for twenty years now.

"Still," said Ben, "the equipment keeps changing all the time."

"I understand that. But the principles—"

"The principles change, too. You know that. We don't edit the same way we did a decade ago, let alone *five* decades ago. The style and pace are different, the *sound* is different." He shook his head. "I wish I could help you, Don. Anything for a fellow Ryerson man—you know that. But . . ." He spread his arms. "Even a guy fresh out of school knows the stuff better than you do. Hell, he knows it better than *I* do."

"But I don't have to be hands-on," said Don. "I mean, the last while, I wasn't much, anyway. I was mostly doing management, and that doesn't change."

"You're exactly right," Ben said. "It doesn't change. Meaning a guy who looks twenty-something isn't going to be able to command respect from men and women in their fifties. Plus, I need managers who know when an engineer is bullshitting them about what the equipment can and can't do."

"Isn't there *anything?*" Don asked.

"Have you tried downstairs?"

Don drew his eyebrows together. "In the lobby?" The lobby— the Barbara Frum Atrium, as it was technically known, and Don was old enough to have actually worked with Barb—contained nothing much except a couple of restaurants, the three security desks, and lots of open space.

Ben nodded.

"The lobby!" Don exploded. "I don't want to be a fucking security guard."

Ben raised his hands, palm out. "No, no. That's not what I meant. I meant—don't take this the wrong way, but what I meant was the museum."

Don felt his jaw go slack; Ben might as well have punched him in the gut. He'd all but forgotten about it, but, yes, in the lobby there was a small museum devoted to the history of the CBC.

"I'm not a bloody *exhibit*," Don said.

"No, no—no! That's not what I meant, either. I just meant that, you know, maybe you could join the curatorial staff. I mean, you know so much of that stuff firsthand. Not just Pellatt, but Peter Gzowski, Sook-Yin Lee, Bob McDonald, all those guys. You knew them and worked with them. And it says here you worked on *As It Happens* and *Faster Than Light*."

Ben was trying to be kind, Don knew, but it really was too much. "I don't want to live in the past," he said. "I want to be part of the present."

Ben looked at the wall clock, one of those broadcasting units with red LED digits in the middle encircled by sixty points of light that illuminated in sequence to mark passing seconds. "Look," he said, "I've got to get back to work. Thanks for dropping by." And he got up and extended his hand. Whether Ben's shake was normally limp and weak, or whether he was being delicate because he knew he was shaking an eighty-seven-year-old's hand, Don couldn't say.

Chapter 18

DON RETURNED TO the lobby. It said something nice about
Canada that anyone could walk around the vast Barbara Frum
Atrium, looking up at the six floors of indoor balconies, and
watch while all sorts of CBC personalities—the Corporation
frowned on the use of the word "stars"—came and went, unac-
companied by security guards or handlers. The little restaurant
Ooh La La!, which had been there forever, had tables spilling out
into the atrium, and there was one of Newsworld's anchors enjoying a Greek salad; at the next table, the lead performer in a
children's show Don had watched with his granddaughter was
sipping coffee; crossing over to the elevators was the woman who
currently hosted *Ideas.* All very open, all very welcoming—of
everyone, except him.

The broadcasting museum was tiny, and tucked off to one
side, clearly an afterthought in designing the building. Some of
the stuff predated Don. The kiddie program *Uncle Chichimus*
was before his time, and *This Hour Has Seven Days* and *Front
Page Challenge* were shows his parents had watched. He *was* old
enough to remember *Wayne and Shuster,* but not old enough to
have ever thought they were funny. But he'd learned his first
French from *Chez Hélène,* and had spent many happy hours with
Mr. Dressup and *The Friendly Giant.* Don took a minute to look at
the model of Friendly's castle, and the puppets of Rusty the
Rooster and Jerome the Giraffe. He read the placard that explained that Jerome's bizarre color scheme of purple and orange

had been selected in the days of black-and-white TV because it had good contrast, and had been left intact when the program switched to color in 1966, giving him a psychedelic look, an unintentional reflection of the times.

Don had forgotten that Mister Rogers had gotten his start here, but there it was, the original miniature trolley from that show, back when it had been called *Mister Rogers' Neighbourhood,* the last word notably sporting a *U.*

No one else was in the museum just now. The emptiness of the handful of rooms was a testament to the fact that people didn't care about the past.

Monitors were showing clips from old CBC shows, some of which he remembered, much of which was cringe-worthy. In the vaults here there must be tapes of dreadful stuff like *King of Kensington* and *Rocket Robin Hood.* Perhaps some things *should* be allowed to pass out of living memory; perhaps some things should be ephemeral.

There was some old radio and television hardware on display, including machines he himself had used early in his career. He shook his head. He shouldn't be curator of a museum like this. He should be on display, a relic of a bygone age.

Of course, he didn't look like a relic—and the Canadian National Exhibition no longer had a freak show; he could just barely remember visiting the Ex as a child and hearing the barkers call out descriptions of fish-tailed men and bearded ladies.

He left the museum, and left the building, going out the Front Street entrance. There were other broadcasters in town, but he doubted he'd have better luck with them. And, besides, he liked working on radio drama and audio documentaries of the kind nobody but the CBC made anymore; as far as other broadcasters would be concerned, his CV might as well have said he painted cave walls at Lascaux.

Don arrived at the entrance to Union Station, which was at the bottom of the U comprising the oldest part of the subway system.

He headed downstairs and passed through the turnstile, paying the normal adult—rather than senior citizen's—fare, and then took the escalator down to the platform. He stood beneath one of those digital clocks that hung from the ceiling. A train came rushing in, and he felt his hair whipping because of its passage, and—

—and he was transfixed, unable to move. The doors opened, making their mechanical drumroll sound, and people jostled in and out. Then the three descending tones sounded, indicating that the doors were closing, and the train started moving again. He found himself stepping right up to the edge of the platform, looking at its departing back.

A little boy, no more than five or six, was staring out the rear window at him. Don remembered when he used to like sitting in the front car as a kid, watching the tunnel speed by; the rear car, looking back, was almost as good. There was a grinding sound as the train banked, turning to go north, and then it was gone. He looked down onto the tracks, maybe four feet below, his toes sticking over the platform's edge. He saw a gray mouse scuttle by, and he saw the third rail, and the notices, covered with grime, that warned of the electrocution danger.

Soon enough, another train was coming down the curving track; its headlights cast mad shadows in the tunnel before it became visible. Don felt the vibration of the train, inches from his face, as it zoomed past him, and felt his hair whipping again.

The train stopped. He looked into the window facing him. Most riders got out at Union, although a few people always rode the train around the bend.

Around the bend.

This *was* the time-honored method to do this, wasn't it? Here, in Toronto, it was the way the despondent had handled things since before he'd been born. The subway trains roared into the station at high speed. If you waited at the right end of the platform, you could jump in front of an incoming one, and—

And that would be it.

Of course, it wouldn't be fair to the train's operator. Don remembered reading years ago, in the *Star,* about how devastating it was for subway drivers when people killed themselves this way. The drivers often had to go on extended leave, and some were so afraid that the same thing would happen again they were never able to return to their jobs. Stations in the downtown core were forty-five seconds apart; there wasn't even time for the drivers to relax between them.

But that had been back when the trains had had human drivers. These days, they were operated by sleek mechanicals, courtesy of McGavin Robotics.

The irony was tempting, and—

And he was trembling from head to toe. Suddenly, his body sprang into action, moving as fast as it could, and—

—and he just barely squeezed through the doors before they rumbled shut. Don clung tightly onto a metal pole for the whole trip home, like a drowning man grasping a log.

Chapter 19

BACK IN 2009, Sarah had spent at least as much time discussing the Dracon questionnaire as she did teaching astronomy,
and the topic often spilled over into evening conversations with
Don. One night, when Carl was down in the basement playing
The Sims 4, and ten-year-old Emily was at her Girl Guides meeting, Sarah said, "Here's an ethical dilemma that came up on the
SETI newsgroup today. Some of the SETI researchers think
they know what the aliens are trying to determine with their survey, which means we could give them the answers they want, in
hopes that they'll keep up contact with us. So, should we lie to get
what *we* want? This is, just how unethical is it to cheat on a survey about ethics?"

"The Dracons are probably at least as clever as we are, no?"
had said Don. "So wouldn't they see through any attempt at de-
ception?"

"That's what I said!" Sarah replied, sounding pleased to be
vindicated. "The instructions for the questionnaire make it quite
clear that the thousand responses we send should be produced in-
dependently and in private. They say there may be follow-up
questions, and any consultation among participants will ruin
those. And I suspect they've actually got some sort of way of de-
termining if the answers are all from one person, instead of the
thousand individuals they'd asked for, or are from a group that
collaborated—you know, by some sort of statistical analysis of
the answers."

They were doing general cleaning up. With both of them working during the days, housework ended up being a low priority. Don was dusting the mantel. "You know what I'd like?" he said absently, looking at the framed Emily Carr print on the wall there. "One of those big sixty-inch flatscreen TVs. Don't you think it'd look great right here? I know they cost a fortune right now, but I'm sure they'll come down in price."

Sarah was gathering up sections of newspaper. "You should live so long."

"Anyway," he continued, "you were saying about the Dracon questionnaire?"

"Yeah. Even if we did want to fake it and have a committee draw up all the answers, for some of the questions we honestly don't know what the 'right' answer is."

He moved on to picking up the used mugs from the coffee table. "Like what?"

"Well, like question thirty-one. You and another person jointly find an object that has no apparent worth, and neither of you desire it. Which of you should keep it?"

Don stopped to ponder, two yellow mugs in his right hand, and one in his left; at sixteen, Carl was learning to drink coffee. "Umm, I don't know. I mean, it doesn't matter, does it?"

Sarah had finished gathering newspapers, and nipped into the kitchen to dump them in the blue box. "Who knows?" she called out. "There's obviously *some* moral point here that the aliens are getting at, but no one I've spoken to can see what it is."

He followed her in, rinsed the mugs under the faucet, and then put them in the dishwasher. "Maybe neither of you should take the object. You know, just leave it where you found it."

She nodded. "That would be good, but that's not one of the allowed answers. The survey is mostly multiple choice, remember."

He was loading a few plates into the dishwasher. "Heck, I don't know. Um, the other guy should take it—'cause, um, 'cause that's me being generous, see?"

"But he doesn't want it," she said.

"But it might turn out to be valuable someday."

"Or it might turn out to be poisonous, or to belong to somebody else who'll be angry over it being taken, and who will exact revenge from whoever stole it."

He shook his head, and put an Electrasol tab into the detergent cup. "There just isn't enough information."

"The aliens think there is, apparently."

He started the dishwasher, and motioned for Sarah to follow him out of the room; the machine was noisy. "Okay," he said, "so you *can't* just give the Dracons the answers that'll make us look good, because you don't know what those are in all cases."

"Right," said Sarah. "And, anyway, even for those questions we *do* understand, there's debate about which answers *would* make us look good. See, some of our morals are rational, and others are based in emotion—and it's not clear which ones the aliens would prize most."

"I thought all morals were rational," Don said. He looked around the living room, gauging if anything else needed tending to. "Isn't that the definition of morality: a rational, reasoned response, instead of a knee-jerk, visceral one?"

"Oh?" she said, straightening the pile of current magazines—*Maclean's, Mix, Discover, The Atlantic Monthly*—that lived on the little table between the couch and the La-Z-Boy. "Try this one on for size. It's a standard puzzle in moral philosophy, a little number called 'the trolley problem.' It's called that because a British philosopher came up with it. Her name, by the way, was Philippa Foot—two fetishes in one, if you stop to think about it. Anyway, she said this: say a streetcar is out of control, rushing along its tracks. And say there are five people stuck on those tracks, unable to get away in time—if the train hits, it'll kill them all. But you happen to be watching all this from a bridge over the tracks, and on the bridge are the switching controls, including a lever that if you pull it will cause the streetcar to be diverted to another track, off to the left, missing the five people. What do you do?"

"Pull the lever, of course," he said. Deciding there was nothing else that needed doing tonight, he sat down on the couch.

"That's what almost everyone says," Sarah said, joining him. "Most people feel a moral obligation to intervene in situations where human life is at risk. Oh, but I forgot to tell you one thing. There's a really big guy stuck on that *other* track. If you divert the streetcar, he'll be killed. Now what do you do?"

He put his arm around her. "Well, um, I'd—I guess I'd still pull the lever."

She leaned her head against his shoulder. "That's what most people say. Why?"

"Because only one person dies rather than five."

He could hear in her voice that she was smiling. "A Trekker to the core. 'The needs of the many outweigh the needs of the few.' No wonder that's what Mr. Spock believes; it's clearly the product of rational thinking. Now, what about this? Say there's no second track. And say instead of being the one hapless fellow stuck on the left, the big guy isn't stuck at all. Instead he's standing right next to you on the bridge. You know for a fact that if you push him off so that he falls in front of the streetcar, hitting him will be enough to make it stop before it hits the five other people. But you yourself are a little guy. The streetcar wouldn't be stopped by hitting you, so there's no point in jumping yourself, but it'll definitely be stopped by hitting this big fellow. Now what do you do?"

"Nothing."

Don could feel her head nodding. "Again, that's what most people say—they wouldn't do a thing. But why not?"

"Because, um, because it's wrong to ... well, ah ..." He frowned, opened his mouth to try again, but then closed it.

"See?" said Sarah. "They're comparable situations. In both scenarios you choose to have one guy die—the same guy, in fact—to save five others. But in the first, you do it by throwing a lever. In the second, you actually push the guy to his death. The rational equation is exactly the same. But the second scenario *feels* different emotionally. For most people, what was judged right in the first scenario is judged wrong in the second." She paused. "The aliens didn't ask that specific question about the streetcar, but there are others for which there's an emotionally ethical response and a logically ethical response. As to which one the Dracons would prefer to see, I'm not sure."

Don frowned again. "But wouldn't advanced beings naturally prefer logic to emotion?"

"Not necessarily. Fairness and a desire for reciprocity seem to be emotional responses: they occur in animals who obviously aren't reasoning in an abstract, symbolic way, and yet those are some of the things we prize most. The aliens might prize them, too, meaning the emotional answers might in fact be what they're looking for. Still, some of my colleagues *do* argue that the logical answers are the better ones, because they denote more sophisticated cognition. And yet giving the purely logical answers wouldn't really portray who we are. I mean, consider this, for instance—the aliens didn't ask about it, but it makes a good point. We've got two kids, a boy and a girl. Suppose when Emily's older, Carl and Emily both went away somewhere for a weekend, and decided to have sex with each other—just once, just to see what it was like."

"Sarah!"

"See, you're immediately disgusted. And, of course, so am I. But *why* are we disgusted? Well, presumably because evolution has bred into us a desire to promote exogamy and avoid the birth defects that often come out of incestuous unions. But say they were practicing birth control—you *know* any daughter of mine will be. That means the concern about birth defects isn't relevant. Plus, say that both were free of venereal disease. Say they only did it that once, and that it caused them no psychological harm at all, and they never told anyone else about it. Is it still disgusting? My gut—and I bet yours, too—says yes, even though we can't articulate a rational reason for the disgust."

"I suppose," he said.

"Right. But for an awfully long time, in a lot of places, homosexual unions were greeted with disgust, too, as were interracial ones. These days, most people don't react negatively to them at all. So, just because something disgusted people once doesn't mean it's universally wrong. Morals change, in part because people can be won over to new positions. It was mostly rational argument, after all, that made the women's rights and civil-rights movements possible. People became convinced that slavery and discrimination were wrong on a principled basis; you educate people about an issue, and their view of what's moral changes. In fact, that's what happens with children. Their behavior gets more moral as their reasoning powers develop. They go from thinking something is wrong simply because they might get caught, to thinking something is wrong in principle. Well, maybe we're grown up enough for the Dracons to want to continue being in contact with us, and maybe we're not, and if we're not there's no way we can guess what the right answers are." Sarah snuggled against him. "No, in the end, I think the only thing we can do is exactly what they asked: send a thousand, independent sets of answers, each done in isolation, each one as honest and truthful as possible."

"And then?"

"And then wait for whatever reply they might eventually send."

Chapter 20

ANOTHER HOT AUGUST day. Don had headed downtown again, but this time it wasn't for a job interview, and so he was actually wearing clothes appropriate for the weather: cutoff denim shorts and a light-blue T-shirt. He was grateful for them as he effortlessly climbed the stairs from the subway station, and exited out into the muggy, searing heat.

Sarah, along with the rest of the SETI community, was still trying to find the decryption key for the second message from Sigma Draconis, and last night an idea had occurred to her. But to try it she needed some old paper records that were stored down at the University.

It was only a short walk from Queen's Park subway station to the McLennan Physical Laboratories tower, which housed the University of Toronto's Department of Astronomy and Astrophysics. On its roof were two observatory domes. Don remembered what he used to think when he saw them: that they couldn't possibly do any good, surrounded by the glare of downtown Toronto. But, to his surprise, as he glanced up at them now, he found himself thinking that they looked like a nice, firm pair of breasts.

As he came out of the elevator on the fourteenth floor of the tower, he saw that along one wall of the corridor there was a display about famous people who had been associated with the department. Included were Dr. Helen Sawyer Hogg, dead for fifty-five years now, whose weekly astronomy columns Don remembered reading as a boy in the Saturday *Star;* Ian Shelton, who discovered Supernova 1987a in the Large Magellanic Cloud; and Sarah herself. He paused and read the placard about Sarah, then looked at her photo, which must have been taken at least forty years ago; she hadn't worn her hair that long since.

Ah, well. Timeworn photos were appropriate here. Universities themselves were an anachronism, bucking the long-established trend to do everything online, everything by telecommuting. Hallowed halls, ivory towers—the synonyms his mental thesaurus provided just underscored how quaint and old-fashioned such institutions were. And yet, somehow, they endured.

He looked again at the photo of Sarah and found himself grinding his teeth. If things had gone the way they were supposed to, his wife would be even younger-looking now. This photo would be of what she'd have had to look forward to, when she gracefully entered middle age for a second time . . . around 2070, he supposed.

He headed around a bend in the corridor, the walls now lined with framed astronomical photos, until he found the door he was looking for. He knocked lightly on it. Old habits die hard, he realized; he'd long ago given up fervent rapping, since it used to hurt his arthritic knuckles, but now he wondered if anyone could have possibly heard him through the thick wood. He was about to knock again, and more loudly, when he heard a female voice call out, "Come in."

He entered, leaving the door open behind him. A young redhead, seated at a computer workstation, looked up at him expectantly.

"I'm looking for Lenore Darby," Don said.

She raised a hand. "Guilty."

He felt his eyebrows going up. Now that he saw her, he did remember that there'd been a redhead among the grad students at the last Christmas party, but he'd forgotten, or, more likely, had failed to notice then, just how pretty she was.

Lenore looked to be twenty-five—a real twenty-five, no doubt. Her orange hair cascaded down to her shoulders, and she had freckled white skin and bright green eyes. She was wearing green denim shorts and a white T-shirt that said "Onderdonk" on it, which he guessed was the name of a musical group. The shirt's lower half had been tied in a knot around her stomach, revealing a couple of inches of midriff that hadn't bunched at all even though she was sitting down.

"Can I help you?" she asked, smiling a perfect smile. So many of Don's contemporaries had spent their whole adult lives, as Don had until recently, with various dental imperfections—misalignments and gaps, overbites and underbites—but young people today almost always had *perfect* teeth, brightly white, totally straight, and completely free of cavities.

He steeled himself for giving the spiel, then: "I'm Don Halifax," he said. "I know I—"

"Oh, my goodness!" exclaimed Lenore. She looked him up and down, causing him to feel embarrassed and awkward, and probably even to blush. "I'd been expecting—well, he must be your grandfather. Are you named for him?"

She'd met an eighty-seven-year-old man back in December named Don Halifax, and she'd been told someone with that name was coming by to pick up some papers for Sarah, so . . .

So, yeah, it was a perfectly reasonable guess on her part. "That's right," he said. Indeed, what she'd suggested was in fact true, just not in the way she meant it. His full name was Donald Roscoe Halifax, and Roscoe had been his father's father's name.

So, why not? It was a harmless enough fiction, and he really hated having to explain his current situation; he certainly didn't want to go over the whole sorry mess with everyone he met. Besides, he'd probably never see this girl again.

"Nice to meet you!" said Lenore. "I've met your grandfather a couple of times. What a charming fellow!"

He was pleased by this assessment, and allowed himself a small smile. "That he is."

"And how is—" Don felt himself holding his breath. If she had finished her sentence with "your grandmother," he doubted he could have gone on with the charade, but she said, "And how is Professor Halifax?"

"She's fine."

"That's good," said Lenore, but then she surprised Don by shaking her head. "I sometimes wish I were older." She smiled and got up, tugging at the tied-up part of her T-shirt after she'd done so to get it to sit properly, which had the effect, for a moment, of emphasizing her breasts. "See, I could have had her as my thesis supervisor. Not that Professor Danylak isn't great, but, you know, it's frustrating studying where the most famous person in my chosen field actually worked and having almost no interaction with her."

"Your specialty is SETI, too?"

She nodded. "Yup. So, as you can imagine, Professor Halifax is a bit of a hero of mine."

"Ah," he said. He looked briefly around the room, because—

Because, he realized, he'd probably been looking too intently, too long, at the very attractive young woman. There were the usual fabric-covered room dividers, and one wall was lined by filing cabinets. The paperless office and the flying car had been a few years in the future for his entire life, but maybe, finally, he'd actually now live long enough to eventually see one or the other become a reality.

He opened his mouth to go on, but caught himself in time. He'd been about to say "Sarah asked me to . . . ," but who the hell calls his own grandmother by her first name? And yet he couldn't bring himself to actually say, "My grandmother." After a second, he fell back on the passive voice. "I've been asked to pick up some old files."

"Oh, I know," said Lenore. "I'm the low person on the totem

pole here; I'm the one who had to dig around for them down in the basement." She was about five-foot-four, although presumably never thought of herself that way; his generation had been the last Canadian one to be taught imperial measures in school. "Let me get them for you."

She walked across the room, and he found his eyes tracking the movement of her rear end through her shorts. Sitting on top of one of the filing cabinets was a stack almost a foot high of papers stuffed into several manila file folders.

Don was worried that his new looks didn't quite stand up to scrutiny; his own appearance these days was so startling to himself that part of him assumed it should be startling to others, too. But as she handed the great pile of paper to him, she gave no sign if she found anything out of the ordinary about him.

For his part, he found himself noticing the gentle hint of fruit fragrance—how wonderful to have his sense of smell back! It wasn't perfume. More likely, he thought, it was her shampoo or conditioner, and it was quite pleasant.

"My goodness," he said. "I didn't expect there to be so much!"

"Do you need a hand getting it all down to your car?" asked Lenore.

"Actually, I took the subway."

"Oh! I can get you a box to put it in."

"Thanks, but . . ." She lifted her orange eyebrows, and he went on. "It's just I was going to go to the Art Gallery this afternoon. They've got a special exhibition of Robyn Herrington blown glass that I want to see."

"Heck, the Art Galley is only a couple of blocks south of here. Why don't you leave the papers here, and pick them up when you're done?"

"I don't want to be a bother."

"Oh, it's no bother at all! I'll be here straight through until 5:00."

"Workaholic, eh? You must really like it here."

She leaned her shapely rump against a nearby desk. "Oh, yes. It's terrific."

"You're doing a Ph.D.?"

"Not yet. I'm just finishing my master's."

"Is this where you did your undergrad?"

"Nah. I went to Simon Fraser."

He nodded. "And is that where home is? Vancouver?"

"Yup. And, no offense, it sure beats this place. I miss the ocean, I miss the mountains, and I can't stand the climate here."

"But don't you get tired of all the rain in Vancouver?"

"I don't even notice it; it's what I'm used to. But the snow here in winter! And the humidity now. I'd die if it weren't for air-conditioning."

Don wasn't much of a fan of Toronto's climate either. He nodded again. "So, are you going to move back after you finish here?"

"Nah, probably not. I want to go somewhere in the southern hemisphere. Not nearly enough SETI searching has been done of the southern skies."

"Anywhere in particular?" asked Don.

"The University of Canterbury has a great astronomy department."

"Where's that?"

"New Zealand. Christchurch."

"Ah," said Don. "Mountains *and* the ocean."

She smiled. "Exactly."

"Have you ever been there?"

"No, no. But someday . . ."

"It's great."

"You've been?" she asked, letting her eyebrows climb her freckled brow.

"Yup," he said, adopting her style of speech. "Back in—" He stopped himself before he said, *Back in 1992.* "Ah, a few years ago."

"*Ooow,*" said Lenore, her lips puckering appealingly as she made the sound. "What was it like? Did you love it?"

He thought he should break eye contact with the young woman again, and his gaze landed on a digital wall clock; it was 1:10. He was getting hungry. That was another thing that had come back along with his sense of smell, now that his body had renewed itself. For so long, he'd been eating tiny meals, always having leftovers to take home from restaurants, and during the rollback, while his body had been rebuilding lost muscle mass, he'd eaten like the proverbial pig. Now, though, his appetite had settled into being what it'd been when he really had been twenty-five, which was still pretty prodigious.

"Anyway," said Don, "thanks for letting me come back later to get the papers. I should be heading off."

"To the Art Gallery?"

"Actually, I thought I'd grab a bite first. Is there anywhere good around here?"

"There's the Duke of York," she said. "It's good. In fact . . ."

"Yes?"

"Well, I really am seriously thinking about applying to New Zealand. I'd love to pick your brain a bit. Mind if I join you for lunch?"

Chapter 21

DON AND LENORE headed outside. The sun was high in the quicksilver sky, the humidity stifling. To the south, the CN Tower shimmered through the haze. The campus had been mostly empty, this being summer, but Bloor Street was packed with what was probably an equal mix of downtown businesspeople and tourists, plus a few robots, all madly hurrying somewhere. Don and Lenore chatted about New Zealand as they walked along.

"It's a great place," he said, "but I'll warn you, they've got this annoying tendency to put a slice of beet on hamburgers, and—oh, look!" There was a car parked at the curb. He pointed at its white and blue license plate: PQHO-294, with the hyphen, as was normal in Ontario, a stylized crown. "Qoph."

Lenore's eyebrows leapt up her forehead. "The name of a Hebrew letter!" she exclaimed with relish. "Do you play Scrabble?" Every serious Scrabble player had memorized the handful of acceptable words that had Q but no U in them.

He smiled. "Oh, yes."

"Me, too," said Lenore. "I'm always practicing with license plates. A few weeks ago, I saw two cars side by side, and their plates were anagrams of 'barf' and 'crap.' I was smiling for days after that."

They continued on, talking some more about New Zealand, and by the time they arrived at the restaurant, they'd exhausted just about everything Don had to say on the topic. The Duke of

York turned out to be a two-story-tall pub-style restaurant on a quiet street north of Bloor. The other buildings on the street, all classy renovated houses, seemed to contain the offices of high-priced lawyers and accountants. They were shown to a booth near the back on the pub's first floor, and settled in. Rock music—or whatever kids today called the stuff they listened to—was playing over the speakers. Mercifully, the place was air-conditioned.

There was a table near theirs, with three men seated at it. A server about Lenore's age, and almost as pretty, wearing a skin-tight black top scooped low to show a lot of cleavage, was taking that group's order for a bottle of wine to go with their meals.

"Red or white?" asked one of the men, looking at his friends.

"Red," replied the fellow on his left, and "red," repeated the guy on his right.

The first man tipped his head up to look at the server, and said, "I'm hearing red."

Lenore leaned over the table and whispered to Don, while indicating the guy who'd just spoken with a tilting of her head. "Wow," she said. "He must have synesthesia."

Don barked a delighted laugh.

The same server turned her attention to them. She was tall, and broad-shouldered, with chocolate brown skin and waist-length blue-black hair. "Can I get you—oh, Lennie! I didn't realize it was you, honey!"

Lenore smiled sheepishly at Don. "I wait tables here two nights a week."

He suddenly had a nice mental picture of Lenore dressed like the server, whose name tag read "Gabby." Gabby put a hand on her rounded hip, appraising him. "So, who's this?" she said, with mock seriousness, as if Lenore's companion had to pass muster with her.

"This is my friend Don," said Lenore.

"Hello," he said. "Nice to meet you."

"You, too," Gabby said. She turned her attention back to Lenore. "See you at the bank on Saturday?"

"For sure."

Gabby took their drink orders. Lenore asked for a glass of white wine; Don ordered his old standby of Diet Coke. He was glad that the Coca-Cola Company and PepsiCo had finally merged; he used to hate that little game of "Is Pepsi okay?" in places that had served only that brand.

"So," he said, after Gabby left, "you're helping her rob a bank?"

Lenore looked a little embarrassed. "Food bank, actually. Gabby helps out there all the time. Me, I'm there most Saturdays." She paused, then, a bit awkwardly, as if she felt a need to offer some further justification: "Working in a restaurant, you see so much food go to waste, and yet people still go hungry."

He looked away, wondering how many—good Christ, how many *millions* of people could have been fed with the money that had been spent rejuvenating him.

Lenore was, as his answering machine had opined, a chatty sort, and he was mostly content to just listen to her ramble on; indeed, it was safer than him doing much talking. She had such an animated face, such a lively voice, that he could have listened to her for hours. Still, he made occasional efforts to keep up his end of the conversation. "So, you like Onderdonk," he said, indicating her T-shirt.

"Oh, they're warp," she replied. He had no idea whether that was good or bad, and kept a poker face. "What about you?" continued Lenore. "What groups do you like?"

Oh, shit, thought Don. He'd set himself up for this. The bands of his youth—ELO, Wings, Supertramp, April Wine—would mean nothing to her, and, for the life of him, he couldn't think of the name of any contemporary group. "I, um, ah . . ." And then, in a flash of brilliance, he pointed at the wall speaker, indicating the group that was playing now—not that he could name it, or the song.

But she nodded, impressed. "Hyperflower," she said. "Skytop." Don tried not to frown. One of those words was probably the name of the group; the other, a favorable reaction to his choice. If it had been her pointing at the speaker and oh, say, "Call Me"—a standard from his own university years—had been playing, he'd have identified the musician first, then added his assessment: "Blondie. Cool." So he assumed "Hyperflower" was the name of the band, and "skytop," a term of praise. *Just like decoding an alien language,* he thought. Sarah would be proud.

"Anybody else?" asked Lenore.

"Umm . . ." After a moment, in desperation, he said, "The Beatles."

"No way!" she squealed. "I love them! What's your favorite song of theirs?"

" 'Yesterday.' "

She murmured appreciatively.

"It's unusual," he said, "liking the Beatles these days." Although once he said it, he was afraid he might be wrong. For all he knew, the Fab Four could be enjoying a general resurgence of interest right now. When he'd been in university, there'd been a huge Bogart revival on campuses, and Bogey's great films had been almost a half-century in the past, even then.

But she nodded enthusiastically. "For sure. Hardly anybody I know has even heard of them."

"How'd you get into them?"

She looked at him quizzically, and he thought that maybe he'd used a dated turn of phrase. But she must have sussed out its meaning because she said, "My grandfather had a collection of them."

Ouch.

She went on. "He used to play them for me whenever I came over as a kid. He had an antique stereo—that was his hobby—and a whole bunch of them on nylon."

It took him a moment to get it; she meant vinyl. But it wasn't polite to correct people when they made innocent mistakes—*his* grandfather had taught him that.

Still, thought Don, there had to be *something* they could discuss that wouldn't put him at such a disadvantage. Of course, they could have talked about the one person they both knew: Sarah. Isn't that what most strangers do? But he couldn't stand to hear another reference to his "grandmother."

Gabby returned with their drinks and took their food order. Don asked for something called "the blue steak salad"—sliced steak on garden greens with crumbled blue cheese. Lenore, who hadn't had to even glance at the menu—working here, she presumably knew it by heart—ordered fish and chips.

Don loved debating politics, but usually avoided it with people he'd just met. But there was a provincial election looming here, and, since Lenore was from British Columbia, she likely didn't have strong feelings about what was happening in Ontario; it was probably a safe topic. "So, who'd you like to see win on Friday?" Don asked.

"I always vote NDP," she said.

That made him smile. He remembered his own socialist days as a student. Still, he was quite impressed with how much Lenore knew about the current scene. But, when history came up—

"Favorite prime minister? I guess I'd have to say Mulroney."

Don really got pissed off by the revisionist history that was popular these days. "Listen," he said, "I remember when Brian Mulroney was prime minister, and he—" He cut himself off when he saw her wide-eyed expression. "I mean," he quickly corrected, "I remember reading about when Brian Mulroney was prime minister, and he was even worse than Chrétien when it came to being sleazy . . ."

Still, why was he leaving his true age a secret? It wasn't as if he could keep it under wraps forever. People would eventually find out—including people at the astronomy department; Sarah was still in touch with several of them, and they had no pact to keep what had happened quiet. Besides, Lenore would probably be fascinated to hear all about his meeting with Cody McGavin, who, after all, was the patron saint of SETI these days. But whenever he contemplated the selective success of the treatment, the guilt cut him from within, like swallowed glass, and—

"Okay," said Lenore, "let's see what you're made of."

He stared at her, completely baffled, as she rummaged in her purse. After a moment, she pulled out her datacom and placed it on the table between them. She pressed a couple of keys, and it projected a holographic Scrabble board onto the wooden tabletop.

"Wow!" Don said. Although he had a nice collection of portable Scrabble boards—fold-up sets, magnetic sets, a set with self-stick vinyl tiles, dedicated electronic devices, even a miniature version that fit on a key chain—he'd never seen one this . . . this *skytop*.

"All right, Mr. Qoph," Lenore said. "Let's play."

Chapter 22

A SPRING EVENING in 2009. "Sweetheart, I'm home!" Sarah called out.

Don came out of the kitchen, crossed through the living room, and stood at the head of the six stairs leading down to the entryway. "How'd it go?"

It was The First International Collaborative Session for Dealing with the Message from Sigma Draconis, a three-day marathon, hosted by the University of Toronto, chaired by Sarah herself, with SETI experts from all over the world having flown in to attend.

"Exhausting," said Sarah, sliding aside the mirrored closet door and hanging up her raincoat; April was Toronto's wettest month. "Contentious. But ultimately worthwhile."

"I'm glad," he said. "I've got a pot roast in the oven, by the way. It should be ready in about twenty minutes."

The door to the house opened again and Carl came in, looking soaked and bedraggled. "Hey, Mom," he said. "How was the conference?"

"Good. I was just telling your father."

"Dinner in twenty minutes, Carl," Don said.

"Great. I'll wash up." Carl managed to get his wet shoes off without bending over or undoing the laces. He didn't take off his wet jacket, but just scooted up the stairs, slipping by Don as he did so.

"So, what happened?" Don asked.

Sarah came up to the living room, and they shared a kiss. "We started with an inventory of the unauthorized messages that we know have already been sent to Sigma Draconis."

"Like what?"

"There's a group that says it managed to render the opening of Genesis in the language the Dracons provided."

"Christ," said Don.

"No," she said. "He doesn't show up until the sequel. Anyway, another group has sent up a library of digitized Islamic art. Somebody else says he's sent a list of the serial numbers of all of the U.S. soldiers killed in Iraq. Another person sent a version of the Mensa admissions test. He said instead of us worrying about passing the aliens' test, they should be worrying about passing one of ours; maybe they're not good enough to join *our* club."

"Huh," said Don.

"And there's been lots of music sent." Sarah moved over to the couch and lay down. He motioned for her to lift her legs so he could sit down at the far end. She did so, then she lowered her feet into his lap, and he began rubbing them for her.

"*Mmmmm,*" she said. "That's nice. Anyway, Fraser Gunn was there—remember him? He argued that sending music was a mistake."

"Why?" asked Don. "Afraid of being sued by the copyright holders?"

"No, no. But, as he said, the only thing we've got to trade with aliens is our culture; that's the only thing you might want from another civilization. And if we give away the best stuff—Bach, Beethoven, the Beatles—we'll have nothing good to offer when the aliens say, hey, what have you got to swap for *our* best work?"

Don knew all about scraping the bottom of the cultural barrel. He was a DVD addict—more so as a collector than as an actual watcher. He'd been thrilled when all the great television of his childhood and teenage years had been released on DVD, and he'd snapped up the boxed sets: *Thunderbirds, All in the Family,*

M*A*S*H, Roots, Kolchak: The Night Stalker, and, of course, the original *Star Trek*. But the last time he'd been in Future Shop, all he'd seen in the new-releases section was forgotten crap like *Sugar Time!*, a seventies sitcom starring Barbi Benton, and *The Ropers*, a spinoff from *Three's Company* whose only virtue was that it proved the original *wasn't* the worst TV show ever made. The studios had gone through their good stuff at a breakneck pace, and were now desperately trying to find anything at all worth releasing.

"Well," he said, "maybe Fraser's right. I mean, the only thing SETI is good for is sending information of one sort or another, no?"

"Oh, I'm sure he *is* right," said Sarah. "But there's nothing we can do about it. People are going to send whatever they want to. It's turned Carl Sagan's old saying on its ear. He used to ask, 'Who speaks for the Earth?' The question really is, 'Who *doesn't* speak for the Earth?'"

"That's our number-one product these days, isn't it?" said Don. "Spam."

He saw her nod ruefully. SETI, as he'd often heard Sarah say, was a mid-twentieth-century idea, given birth to by Morrison and Cocconi's famous paper, and, as such, it carried a lot of quaint baggage. The notion that governments, hopefully cooperating internationally, would control the sending and receiving of signals was a fossil of an earlier age, before cheap, mass-produced satellite dishes became common, allowing everyone everywhere to watch ESPN and the *Playboy* channel.

No, these days anybody who wanted to cobble together the equipment from off-the-shelf parts could build their own radio-telescope array. Using home-computer astronomy software to drive them, consumer satellite dishes could easily track Sigma Draconis across the sky. Such dishes separated by wide distances could be linked via the Internet, and with the aid of error-correcting and noise-canceling software, groups of them effectively formed much bigger dishes. The phrase "SETI@home" had taken on an all-new meaning.

Of course, the American FCC, and comparable bodies in other jurisdictions, had the authority to limit private radio broadcasting. At the urging of the SETI community, the FCC was trying to prosecute many of the individuals and groups that were beaming unofficial replies to Sigma Draconis. But those cases were almost certainly all going to be lost because of First Amendment challenges. No matter how powerful they were, tight-beam transmissions aimed at one tiny point in the sky had no impact on the normal use of the airwaves, and attempts to ban such narrowcasts were therefore an unwarranted infringement of free speech.

Don knew that some religious organizations, including a few new cults that had sprung up, had already built their own vast dishes, dedicated to beaming signals to Sigma Draconis. Some did it twenty-four hours a day; Sigma Drac never set in the sky for anyone whose latitude was greater than twenty degrees north.

And for those who just wanted to send one or two messages— crackpot theories, execrable poetry, political tracts—there were private-sector firms that had built dishes and offered various transmission plans. One of the best-known was Dracon Express, whose slogan was "When it absolutely, positively has to be there 18.8 years from now."

Nine-year-old Emily appeared, having come up from the basement. "Hi, sweetheart," Don said. "Just a few minutes to dinner. Set the table, will you?"

Emily looked petulant. "Do I *have* to?"

"Yes, dear, you do," he said.

She let out a theatrical sigh. "I have to do *everything!*"

"Yes, you do," Don said. "After dinner, you have to go out and plow the fields for a few hours. And when you're done with that, you'll need to sweep all the streets from here to Finch Avenue."

"Oh, Daddy!" But she was grinning now as she headed off

into the kitchen. He turned back to his wife, who was visibly try-ing not to wince every time Emily banged the plates together.

"So," he said, "did your group figure out precisely *why* the aliens are interested in our morality?"

She shook her head. "Some paranoid types think we're being tested, and, if found wanting, will be subject to retribution. Someone from France went so far as to suggest we were undergo-ing an evaluation by the Sigma Draconian equivalent of PETA, wanting to determine, before they came to eat us, whether we had the higher moral and cognitive standing of true intelligences, or were just dumb cattle."

"I thought it was an article of faith in SETI circles that aliens only communicated; they never actually go places."

"Apparently they didn't get that memo in Paris," said Sarah. "Anyway, someone else suggested that we're just one data point in some wider survey, the kind that would be summarized in multicolor pie charts in the Dracon counterpart of *USA Today*."

A timer sounded in the kitchen. Don patted her legs, indicat-ing she should let him up. She did so, and he headed in. He rinsed his hands, then opened the stove, feeling a rush of hot air pouring out. "And what about orchestrating the replies?" he called out. "What did you guys decide about that?"

Sarah called back, "Hang on, I'm going to wash up."

He got the oven mitts and removed the pot, placing it on the stove top.

"Where are the napkins?" Emily asked.

"In that cupboard," he said, indicating it with a movement of his head. "Just like yesterday. And the day before."

"Stacie said she saw Mommy on TV," Emily said.

"That's pretty cool, isn't it?" he said, opening the pot and stir-ring the vegetables surrounding the meat.

"Yeah," said Emily.

Sarah appeared in the doorway. "Something smells good."

"Thanks," said Don, then, shouting, "Carl! Dinner!"

It took a few minutes to get everyone seated and served, and then Don said, "So, what *are* you going to send the aliens?"

"We're going to do what they asked. We're going to set up a website, based at U of T, and let people from all over the world answer the questions the aliens asked. We'll pick at random a thousand completed surveys, and send them off."

Carl was reaching for the dinner rolls. "Hey," Don said, "come on, Carl. Don't reach halfway across the table. Ask your sister; she'll pass them."

Carl sighed. "Can I have the rolls?"

"Say please," Emily said.

"Dad!"

Don was tired. "Emily, give your brother the rolls."

Scowling, she did so.

"Why do you suppose they want a thousand sets of responses?" continued Don. "Why not just, you know, send a summary—like, X percent chose answer A, Y percent chose B, and so on."

"This isn't *Family Feud*," said Sarah.

Don chuckled.

"Seriously," said Sarah, "I suspect it's because if you summarize it all, you'd never see the seemingly contradictory stuff. You know, saying that X percent are against abortion and Y percent are for the death penalty doesn't let you draw out the fact that, often, it's the same people who are pro-life and also pro-capital punishment. Or, for that matter, the aliens might consider my own beliefs to be bizarrely contradictory. Being both pro-choice and anti-capital punishment could be interpreted as meaning you're in favor of murdering innocent children but against killing those who could be said to deserve it. I'd never put it that way, of course, but combinations like that are interesting, and I guess they don't want them to get lost in the data."

"Sounds like a plan," Don said, while carving another piece of roast for Carl. "But what about your own answers?"

"Sorry?"

"You figured out that it was a survey," he said. "Surely one of the thousand sets of answers sent should be yours."

"Oh, I don't know about that . . ." Sarah said.

"Sure, Mom," said Carl. "You've got to include your own answers. It's your right."

"Well, we'll see," said Sarah. "Emily, would you please pass the peas?"

Chapter 23

AFTER LUNCH, LENORE headed back to the University, and Don made his way down to the Art Gallery. He'd been impressed by the young lady's Scrabble play. She had a terrific vocabulary, a good strategic sense, and didn't take too long to make her moves. Although he did ultimately win, she had the best single turn, placing *oxlip* vertically starting at the triple-word-score square in the upper-left corner of the board.

The Art Gallery of Ontario had the world's largest collection of Henry Moore sculptures, as well as major collections of European Old Masters and Canada's Group of Seven, plus a permanent exhibition of Helena van Vliet watercolors—and although Don had seen all of those before, he enjoyed looking at them again. But it was the traveling exhibition of blown glass by Robyn Herrington that had really brought him here today, and he took his time admiring each piece. He had a fondness for art forms that required genuine manual skill; so often, today's digital arts substituted patience for real talent.

The AGO was popular with tourists, and he had to put up with being jostled a fair bit—but at least it didn't actually hurt to be bumped by people anymore; until recently, he often used to ache for hours after colliding with a wall or another person.

His favorite Herrington piece, he decided, was a yellow fish with big blue eyes and giant pink lips; somehow, out of molten glass, the artist had imbued great personality into it.

After he'd seen his fill, Don headed outside and started making his way back to the university to pick up the pile of papers. Rush hour had begun and the traffic on the streets was already bumper-to-bumper. By the time he got back to the fourteenth floor of the McLennan tower, it was a quarter to five, but, as promised, Lenore was still there.

"Hi, Don," she said. "I was beginning to think you'd fallen into a black hole."

He smiled. "Sorry. Lost track of time."

"How was the exhibition?"

"Terrific, actually."

"I put your papers into a couple of bags for you, so they'd be easier to carry."

And who said young people today were inconsiderate? "Thanks."

"It's too bad it's so late," Lenore said. "The subway will be jam-packed, at least for the next ninety minutes. Sardine City."

"I hadn't thought about that," he said. It had been years since he'd had to come home from downtown in rush hour. A tin can full of sweaty, exhausted people didn't sound very pleasant.

"Look," said Lenore, "I'm about to head back to the Duke of York."

"Again?" said Don, astonished.

"I get a discount there. And it's Tuesday night—that's wing night. Me and a few other grad students meet there every week. Why don't you come along? You can hang with us until the subway traffic dies down a bit."

"Oh, I don't want to intrude."

"It's no intrusion."

"I, um . . ."

"Think about it. I'm going to have a pee before I head out." She left the office, and Don looked out the little window. In the distance, beyond the campus, he could see gridlocked streets. He reached into the pocket of his shorts, and pulled out his datacom. "Call Sarah," he said to it, and a moment later he heard her saying, "Hello?"

"Hey, hon," he said. "How are you?"

"Fine. Where are you?"

"Actually, down at your old stomping grounds. Just picking up the papers you wanted."

"How was the exhibit at the AGO?"

"Good; I'm glad I saw it. But, listen, I really don't want to face the rush-hour crush on the subway."

"No, you shouldn't."

"And Lenore here, and a few other grad students, are going out for chicken wings, and—"

"And my husband loves his wings," Sarah said, and Don could hear the smile in her voice.

"So would you mind if . . . ?"

"No, not at all. In fact, Julie Fein just called. They've got theater tickets for tonight, but Howie's not feeling up to going, so she wanted to know if I wanted to go; I was just about to call you."

"Oh, for sure. Go. What are you going to see?"

"*Fiddler on the Roof,* at Leah Posluns." Just a few blocks from their home.

Don did a decent Topol impersonation, and he sang a few bars of "If I Were a Rich Man"—he liked any song that properly employed the subjunctive. Then he added, "Have a wonderful time."

"Thanks, dear—and enjoy your wings."

"Bye."

"Bye."

Just as Don was closing up his datacom, Lenore came back into the room. "So, what's the verdict?" she asked.

"Thanks," he said. "Wings sound great."

WHEN DON AND Lenore arrived back at the Duke of York, Lenore's friends had already shown up. They were seated in a small room to the left on the ground floor, an area Lenore said was called "the snug."

"Hey, everybody," Lenore said, pulling out a captain's chair and sitting down. "This is my friend Don."

Don took a seat, as well. Two small round tables had been shoved together.

Lenore indicated a lanky Asian man in his twenties. "Don, this is Makoto. And this is Halina" (petite, with brown hair) "and Phyllis" (a blond who looked like she'd be quite tall, if she were standing up).

"Hi, everybody," Don said. "Thanks for letting me join you." A moment later, Gabby, who was still on duty, came by. He listened as she recited what was on draft, and he ordered an Old Sully's Light, the only low-carb beer on the list.

Lenore immediately dove into the current topic of conversation, something about a guy they knew having gotten into a fight with his girlfriend. Don settled into his chair and tried to get a handle on the personalities. Halina didn't seem to ever speak, but she had an expressive face that reacted—indeed, overreacted—to whatever the others were saying: eyebrows shooting up, jaw dropping, big smile, bigger frown; she was a living series of emoticons. Phyllis had what seemed to Don to be a juvenile and bawdy sense of humor, and she made liberal use of the F-word. Makoto looked unhappy that Don was there; perhaps he'd been counting on being the only guy with three beautiful women.

Don mostly just listened to the conversation for the next little while, laughing a bit at those jokes he got, and drinking beer. He knew he could have joined in the discussion, but what they were talking about was so trivial, and they seemed to blow their little life crises out of any reasonable proportion: being away from home for the first time, petty social dynamics, and so on. Makoto, Halina, and Phyllis didn't have a ghost of an idea what it was like to have lived a life, to have raised kids and had a career. Lenore *did* have interesting things to say, and he paid attention when she was speaking, but when the others were talking he found himself mostly eavesdropping on the middle-age couple at the next table, who were having a spirited discussion about how they thought the Conservative party was going to rout the Liberals in the upcoming election, and—

"Did you see Sarah Halifax on TV last week?" Makoto said to the others. "A fucking corpse walking. She must be like a hundred and ten."

"She's only eighty-seven," Don said evenly.

"'Only,'" said Makoto, as if repeating a punch line for the benefit of those who might not have heard it.

Lenore spoke up. "Makoto, Don is—"

Don cut her off. "I'm just saying, Sarah Halifax is not that old."

"Yeah, well, she looks like Gollum," said Makoto. "And she must be completely senile."

Halina nodded vigorously but said nothing.

"Why do you say that?" Don said, trying to keep his voice even.

"Don't get me wrong," said Makoto. "I know she figured out what the first message meant. But the TV thing said Cody McGavin thinks the old bat is going to figure out the new message, too." He shook his head in a "can-you-imagine" sort of way.

"Speaking of messages," said Lenore, gamely trying to change the topic, "I got a call the other day from Ranjit at CFH. He says—"

But Don couldn't help himself. "Professor Halifax understands the Dracons better than anyone."

Makoto waved a hand dismissively. "Oh, she might have back in her day, but—"

"This is *still* her day," said Don. "She's Professor Emerita, remember—and without her, we wouldn't be communicating with the Dracons at all."

"Yeah, yeah," said Makoto. "But if McGavin would put some of his money behind someone who's got a chance—"

"You mean you," Don snapped.

"Why not? Better someone born this century, this millennium, than a dried-up old fossil."

Don looked down at his half-empty beer bottle, trying to remember if he was on his second or third. "You're being unfair," he said, without looking up.

"Look, Dan," Makoto said, "this isn't your field. You don't know what you're talking about."

"It's Don," Lenore said, "and maybe he should tell you who—"

"I *do* know what I'm talking about," said Don. "I've been to Arecibo. I've been to the Allen."

Makoto blinked. "You're full of shit. You're not an astronomer."

Damn. "Forget it." He got up, his chair making a loud wooden *whack* as it collided with the table behind them. Lenore looked at him in horror. She clearly thought he was going to take a swing at Makoto, and Makoto had a "just-try-it" scowl on his face. But he simply said, "I'm going to the john," and he squeezed his way past Halina and Phyllis, and headed for the stairs leading down to the basement.

It took a while to empty his bladder, which was probably just as well; it gave him some time to calm down. Christ's sake, why couldn't he have just kept his mouth shut? And he knew what conversation was going on back in the god-damn snug. "Shit, Lenore, that friend of yours is—" and Makoto would plug in whatever term kids today used for "touchy" or "crazy."

Kids today. The urinal flushed as he turned around and walked to the sink. He washed his hands, avoiding looking at his reflection, then he climbed back upstairs. When he sat down, Lenore glared expectantly at Makoto.

"Look, man," Makoto said, "I'm sorry. I didn't know she was your grandmother."

"Yeah," said Phyllis. "We're sorry."

He couldn't bring himself to respond in words, so he just nodded.

There was more conversation, although Don didn't say much, and lots of wings were eaten; the primal tearing of flesh from bone with his teeth actually helped calm him down. Finally, the bill came. After paying his share, Makoto said, "Gotta motor." He looked at Don. "Nice to meet you."

Don managed a calm tone. "And you."

"I should go, too," said Phyllis. "Got a meeting with my supervisor first thing in the morning. You coming, Halina?"

"Yeah," said Halina, the only word Don had heard from her all evening.

When they were alone, he looked at Lenore. "I'm sorry," he said.

But she lifted her rusty eyebrows. "For what? For defending your grandmother who wasn't here to defend herself? You're a good man, Donald Halifax."

"I'm sure I spoiled your fun. I'm sorry your friends don't like me, and—"

"Oh, they do. Well, maybe except for Makoto. But while you were in the washroom, Phyllis said you were gallant."

He felt his jaw go slack. "Gallant" wasn't the sort of word one normally applied to a twenty-five-year-old.

"I guess I should be going, too," he said.

"Yeah," she said. "Me, too."

They headed out the pub's doors, Don carrying his two plastic bags full of file folders. To his surprise, it was now dark; he hadn't realized how long he'd been in the pub. "Well," he said, "that was fun, thanks, but—"

Lenore seemed surprised that it had grown dark, too. "Walk

me home?" she asked. "It's only a few blocks, but my neighborhood's a bit rough."

Don looked at his watch again. "Um, sure. Okay."

She took one of the bags, and they made their way along, Lenore chatting in her animated way. It was still hot and sticky as they came to Euclid Avenue, a tree-lined downtown street filled with crumbling, ancient houses. Two beefy guys passed them. One, with a shaved head that glistened in the light of the streetlamps, had an animated tattoo of the grim reaper on his bulging right biceps. The other had laser scars on his face and arms that could easily have been erased; he was presumably wearing them as badges of honor. Lenore cast her gaze down at the cracked and broken sidewalk, and Don followed her example.

"Well," she said, a hundred meters or so farther along, "here we are." They were standing in front of a dilapidated house with dormer windows.

"Nice place," he said.

She laughed. "It's scuzbum. But it's cheap." She paused, and her face grew concerned. "Look at you! You must be parched in this heat, and it's a long walk back to the subway. Come on in. I'll give you a Diet Coke to take with you."

They walked around to the side of the house, and some animal—a raccoon, maybe—quickly moved out of their way. Lenore opened the side door and led them down the stairs.

He braced himself for the place to be a mess—he remembered his own student days—but her apartment was tidy, although the furniture was a mismatched array, presumably of garage-sale acquisitions.

"Very pleasant," said Don. "It—"

Her mouth was on his. He felt her tongue pressing against his lips. His mouth opened, and his penis grew instantly hard. Suddenly her hand was on his zipper, and—*Oh, my!*—she was on her knees, taking him into her mouth . . . but only for a few spectacular seconds. She rose to her feet, took his hands, and, walking backward, facing him, a lascivious smile on her face, she started pulling him toward the bedroom.

He followed her in.

Don was terrified that he'd come too soon. This was, after all, more excitement and stimulation than he'd had in years. But the old boy kept himself in check as he and Lenore rolled around— now him on top, now her on top—until finally he did come. He immediately went back to work until, at last, she had a shuddering orgasm, too.

"Thank you," she said, smiling at him, as they now lay side by side, each facing the other.

He lightly traced the line of her check with his index finger. "For what?"

"For, um, making sure that I . . ."

His eyebrows went up. "Of course."

"Not every guy, you know, cares . . ."

She was totally naked, and the room's lights were on. He was delighted to see that the freckles were everywhere, and that her pubic hair was the same coppery shade as the hair on her head. She seemed totally at ease with her nudity. Now that they were done, he wanted to scoot under the sheet. But her body was pinning the sheet in such a way that he couldn't get under without making a big deal out of it. But as her finger played with the hair in the middle of his chest, he was uncomfortably conscious of her scrutiny.

"No scars," she said, absently.

The dermal regeneration had gotten rid of all Don's old ones. "Just lucky, I guess."

"Well," said Lenore, whapping him playfully on the arm, "you certainly got lucky tonight." And she made a big O with her mouth.

He smiled at her. It had been *amazing*. Tender yet spirited, gentle and vigorous all at once. It wasn't quite sleeping with a supermodel—but it would do! Oh, yes, it would do!

His hand found her nipple, and he tweaked it lightly between thumb and forefinger. "The pallid bust of Pallas," he said softly, smiling at her.

Her eyes went wide. "You're the first guy I've met who knows more of that poem than just the 'nevermore' part. You don't know how sick I got of people intoning 'nevermore, nevermore' at me."

He stroked her breast gently, and said:

And the raven, never flitting
still is sitting, still is sitting

On the pallid bust of Pallas
just above my chamber door;

And his eyes have all the seeming
of a demon's that is dreaming,

And the lamp-light o'er him streaming
throws his shadow on the floor;

And my soul from out that shadow
that lies floating on the floor

Shall be lifted—nevermore!

"Wow," said Lenore, softly. "I've never had a guy recite poetry to me."

"I've never had a girl challenge me to Scrabble before."

"And I want a rematch!" she said.

He raised his eyebrows. "Now?"

"No, not now, silly." She pulled herself closer to him. "In the morning."

"I—I can't," he said. He felt her stiffen against him. "I, um, I've got a dog."

She relaxed. "Oh. Oh, okay."

"Sorry," he said. He meant "for lying," but let her take it to mean "for not being able to stay." He scanned around the room for a clock, saw one, and his heart jumped. "Look," he said, "I, um, I really do have to get going."

"Oh, all right," said Lenore, sounding not at all happy about it. "But call me! I'll give you my number . . ."

Chapter 24

DON FONDLY REMEMBERED the trip he and Sarah had taken to New Zealand in 1992. But Carl had been conceived on that trip, and his birth had put an end to them doing much traveling together for the next couple of decades; Sarah still went all sorts of places to attend conferences, but Don stayed home. He'd been quite sad to miss out on going to Paris with her in 2003 for a symposium with the nifty name "Encoding Altruism: The Art and Science of Interstellar Message Composition." But he *had* gotten to go to Puerto Rico with her in 2010 for the transmission of the official reply to Sigma Draconis. His brother Bill looked after Carl and Emily while they were away.

The city of Arecibo is about seventy-five minutes west of San Juan, and the Arecibo Observatory is ten miles south of the city, although it seemed much farther, Don had thought, as they were driven there on the twisting mountain roads. The landscape was all karst, said the driver: limestone that had been eroded to produce fissures, underground streams, caverns, and sinkholes. The Caverns Rio Camuy, one of the most spectacular cave systems in the world, were southwest of the observatory. And the great radio-telescope dish itself had been built here because nature had kindly provided a thousand-foot-wide sinkhole, perfectly shaped to hold it.

Don had been surprised to see that the dish wasn't solid. Instead, it was made of perforated aluminum slats with gaps between them, all held in place by steel guys. And beneath the dish, in the partial shade, was plenty of lush vegetation, including ferns, wild orchids, and begonias. Around the observatory grounds, Don was delighted to see mongooses, lizards, fist-sized toads, giant snails, and dragonflies.

He and Sarah were put up in one of the VSQs—"Visiting Scientist Quarters"—a wooden cabin on a hill, raised up above the uneven ground on ten cement-block pillars. The cabin had a small porch (excellent, they discovered, for watching the afternoon thunderstorms), a tiny kitchen, one little bedroom, a small bathroom, and a rotary phone. A boxy air conditioner was installed just below one of the windows, all of which were covered on the outside by wooden shutters.

Besides being technically a good choice for sending the message, Arecibo was also good symbolically. Seventy-nine-year-old Frank Drake was on hand in the control room overlooking the great dish when Sarah used a USB cable to connect her Dell notebook computer, containing the master version of the response, to the transmitter. Drake's message to M13—until this moment, the most famous SETI broadcast—had been sent from here thirty-six years previously.

As planned, the response contained a thousand completed surveys, chosen at random from the 1,206,343 sets of responses that had been uploaded to the website Sarah had helped create. Well, actually, truth be told, 999 of the sets were randomly chosen; the one thousandth was Sarah's own set, shuffled into the middle. Not that she'd snuck it in. Rather, after Don and Carl had put the notion in her head, she'd broached the topic of including her own answers at a meeting, and the PR officer for the SETI Institute had loved the idea. It made for a great human-interest angle, he said.

At the transmission ceremony, commemorative CD-ROMs containing archival copies of the message were distributed to key researchers, but the actual responses people had given weren't being made public. As per the Dracons' request, the answers were still being kept secret, so that the participants wouldn't be influenced by each others' responses when dealing with follow-up questions that might come at some point.

The control room had large floor tiles set on the diagonal, alternating in a checkerboard of beige and brown; it made Don more dizzy to look at them than it did to look out the angled window at the gigantic dish, and the 600-ton triangular instrumentation platform mounted above it.

Scientists, press, and a few other spouses were jammed into the control room. Electric fans were sitting on pieces of equipment or clamped to them, but, even though it was still early in the morning, the heat was oppressive. Don looked on as Sarah sat down at the central L-shaped desk and brought up the response on her notebook. He'd suggested she come up with a memorable phrase—her own "one small step" speech—but she'd declined; the important message was what was going to be transmitted, not anything she said. And so, with nothing more than an "All right, here we go!," Sarah clicked the on-screen button, and the word "Transmitting" appeared on the notebook's display.

Shouts went up and champagne appeared. Don stood at the periphery, enjoying seeing Sarah so happy. After a bit, the beefy, silver-haired representative of the International Astronomical Union started tapping on the side of his champagne glass with a Mont Blanc pen until he had everyone's attention.

"Sarah," he said, "we've got a little something for you." He opened one of the metal lockers mounted to the walls. Inside was a trophy, with a marble base, a central column with blue silk inserts, and, on top, winged Athena stretching toward the stars. The man bent down, picked it up, and held it at an angle in front of him, as though he were appraising a large bottle of wine. And then, in a loud, clear voice, he read out the inscription on the plaque for all to hear. " 'For Sarah Halifax,' " he said, " 'who figured it out . . .' "

DON CLIMBED UP the stairs, leaving Lenore's basement apartment. It was past 11:00 p.m., and as Lenore had said, it was a rough neighborhood. But that wasn't why his heart was pounding.

What had he done?

It had all happened so quickly, although he supposed he was naïve to not have realized how Lenore had expected the evening to turn out. But it had been sixty years since he'd really been in his twenties, and, even then, he'd missed the sexual revolution by a decade. The free love of the 1960s had been a little too early for him; like Vietnam and Watergate, they were things he had only vague childhood recollections of, and certainly no firsthand experience.

When, at fifteen, he'd started his own fumbling forays into sexuality—at least, with a partner—people had been afraid of disease. And already one girl in his class at Humberside had gotten pregnant, and that had also had a chilling effect on promiscuity. And so, even though the morality of sex had not been at issue back then—everyone of Don's generation wanted to do it, and few, at least in the middle-class Toronto suburb he grew up in, thought there was anything wrong with doing it before getting married—the act itself was still treated as a big deal, although, given what was to come a decade later, the fear of getting gonorrhea or crabs seemed downright quaint.

But how did the saying go? *Everything old is new again.* AIDS had been conquered, thank God—just about everyone Don's age knew someone who had died from that miserable plague. Most other forms of sexually transmitted disease had been wiped out, or were trivial to cure. And safe, virtually infallible, over-the-counter birth-control drugs for men and women were available here in Canada. That, coupled with a general loosening up, had led to a second era of sexual openness not seen since the heyday of Haight-Ashbury, Rochdale College, and, yes, the Beatles.

But, as Don continued along the cracked sidewalk, he knew all of that was rationalization. It didn't matter what the morality of young people today was; that wasn't his world. What mattered was what his generation—his and Sarah's—thought. He'd managed sixty years without ever once straying, and now, suddenly—*boom!*

As he rounded off of Euclid onto Bloor, he took out his datacom. "Call Sarah," he said; he needed to hear her voice.

"Hello?"

"Hi, sweetheart," he said. "How—how was the play?"

"It was fine. The guy playing Tevye didn't have a strong enough voice, I thought, but it was still good. How were your wings?"

"Great. Great. I'm just heading to the subway now."

"Oh, okay. Well, I won't wait up."

"No, no. Don't. Just leave my pajamas in the bathroom for me."

"Okay. See you later."

"Right. And . . ."

"Yes."

"I love you, Sarah."

She sounded surprised when she replied. "I love you, too."

"And I'm on my way home."

Chapter 25

"BUT I STILL don't get it," Don had said, back in 2009, after Sarah had figured out that the first message from Sigma Draconis was a survey. "I don't see why aliens should care what we think about morals and ethics. I mean, why would they give a damn?"

Sarah and Don were out for another one of their nightly walks. "Because," Sarah said, as they passed the Feins' place, "all races *will* face comparable problems as time goes on, and if the race has any individual psychological variation—which it will, unless they've done as you suggest and become a hive mind—they'll be debating those issues."

"Why do you say they must have psychological variation?" he asked.

"Because variation is the *sine qua non* of evolution: without variation, there's nothing for natural selection to act upon, and without natural selection, there's nothing to lift a species up out of the slime. Psychology is no different from any other complex trait: it's going to show variation, everywhere in the universe. And that means there'll be arguments over fundamental issues."

"Okay," he said. There was a cool breeze; he wished he'd worn a long-sleeve shirt. "But the moral issues *they* argue about and the ones *we* argue about aren't going to be the same."

Sarah shook her head. "Actually, I bet they *will* be facing the same sorts of questions we are, because advances in science will always lead to the same basic moral quandaries."

He kicked a pebble. "Like what?"

"Well, consider abortion. It was advancing science that propelled that into being a mainstream issue; the technology to reliably terminate a fetus without killing or maiming the mother is a scientific innovation. We *can* do this now, but *should* we do it?"

"But," he said, "suppose the Dracons really are dragons—you know, suppose they're reptiles. I know they probably aren't; I know the name refers to the constellation they happen to be in from our point of view. But bear with me. If you had a race of intelligent reptiles, then abortion isn't a technological issue. Smashing the egg in the nest doesn't physically harm the mother in any way."

"Yeah, okay, granted," she said. The pebble Don had kicked was now in her path, and she sent it skittering ahead. "But that's not the counterpart of abortion; the counterpart of abortion would be destroying the fertilized egg before it's laid while it's still inside the mother."

"But some fish reproduce by having the female eject unfertilized eggs into the water, and the male eject semen into the water, so that fertilization takes place outside the female's body."

"Okay, all right," said Sarah. "Beings like that wouldn't have the abortion issue in precisely the same way, but, then again, like I said on *As It Happens,* aquatic beings probably don't have radio or other technology."

"But, still, *why* is abortion a moral issue? I mean, it is for people here because we believe at some point a soul enters the body; we just can't all agree on *what* that point is. But the alien message made no mention of souls."

" 'Souls' is just a shorthand for discussing the question of when life begins, and that *will* be a universal debate—at least among those races who practice SETI."

"Why?"

"Because SETI is an activity that says life, as opposed to nonlife, is important, that finding life is meaningful. If you didn't care about the distinction between life and nonlife, all you'd do would be astronomy, not SETI. And where to draw that distinction will always be of interest to people who value life. I mean, most people would agree it's wrong to kill a dog for no reason, because a dog is clearly alive—but is an embryo alive? *That's* debatable; every race will have to define when life begins."

"Well, it either begins at conception or at birth, no?"

Sarah shook her head. "No. Even here on Earth, there are cultures that don't name kids until they've lived forty days, and I've even heard it argued that babies aren't people until they turn three or so—until they begin to form long-term, permanent memories. And even then, there's still room for moral debate. We know the Dracons reproduce sexually, shuffling their genes while doing so; that was clear from their message. And I rather suspect, by the way, that that sort of reproduction will be common throughout the universe: it provides a huge kick to evolution, getting a new genetic hand dealt with every generation instead of having to wait around for a cosmic ray to induce a random mutation in a being that otherwise just reproduces exact copies of itself. Remember, life first appeared on this planet four billion years ago, and it spent the first three and a half billion of those years basically the same. But when sex was invented half a billion years ago, in the Cambrian explosion—*boom!*—suddenly evolution was proceeding by leaps and bounds. And any race that reproduces sexually might very well still argue about the ethics of destroying a unique combination of genetic material even if they've always held that such a thing wasn't alive until the moment of birth."

Don frowned. "That's like saying it's a moral quandary to worry about destroying snowflakes. Just because something is unique doesn't make it valuable—especially when *everything* in that class of entities is unique."

A chipmunk scampered across the road in front of them. "Besides," continued Don, "speaking of evolution, doesn't the abortion issue ultimately take care of itself, given enough time? I mean, natural selection obviously would favor those people who actually put into practice being pro-life over those who actually choose to personally have abortions, because every fetus you abort is one less set of your genes around. You wait enough generations, and being pro-choice should be bred out of the population."

"Good grief!" Sarah said, shaking her head. "What a revolting thought! But, even so, that's only true if the desire for reproductive choice is merely one of passing convenience, and has nothing to do with whether the kid will make it to reproductive age without too many resources being invested. I mean, look at Barb and Barry—they've essentially devoted their whole lives to raising Freddie." Barb was Sarah's cousin; her son was severely autistic. "I love Freddie, of course, but in effect, he's replaced potential siblings who would have required a fraction of the investment and would have been far more likely to provide Barb and Barry with grandchildren."

"You know as well as I do that a vanishingly small number of abortions are because the fetus is defective," said Don. "Hell, we've had abortion for centuries, and only had prenatal screening for decades. Infanticide, that's another thing, but . . ."

"Postpartum depression has its evolutionary roots in the mother recognizing that she has insufficient resources to insure that this particular offspring will survive to reproductive age, and so the mother conserves her parental investment by cutting her losses and failing to bond with the infant. No matter how you slice it, evolution *will* conserve mechanisms that don't always lead to simply having the most offspring. Anyway, setting aside abortion, I still think most races *will* face very similar moral issues as they develop technology that expands their powers. I know the aliens didn't mention God—"

"That's right," Don said smugly.

"—but every race that survives long enough will eventually struggle with the ramifications of getting to *play* God."

It was growing dark; the streetlights flickered on. "'God' is a very loaded term," he said.

"Maybe so, but we don't have a lot of synonyms for the concept: if you define God as the creator of the universe, all races that live long enough eventually become Gods."

"Huh?"

"Think about it. We'll eventually be able to simulate reality so well that it will be indistinguishable from . . . well, from reality, right?"

"One of my favorite authors once said, 'Virtual reality is nothing but air guitar writ large.'"

She snorted, then continued: "And a sufficiently complex virtual reality could simulate living beings so well that they themselves will actually think they're alive."

"I suppose," he said.

"For sure. Have you seen that game *The Sims* that Carl likes to play? The simulations of reality we can make today are already amazing, and we've only had digital computers for—what?—sixty-five years now. Imagine what sort of reality you could simulate if you had a thousand or a million or a billion times more computing power at hand—which we, or any technological race that lives long enough, eventually will. Again, where do you draw the line between life and nonlife? What rights do those simulated lifeforms have? Those are moral issues all races will have to face."

Another couple, also out for a walk, was coming toward them. Don smiled at them as they passed.

"In fact," she continued, "you could argue there's even some evidence that we ourselves are precisely that: digital creations."

"I'm listening."

"There's a smallest possible length in our universe. The Planck length: 1.6×10^{-35} meters, or about 10^{-20} times the size of a proton, you can't measure a length any smaller than that, supposedly because of quantum effects."

"Okay."

"And," she said, "there must be a smallest unit of time, too, if you think about it: since a particle of light has to be either *here*, at Planck length unit A, or *next to it*, at Planck length unit B, then the time it takes to move from one unit to the next—the time it takes a photon to click over from being in *this* Planck space-unit to *that* Planck space-unit—is the smallest possible bit of time. And that unit, the Planck time, is 10^{-43} seconds."

"The Clock of the Short Now," said Don, pleased with himself.

"Exactly! But think about what that means! We live in a universe made up of discrete little bits of space that's aging in discrete little chunks of time—a universe that has pixels of distance and duration. We *are* digital at the most fundamental level."

"Quantum physics not as the basic nature of reality, but rather as the—how would you put it?—as a by-product of the level of resolution of our simulated world." He made an impressed face. "Cool."

"Thanks," she said. "But that means our world, with its pixels of time and space, might be nothing more than some far-advanced civilization's version of *The Sims*—and *that* would mean there's a programmer somewhere."

"I wonder what his email address is," Don said. "I've got some tech-support questions."

"Yeah, well, just remember once you open the seal on the universe, you can't get your money back." They turned a corner. "And speaking of making universes, with particle accelerators we may eventually be able to create daughter universes, budding off from this one. Of course, we won't create a full-blown universe, with stars and galaxies; we'd just create an appropriate singularity, like the one that our universe burst forth from in the big bang, and then the new universe will make itself from that. Physics says it's possible—and I rather suspect it's only a matter of time before someone successfully does it."

"I get it," said Don. "If you take a step back, that means *we* could be living in a universe created by a scientist in some parent universe's particle accelerator."

"Exactly!" said Sarah. "And, look, you know I love following all those debates in the U.S. about the teaching of evolution and intelligent design. Well, I'm an evolutionist—you know that—but I don't agree with the testimony that the scientists on the evolution side keep giving. They keep saying that science cannot admit supernatural causes, by which they mean that any scientific explanation has to, by definition, be limited to causes intrinsic to this universe."

"What's wrong with that?"

"*Everything* is wrong with it," she said. "That definition of science prevents us from ever concluding that *we* are the product of the work of other scientists, working in a reality above this one. It leaves us with the cockeyed mess of having a scientific worldview that on the one hand freely acknowledges that we will eventually be able to simulate reality perfectly, or maybe even create daughter universes, but on the other hand is constrained against ever allowing that we ourselves might exist in one of those things."

"Maybe science isn't interested in that question simply because it doesn't really answer anything," Don said. "I suspect somebody like Richard Dawkins would say, so what if we are the creation of some other intelligent being? That doesn't answer the question of where that other intelligent being came from."

"But science—and in particular, evolutionary science, which is Dawkins's forte—is largely about tracing lineages, and filling in the stages. If you took a comparable view of evolution, you'd have to say that wondering whether birds really evolved from dinosaurs is a dumb question to bother with, as is wondering whether Lucy was one of our ancestors, since the only truly interesting question is how the original, common ancestor of all life came into being. That's wrong; it's *one* interesting question, but it's hardly the only one worth asking. Whether we live in a created universe *is* an inherently interesting question, and it's worthy of scientific investigation. And if a creator does exist, or if a race becomes such a creator itself, that immediately raises the moral question of what, if any, accountability or obligation the creations have to that creator—and the flipside, and the part that I think we don't spend nearly enough time debating, which is what if any accountability or obligation our possible creator has to *us*."

Don took a big step sideways, and looked up at the dark sky. "Hey, God," he said, "be careful with your aim . . ."

"No, seriously," said Sarah. "Technology gives a species the power to prevent life, to create life, to take life on scales small and large; technology ultimately gives the power to be what we would call Gods, and, even if our definition of science is blind to it, it raises the possibility that what we are is the result of the work of some other being that would, by virtue of having created us, also deserve that term God. Doesn't mean we have to worship it—but it *does* mean that we, and any other technologically advanced race, will have to deal with ethical questions related both to potentially being Gods ourselves and potentially being the children of Gods."

They jogged across the street, beating an oncoming car. "And so the aliens from Sigma Drac wrote to us asking for our *advice?*" asked Don. He shook his head. "Heaven help them."

Chapter 26

SARAH HAD SAID one of the appeals of becoming young again would be having time to read all the great books. Don couldn't quite say that the book he was looking at now—a thriller of the type that would have been sold in drug-store spinner racks when he'd been young the first time—was great, but it was a pleasure to be able to read for hours without getting eye fatigue, and without having to put on his cheaters. Still, eventually, he did get bored with the book, and so he had his datacom scan the TV listings for anything that might interest him, and—

"Hey," he said, looking up from the list the device had provided, "Discovery is showing that old documentary about the first message."

Sarah, seated on the couch, looked over at him; he was leaning back in the chair. "What old documentary?" she said.

"You know," he said, a little impatiently, "that hour-long thing they did when you sent the initial reply to Sigma Draconis."

"Oh," said Sarah. "Yeah."

"Don't you want to watch it?"

"No. I'm sure we've got a recording of it somewhere, anyway."

"Doubtless in some format we can't read anymore. I'm going to put it on."

"I wish you wouldn't," she said.

"Oh, come on!" said Don. "It'll be fun." He looked at the panel above the fireplace. "TV on; Discovery Channel." The picture was razor-sharp and the colors vibrant. Don had forgotten they'd had high-definition TV that long ago; he found lots of older shows unwatchable now, because they'd been videotaped in low-res.

The documentary was already under way. Some aerial footage of the Arecibo radio telescope was being shown, and the voice of a Canadian actor—was it Maury Chaykin?—was doing the narration. Soon, that was replaced with a potted history of SETI: the Drake equation, Project OZMA, the *Pioneer 10* plaque, the *Voyager* records—which, it was duly noted, this being the Canadian version of Discovery Channel, had been designed by Toronto's own Jon Lomberg. Don had forgotten how much of the documentary *wasn't* about Sarah and her work. Maybe he'd go into the kitchen to get a drink, and—

And suddenly, there she was, on the screen, and—

And he looked over at his wife, seated on the couch, then back at the monitor, then shifted his gaze between the two once more. She was steadfastly staring at the fireplace, it seemed, not the magphotic panel above it, and she was red in the face, as if embarrassed, because—

Because she looked so much younger, so much less frail, on the monitor. After all, this had been recorded thirty-eight years ago, back when she was forty-nine. It was a sort of rollback, a regressing to a younger state; oh, to be sure, not nearly as far back as he had gone, but still a bitter taste of what might have been.

"I'm sorry, sweetheart," he said, softly, and then, more loudly, into the air: "TV off."

She looked over at him, her face expressionless. "I'm sorry, too," she said.

AS THE DAY wore on, Sarah went up to Carl's old room, to work through the giant stack of papers Don had brought her from the University.

Don, meanwhile, went down to the basement. He and Sarah had almost given up on using the rec room as they'd gotten older.

The stairs down to it were particularly steep, and there was a banister only on the wall side. But he now had no trouble going down there, and, on these hot summer days, it was the coolest place in the house.

Not to mention the most private.

He sat on the old couch there, and looked about, a fluttering in his stomach. History had been made here. Right over there, Sarah had figured out the meat of the original message. And history might be made in this house again, if she could decrypt the Dracons' latest transmission. Perhaps someday there'd be a plaque on their front lawn.

Don was holding his datacom tightly in his hand, and its plastic shell was now moist with his perspiration. Although he'd fantasized about seeing Lenore again, he knew that could never happen. But she'd made him promise to call, and he couldn't just ignore her, couldn't leave her hanging. That would be wrong, mean, petty. No, he had to call her up and say good-bye properly. He'd tell her the truth, tell her there was someone else.

He took a deep breath, let it out slowly, opened the datacom, snapped it immediately shut, and then, at last, opened it once more, gingerly, as though lifting the lid on a coffin.

And he spoke to the little device, telling it who he wanted to contact, and—

Rings. The tolling of a bell. And then—

A squeaky voice. "Hello?"

"Hi, Lenore," he said, his heart jackhammering. "It's Don."

Silence.

"You know, Don Halifax."

"Hello," Lenore said again, this time her tone icy cold.

"Look, I'm sorry I haven't called you, but . . ."

"It *has* been three days."

"Yes, I know, I know, and I'm sorry. I really did mean to call. I didn't want you to think I was one of those guys who . . . well, you know, one of those guys who doesn't call."

"Could have fooled me," she said.

He cringed. "I'm sorry. You deserve way better—"

"Yes, I do."

"I know. But, look, I—"

"Didn't you have a good time?"

"I had a great time," he said. And he had—just about the only time he'd been happy for weeks now. Not just the sex, but just being with someone who could keep up with him, and—

Lenore sounded relieved. "Good. 'Cause, I did too. You . . . you're really something."

"Um, thanks. So are you. But, um . . ."

"Look," she said, her tone conveying that she was making a special dispensation, "I'm busy at the food bank tomorrow. But I'm free on Sunday. Maybe we could get together then?"

No, thought Don.

"What did you have in mind?" he said, astonished to hear himself speak the words.

"The forecast says it's going to be gorgeous. Why don't we go down to Centre Island?"

I cannot do this, he thought. *I will not do this.*

"Don?" said Lenore, into what had become an uncomfortable silence.

He closed his eyes. "Sure," he said. "Sure, why not?"

DON HAD ARRIVED at the ferry docks at the foot of Bay Street about ten minutes early, and he kept scanning the crowds, looking for—

Ah, there she was: the rare and radiant maiden whom the angels named Lenore. She came running over to him, in white short-shorts and a loose-fitting white top, clutching a giant sun hat. She stretched up and kissed him quickly on the mouth, and then pulled back, smiling, and—

And he was stunned. In his mind, he'd aged her forward: he'd been picturing her as being in her mid-thirties, which seemed a more appropriate age for someone he might want to talk to, but here she was, freckled and fresh-faced, looking ten years younger than that.

They boarded the *Max Haines*, a white, double-decker ferry, and took the kilometer-and-a-half journey to Centre Island, with its boardwalks, beaches, amusement park, and gardens.

Lenore had wanted to come down here, she said, because she missed the water. But the result was not proving entirely satisfactory: gulls eating garbage were no substitute for Vancouver's great blue herons, and, besides, there was no salt tang to the air. Once they'd docked, they jogged for about half an hour. Don found that exhilarating, and he loved to feel his hair—yes, hair!—whipping in the breeze.

After that, they just strolled along a paved walkway, gingerly trying to avoid all the goose droppings. Off to their right was the bay, and across it was Toronto itself, with the skyline that Don had watched grow and spread over the better part of a century. It was still dominated by the CN Tower, once, but certainly no longer, the tallest freestanding structure in the world; as a teenager, he had gone downtown with his friend Ivan to watch a Sikorsky Skycrane assemble its huge components. Blockish skyscrapers, like the elements of a bar chart, trailed off left and right from the Tower. He recalled when Toronto's downtown had been a tiny cluster of tall buildings, but now it went on and on along the lakeshore, west toward Mississauga, and east until the Scarborough Bluffs forced it to stop.

More than just the skyline had changed during Don's lifetime—and yet some things *hadn't* changed nearly as much as he'd expected. He remembered seeing *2001: A Space Odyssey* with his dad when it had come out, back in 1968. The nice thing about being born in a year that ends in a zero was that it made math simple. Even as a kid, he knew he'd be forty-one in 2001, and his father, sitting next to him at Toronto's Glendale Theatre, had been forty-three then, meaning Don would be younger than him when the wonders that film portrayed were supposed to come to pass: Pan Am space planes, giant wheel-shaped space stations with Howard Johnson hotels, cities on the moon, humans traveling out to Jupiter, cryogenic suspended animation, and—*Open the pod-bay doors, Hal*—true artificial intelligence.

But by the time the actual 2001 had rolled around, none of those things were realities. So perhaps Don shouldn't have been too surprised that the extravagant wonders predicted in the science fiction of the first decade of the new millennium likewise hadn't materialized. The technological singularity had never happened; extreme body modification, either through genetic engineering or with artificial parts, never became popular; the nanotech assembler that could turn anything into anything else was still the stuff of dreams.

Don looked out over the water, back at the city he'd been born in. Nestled at the foot of the CN Tower was the stadium where the Blue Jays played. He pointed at it. "See? The roof's open on SkyDome."

Lenore looked at him as though he were speaking a foreign language, and—

Oh, shit. *He* still referred to it as SkyDome; so did lots of people his age. But that hadn't been its name for over forty years. Christ, the gap between them was everywhere, in everything. "The Rogers Centre, I mean. The, um, the roof is open." It was such a trivial observation, he was sorry now he'd made it.

"Well, it *is* a lovely day," said Lenore. It buoyed him that she made no further comment on what he'd said.

They were holding hands as they walked, skateboarders, hoverpadders, rollerbladers, and joggers passing them in both directions. She was wearing her big, floppy hat; with her pale skin, she doubtless burned easily. For his part, he was enjoying being out in the sun *without* having to wear a hat. After four decades of baldness, it was wonderful to have his own built-in protection.

They'd talked about this and that: a lively, animated conversation, so unlike—what had one of his friends called it?—the companionable silence of old married people who had, decades ago, run out of points of view to share or jokes to tell or issues to explore.

"Do you play tennis?" Lenore asked, as they passed a couple of people carrying racquets.

"I haven't since . . ." *Since before you were born.*

"We should play sometime. I can get you a guest pass to Hart House."

"That'd be great," Don said. And he meant it. He'd been sedentary the first time he'd been this age; now, he was loving the sheer physicality of being alive. "You realize I'm going to beat your pants, off, though. I mean, I'm medically enhanced."

She grinned. "Oh, yeah?"

"Sure. Just call me Bjorn Borg."

She looked at him, totally baffled, and his heart fell a bit. Sarah would have gotten the joke.

"Um," he said, painfully aware of Johnny Carson's dictum that it isn't funny if you have to explain it, "Bjorn Borg was a famous tennis player; won Wimbledon five times in a row. And the Borg, well, they're this alien race on an old TV show called *Star Trek*. The Borg augment their bodies with technology, so, um . . ."

"You are a supremely silly man," Lenore said, smiling warmly at him.

He stopped dead in his tracks, and looked—*really* looked, for the first time—at Lenore.

She was a grad student studying SETI.

She liked to eat in restaurants, to talk about philosophy and politics.

She was confident and funny and a joy to be with.

And now she was even *talking* like—

But he'd missed putting it together until just now. She reminded him of—

Of course. Of course.

She reminded him of Sarah as *she'd* been back in her twenties, back when Don had fallen in love with her.

Oh, true, they looked nothing alike physically, and perhaps that's why he'd failed to notice all the other similarities when they'd been together before. Lenore was shorter than Sarah, or, at least, shorter than Sarah had been in her prime. And Sarah had originally had brown hair, and still had blue-gray eyes, while Lenore was redheaded, freckled, and green-eyed.

But in spirit, in attitude, in the joy they took in life, they were kindred spirits.

Coming toward them was a young couple: an Asian woman and a white man, the man pushing a stroller. Don was wearing sunglasses—as was Lenore—so he felt no compunction about looking at the beautiful young woman, with long black hair, wearing pink shorts and a red tank top.

"Cute kid," said Lenore.

"Um, yeah," said Don. He hadn't even noticed.

"Do you—do you like kids?" Lenore asked, a tentative note in her voice.

"Sure. Of course."

"Me, too," she said.

There was a park bench on the grass a short distance from the walkway, facing back across the water toward the city. Don pointed at it with his chin, and they went over and sat. He put his arm around her shoulders, and they stared out at the water, watching a ferry coming toward them.

"Do you want to have kids of your own?" he asked.

"Oh, yeah. Definitely."

"How soon?"

She leaned her head against his shoulder. Her hair was blowing a bit in the breeze, occasionally gently slapping his cheek. "Oh, I don't know. By the time I'm thirty, I suppose. I know that's a long time from now, but . . ."

She trailed off, but he found himself shaking his head. Five years would go by like *that*; it seemed only yesterday he'd been in his seventies. Hell, it hardly seemed that long ago that he'd been in his sixties. The years just fly by, and—

And he wondered if that would still be true. He'd certainly experienced the phenomenon of time seeming to pass more quickly as he'd gotten older, and he'd read the pop-psychology explanation for it: that, when you're a kid of ten, each year is a whopping ten percent of your life to date, and so seems ponderously long, but by the time you're fifty, each year is just two percent of your life, and so passes in the wink of an eye. He wondered what would happen to his time sense now that he was young again. He'd be one of the first people ever to get to test the validity of the standard explanation.

Lenore said nothing more; she just looked out at the lake. Still, it was ironic, he realized. She was thinking farther into the future than he was. But he'd thought he was *done* with the future, and, although he knew that poem, too, he hadn't planned on raging against the dying of the light . . .

In five years, Lenore would likely have a Ph.D., and be well on her way in her career.

And in five years, Sarah would probably be . . .

He hated to think about it, but it was all but inevitable. By 2053, Sarah would almost certainly be gone, and he'd—

He'd be alone. Unless—

Unless he . . .

Unless he found somebody else.

But he'd seen at the grad students' wing night just how vapid most twenty-five-year-olds were. People who shared his apparent physical age would never appeal to him intellectually, emotionally. Lenore, somehow, was different, and—

And it was way too soon to go further with this conversation, but the reality was clear: his future with Lenore, or, he imagined, with just about any woman who was as young as he looked, would depend on his being willing to be a father again.

But, God, to have more kids! Could he face late-night feedings, and changing diapers, and being a disciplinarian?

And yet . . .

And yet perhaps people would forgive him his transgressions if someday he did start a second family. He knew that no matter how *logical* it might be for him to want the company of someone so much younger than Sarah, in the eyes of his friends and family that would be seen as tawdry, thinking with his dick instead of his brain. But if they thought his desire was to be a father again, well, then maybe that wasn't quite so bad.

In this age of open sexuality online and off, it was probably no longer true, but in Don's day, many men he knew had had a favorite *Playboy* Playmate, and his had been Vicki Smith, or, at least, that had been the name he'd first encountered the five-foot-eleven, Rubenesque Texan under, when she was Miss May 1992. But by the time she'd been named Playmate of the Year in 1993, she'd changed her stage name to Anna Nicole Smith. And she became even more famous when, at twenty-six, she married a billionaire who was almost ninety.

That's the comparison people of his generation would make, he knew. Except that he wasn't a billionaire, although he'd gotten what that crazed old coot doubtless would have traded his entire fortune for. And it was he, not the woman, who was fake. Anna Nicole Smith had had an A-cup before breast implants pushed her three letters down the alphabet. But Lenore was natural—well, as natural as anyone these days. It was Don who'd had himself remade, although somehow, at least to him, gene therapy and the lengthening of telomeres seemed less creepy than having your chest carved open and bags of silicone shoved inside.

Still, an eighty-seven-year-old man and a twenty-five-year-old woman! The things people would say! But if he eventually had more kids, became a dad to little ones again, well, then, that was good and normal and right, and maybe everyone would understand, everyone would forgive.

Of course, that was no reason to become a father, but, hell, he hadn't given it *any* thought the first time; it hadn't taken any justification. It had just seemed the most natural thing in the world when he and Sarah had gotten married.

Three ducks landed on the lake, small wakes appearing behind them. Lenore snuggled closer to Don. "It's such a beautiful day," she said.

He nodded, and stroked her shoulder gently, wondering what the future might hold.

Chapter 27

DON HAD HAD a truly wonderful time both down at the Island and afterwards, back at Lenore's. But she had a lot of reading to do for a seminar tomorrow, so extricating himself at the end of the day had not been an issue. Sarah, meanwhile, had said she was going to stay in all day—she was still sorting through the mountain of paper records about the first message—and as Don headed toward the subway, he was startled that the answering machine picked up when he tried to call his house. Of course, Sarah's hearing wasn't what it used to be; she might simply have not heard the phone ringing, or she might be out, or—

"Where is Sarah's datacom?" he said to his own unit.

"At home," the device replied, after connecting with its twin. "On her nightstand."

Don felt himself frowning; she wouldn't have gone out without it, and he'd tried now calling both her datacom and their landline household phone. Something was wrong; he just knew it.

He started jogging toward St. George subway station; the parts between here and that station, and between his home station of North York Centre and his front door, were the only segments of the journey he could speed up. The rest would happen at what he was sure would seem the snail's pace of the Toronto Transit Commission's trains—taking a taxi all the way up to North York would cost a fortune and would be no faster.

As luck would have it, he got through the turnstile and down the escalator just in time to see the doors close on the eastbound train, and he had to wait an interminable time—this being Sunday evening—for the next one to pull into the station.

His datacom worked just fine down in tunnels, but each time he called, his household phone rang and rang until his own voice—his own *previous* voice, the thin, weary version of it that sounded so different from the way he currently did—came on, saying, "Hello. Neither Sarah nor I can come to the phone right now . . ."

Don sat, looking down at the gray, dirty floor, holding his face up with his hands.

Finally, after an eternity, the subway arrived at North York Centre, and he bounded out of the car. He ran up the escalator, through a turnstile, and exited onto Park Home Avenue, which was dark and deserted. He jogged the three blocks to his house, trying once more to call along the way, but to no avail. At last, he opened his front door, and—

She was lying facedown on the scuffed hardwood floor in front of the mirrored closet. "Sarah!"

Her limbs were splayed, and the lightweight summer dress she was wearing had billowed about her like a shroud. It seemed clear that she'd taken a tumble coming down the stairs to the entryway. "Sarah, are you all right?"

She stirred, lifting her head a little.

"No," said Don. "No, no. Don't move!"

"My leg," she said softly. "My God, you should have heard the *snap* . . ."

He'd learned some first aid years ago. "This one?" he said, touching her right leg.

"No. The other one."

He shifted the dress so that he could see her leg, and the bruising and swelling were obvious. He touched it gingerly, and he saw Sarah wince. There was no phone in the entryway; Sarah would have had to have pulled herself up the six stairs to the living room to call him; she had neither the sense of balance nor the strength in her other leg to hop. He got out his datacom, and said to it, "Nine-one-one," a term now used as a name in this post-phone-number age.

"Fire, police, or ambulance?" asked the operator.

"Ambulance," Don said. "Please hurry!"

"You're calling from a mobile device," the operator said, "but we have the GPS coordinates. You're at—" and she read the address to him. "Correct?"

"Yes, yes."

"What's happened?"

He gulped for air. "My wife—she's eighty-seven, and she's fallen down some stairs."

"I've dispatched the ambulance," said the operator. "The data-com you're calling from is registered to Donald R. Halifax; is that you?"

"Yes."

"Is your wife conscious, Mr. Halifax?"

"Yes. But her leg is broken. I'm sure of it."

"Don't move her, then. Don't try to move her."

"I won't. I haven't."

"Is the door to your house unlocked?"

He looked up. The door was still wide open. "Yes."

"All right. Don't leave her."

Don took his wife's hand. "No, no, I won't." God, why hadn't he been here? He looked into her pale blue eyes, which were bloodshot and half-closed. "I won't leave her. I swear I won't ever leave her."

He finished with the operator, and put the datacom down on the floor. "I'm sorry," he said to Sarah. "I'm so sorry."

"It's all right," she said, weakly. "I knew you'd be home soon, although . . ."

She left the thought unspoken, but doubtless she'd been think-ing he should have been home earlier than this.

"I'm sorry," Don said again, his gut clenching. "I'm sorry, I'm sorry, I am so sorry . . ."

"It's okay," insisted Sarah, and she managed a small smile. "No permanent damage done, I'm sure. After all, this is the age of miracle and wonder." A song lyric, from their youth. Don recognized it, but shook his head slightly, lost. She gestured with her head at him, and, after a moment, he got it: she was referring to his new, younger form. Now *she* was holding *his* hand, comforting him. "It'll be all right," she said. "Everything will be fine."

He couldn't meet her eyes as they waited and waited until, at last, the ambulance's siren drowned out the thoughts that were torturing him, and everything was bathed in strobing red through the open front door.

Chapter 28

FORTUNATELY, IT WAS a clean, simple fracture. Orthopedics had come a long way since Don had broken his own leg in 1977, during a high-school football game. The pieces of Sarah's femur were aligned, some of the excess fluid was drained off, Sarah was given the calcium infusion into her legs that she would have received anyway had the rejuvenation process worked on her, and a small external support was erected around her leg—these days, only dinosaur bones were wrapped in plaster. The doctor said she'd be fine in two months, and, with the support, which had its own little motors, she wouldn't even need crutches while she healed, although a cane was advisable.

Fortunately, too, their provincial health plan covered all this. Most of the crises in Canadian health care had passed. Yes, there'd been a period when biotechnology had been young during which costs had spiraled out of control, but all technologies come down in price with time, even medical ones. Procedures that cost hundreds of thousands of dollars in Don's youth now cost a tiny fraction of that. Even sophisticated pharmaceuticals were so inexpensive to develop and produce that governments could give them away in the Third World. Why, someday, even the magic of rejuvenation would be available to all those who wanted it.

Once they got home from the hospital, Don helped Sarah get ready for bed. Within minutes of lying down, she was asleep, helped into the arms of Morpheus, no doubt, by the painkillers the doctor had prescribed.

Don, however, couldn't sleep. He just lay on his back, staring up in the dark at the ceiling, an occasional band of light caused by a passing car sweeping across it.

He loved Sarah. He'd loved her for almost his entire life. And he never, ever wanted to hurt her. But when she'd needed him, he wasn't there for her.

He heard a siren in the distance; someone else with their own crisis, just like the one they'd faced today.

No. No, *they* hadn't faced it. *Sarah* had faced it—facedown, on the hard wooden floor, waiting hour after hour for him to return while he fucked a woman less than half—Christ, less than a third!—his age.

He rolled onto his side, his back to the sleeping Sarah, his body tucked into a fetal position, hugging himself. His eyes focused on the softly glowing blue numerals of a digital clock on his nightstand, and he watched the minutes crawl by.

FOR THE FIRST time in years, Sarah was sitting in the La-Z-Boy with it reclined. It was, she said, easier and more comfortable to have her injured leg stretched out.

Despite hardly sleeping at all the previous night, Don was unable to rest; he kept pacing. She had once quipped that they'd both fallen in love with this house at first sight—her because of the fireplace, him because of the long, narrow living room that just cried out for someone to march back and forth in it.

"What are you going to do today?" Sarah asked him. The foot-high digits on the wall monitor showed 9:22 a.m. The windows on either side of the fireplace had polarized, reducing the August sunshine to a tolerable level.

He halted in his pacing for a moment and looked at his wife. "Do?" he said. "I'm going to stay here, look after you."

But she shook her head. "You can't spend the rest of your life—the rest of *my* life—as a shut-in. I see how much energy you've got. Look at yourself! You can't sit still."

"Yes, but—"

"But what? I'll be fine."

"You weren't fine yesterday," he said, and he resumed walking. "And . . ."

"And what?" said Sarah.

He said nothing, his back to her. But people who'd been married so long could finish each other's sentences, even when one of them didn't want the other to do so. "And it's only going to get worse, right?" said Sarah.

Don tilted his head, conceding that she'd guessed correctly. He looked out the brown-tinged window. They'd bought this place in 1988, just after getting married, his parents, and Sarah's, too, helping with the down payment. Back then, Betty Ann Drive had had a few skinny trees here and there, plus one or two large blue spruces. Now, those skinny trees, planted for free by the City of North York, a municipality that didn't even exist anymore, had grown to be tall, luxurious maples and oaks.

He continued walking, now approaching her. "You need me here," he said, "to take care of you."

She looked down at her leg encased in the armature. "I need *someone,* yes. Maybe Percy—"

"Percy starts grade eight in two weeks," he said. "He'll be too busy. And Carl and Emily both work during the day. And we can't afford to hire a home-care worker."

"We could if . . ." she began, and he mentally finished *that* sentence: *if we sold the house.*

He looked out one of the windows again. Yes, this house, small though it was, was bigger than they needed, and had been since Emily had moved out more than twenty years ago. Maybe they *should* sell it. As was now painfully obvious, Sarah was having real trouble with the stairs. Moving to an apartment would free up money *and* deal with that problem.

He'd reached the far end of the room and turned around, facing his wife again, and he saw her expression brighten. "You know what we need?" she said. "A Mozo."

"Mozo?" He said it the way she had, with two long-O sounds.

She nodded. "You know what that is?"

"I know it's worth fifteen points."

Sarah frowned. "It means 'male servant,'" she said. "It's from the Spanish. But it's also the brand name for a line of robots designed to help the elderly."

Don narrowed his eyes. "They make such things?"

"See what I mean?" said Sarah. "You have *got* to get out more. Yes, they make such things, if by 'they,' you mean McGavin Robotics."

He stopped pacing. "Even a low-end bot costs a fortune."

"Sure. But Cody thinks I've got some special insight into decrypting the response from Sigma Drac. I'll tell him I need a Mozo. It wouldn't be a lie. I could easily get more done with someone to serve as a research assistant, get me coffee, and so on. And it would mean I'd never be alone. You could go out without worrying about me."

He thought about complaining that the last time they'd taken charity from McGavin, it hadn't worked out so well. But Sarah was right. He'd go nuts if he had to stay home all the time, and, well, a housebot would make a lot of things easier, wouldn't it?

Chapter 29

IT WAS AS though Ikea sold mechanical men. The Mozo arrived disassembled in a cubic crate that measured about a meter on a side. Don found it disconcerting seeing the head in a plastic bag, and it took him a good five minutes to figure out how to connect the legs (which were stored folded in half at the knee). But, at last, it was done. The robot was sky blue trimmed with silver; its body was covered with a soft material like that used to make wet suits. It had a round head about the size of a basketball, with two glassy eyes. And it had a mouth, of sorts. He had seen similar things on some other robots he'd run into: a horizontal black line beneath the eyes that could animate to match speech patterns. Although the market for robots that looked more or less human was small, people did like robots to have some facial expression.

Don couldn't help comparing their new robot to the fictional bots of his youth. He decided that, except for the mouth, it looked most like one of those from the old Gold Key comic *Magnus, Robot Fighter*. And, he had to admit, it *was* way cool having one, and not just because it let him put a check mark beside another of those twenty items on his old high-school list of things to do.

He looked at the Mozo, another modern miracle they couldn't afford. "Well," he said, hands on his hips, "what do you think?"

"It looks nice enough," said Sarah. "Shall we turn it on?"

Don was amused to see that the switch was a recessed button in the middle of the robot's torso; their Mozo had an innie. He pressed the switch, and—

"Hello," said a plain male voice. The mouth outline moved in a cartoonish approximation of the shapes human lips would have made. "Do you speak English? *Hola. Habla Español? Bonjour. Parlez-vous français? Konichi-wa. Nihongo-o hanashimasu-ka?*"

"English," said Don.

"Hello," said the robot again. "This is the first time I've been activated since leaving the factory, so I need to ask you a few questions, please. First, from whom do I take instructions?"

"Me and her," Don said.

The robot nodded its basketball head. "By default, I will call you ma'am and you sir. However, if you prefer, I can address you any way you like."

Don grinned. "I am the Great and All-Powerful Oz."

The robot's mouth outline moved in a way that suggested the machine knew Don was kidding. "A pleasure to meet you, Great and All-Powerful Oz."

Sarah looked at the robot with a "see what I have to put up with" expression. Don smiled sheepishly, and she said, "Call him Don. And you can call me Sarah."

"A pleasure to meet you, Don and Sarah. What you are hearing is my default voice. However, if you prefer me to use a female voice or a different accent, I can. Would you like that?"

Don looked at Sarah. "No, this is fine," she said.

"All right," said the robot. "Have you chosen a name for me yet?"

Sarah lifted her shoulders and looked at Don. "Gunter," he said.

"Is that G-U-N-T-H-E-R?" asked the robot.

"No *H*," said Don. And then, unable to help himself, "Get the *H* out."

"My little boy," Sarah said, smiling at Don. She'd said that often enough over the years, but, just now, it seemed to hit a little too close to home. She must have noticed his quickly suppressed wince, because she immediately said, "Sorry."

Still, he thought, she was right. He *was* a kid at heart, at least when it came to robots. And his absolute favorite when he was growing up, as Sarah well knew, was the robot from *Lost in Space*. He got miffed whenever people called that robot Robby, although Robby, the robot from the movie *Forbidden Planet*, did bear a passing resemblance to the one from *Lost in Space*—not surprising, given that they were both designed by the same person, Robert Kinoshita. The *Jupiter 2*'s robot was mostly just referred to as "the Robot" (or the "bubble-headed booby" and a hundred other alliterative insults by Dr. Smith). Still, many hardcore *Lost in Space* fans called it B-9, which was the model number it gave for itself in one episode. But Don had always contended that the barrel-chested automaton with vacuum-cleaner hoses for arms was actually named GUNTER, because another episode contained a flashback, showing the robot in its original packing crate, which was labeled "General Utility Non-Theorizing Environmental Robot." Despite pointing this out to people for—God, for over seventy years now—Don hadn't won many converts. But at least now there was a robot in the world who indisputably had that name.

Of course, thought Don, Sarah understood all this. She'd grown up watching *Lost in Space*, too, although what she'd loved most about it were the photos of real nebulas and galaxies used in space scenes ("Astronomical Photographs Copyrighted 1959 by the California Institute of Technology," the card on the ending credits said). But, he realized sadly, none of this would mean anything to Lenore or anyone else who was as young as he felt.

They continued responding to Gunter's questions for about half an hour, outlining the sorts of duties he was to perform, whether he should answer the phone or door, advising him not to enter the bathrooms when they were occupied unless he heard a call for help, and so on.

But Gunter's principal job was making sure Sarah was safe and well. And so Don said, "Do you know CPR?"

"Yes."

"What about the Heimlich maneuver?" asked Sarah.

"That, too. I'm fully trained in first aid. I can even perform an emergency tracheotomy, if need be, and my palms have built-in defibrillator pads."

"See!" said Don. "He is like Gunter. The real Gunter could shoot lightning out of his claws."

Sarah looked at Don with an affectionate grin. "The *real* Gunter?"

Don laughed. "You know what I mean." He looked at the blue machine. "What do we do with you when we go to bed?" he asked. "Do we turn you off?"

"You may if you wish," said Gunter, and he smiled reassuringly. "But I suggest you leave me on so that I can respond instantly to any emergency. You can also set me tasks to perform while you're sleeping: I can dust and do other chores, and have a hot breakfast ready for you when you get up."

Don looked around the living room, and his eyes landed on the fireplace. "Do you know how to make a fire?"

The robot tilted his head a little to one side, and, if glass lenses could be said to have a faraway look, Gunter's did for a second. "I do now," he said.

"Great," said Don. "We'll have to get some wood, come winter."

"Do you get bored if you have nothing to do?" asked Sarah.

"No," said the robot, and he smiled that reassuring smile again. "I'm content just to relax."

"An admirable trait," said Sarah, glancing at Don. "I wonder how we ever got along without one."

Chapter 30

DON FOUND HIMSELF feeling more and more confused with each passing day. He'd had a handle on life, damn it all. He'd understood its rhythms, its stages, and he'd moved through them all, in the proper sequence, surviving each one.

Youth, he knew, had been for education, for the first phase of professional development, for exploring sexual relationships.

Mature adulthood had meant a committed marriage, raising children, and consolidating whatever material prosperity he had been entitled to.

After that had come middle age, a time for reevaluation. He'd managed to avoid the affair and sports car then; his midlife crisis, precipitated by a minor heart attack, had finally spurred him to lose weight, and hearing so many women—and some men— tell him how good he looked, how he was hotter at forty-five than he'd been at thirty, had been tonic enough to help him weather those years without needing to do anything more to prove he was still attractive.

And, finally—or so it should have been—there had been the so-called golden years: retirement, becoming a grandparent, taking it easy, an epoch for acceptance and reflection, for companionship and peace, for winding things up as the end approached.

The stages of life; he knew them and understood them: collectively, an arc, a storyline, with a predicable, clichéd beginning, middle, and end.

But now there was suddenly *more;* not just an epilogue tacked on, but a whole new volume, and a totally unplanned one, at that. *Rollback: Book Two of the Donald Halifax Story*. And although Don understood he was its author, he had no idea what was supposed to happen, where it was all supposed to lead. There was no standard plot skeleton to follow, and he didn't have a clue how it was going to end. He couldn't begin to visualize what he should be doing decades down the road; he wasn't even sure what he should be doing in the present day.

But there *was* one thing he knew he had to do soon, although he was dreading it.

"I HAVE SOMETHING to tell you," Don said to Lenore the next time he saw her.

Lenore was lying naked in bed next to him, in her basement apartment on Euclid Avenue. She propped her head up with a crooked arm and looked at him. "What?"

He hesitated. This was more difficult than he'd thought it would be, and he'd thought it would be *very* difficult. How'd he ever get into a situation in which telling his . . . his . . . his whatever Lenore was . . . that he was married would be the *easy* part?

He let the air out of his lungs through a small opening between his lips, puffing his cheeks out as he did so. "I—um, I'm older than you probably think I am," he said at last.

Her eyes narrowed a bit. "Aren't you the same age as me?"

He shook his head.

"Well, you can't be any more than thirty," she said.

"I'm older than that."

"Thirty-one? Thirty-two? Don, I don't care about six or seven years. I've got an uncle who is *ten* years older than my aunt."

I can do ten years for breakfast, he thought. "Keep going."

"Thirty-three?" Her tone was getting nervous. "Thirty-four? Thirty—"

"Lenore," he said, closing his eyes for a moment. "I'm eighty-seven."

She made a small raspberry sound. "Jesus, Don, you—"

"*I'm eighty-seven,*" he said, the words practically exploding from him. "I was born in 1960. You must have heard about the rejuvenation process they've got now. I underwent a rollback earlier this year. And this"—he indicated his face with a counterclockwise motion of his hand—"is the result."

She scuttled sideways on the bed, like a crab on hot sands, increasing the distance between them. "My . . . God," she said. She was peering at him, studying him, clearly looking for some sign, one way or the other, of whether it was true. "But that procedure, it costs a fortune."

He nodded. "I, um, had a benefactor."

"I don't believe you," Lenore said, but she sounded as though she were lying. "I—I mean, it can't . . ."

"It's true. I could prove it in a hundred different ways. Do you want to see some photo ID, the way I looked before?"

"*No!*" An expression of . . . of disgust, perhaps, had fleetingly passed over her face. Of course she didn't want to see the old man she'd just had inside her.

"I should have told you sooner, but—"

"You're damn right you should have. Shit, Don!" But then, perhaps the thought occurring because she'd just uttered his name, a glimmer of hope appeared in her eyes, as if she'd realized that this might all be some elaborate put-on. "But, wait, you're Sarah Halifax's grandson! You told me that."

"No, I didn't. You *guessed* that."

She pulled even farther away, and managed to cover her breasts with the sheet, the first hint of modesty he'd ever seen from her. "Who the hell are you?" she said. "Are you even *related* to Sarah Halifax?"

"Yesss," he said, protracting the word into a gentle hiss. "But"—he swallowed hard, trying to keep it all together—"but I'm not her grandson." He found himself unable to meet her eyes, and so he looked down at the rumpled bedspread between them. "I'm her husband."

"Fuck," said Lenore. "Shit."

"I am *so* sorry. Really, I am."

"Her husband?" she said again, as if perhaps she'd misheard the first time.

He nodded.

"I think you should leave."

The words tore into his heart, like bullets. "Please. I can—"

"What?" she demanded. "You can *explain?* There's no fucking explanation for this."

"No," he said. "No, I can't explain. And I can't justify it. But, God, Lenore, I never wanted to hurt you. I never wanted to hurt *anyone.*" His stomach was churning, and he felt disoriented. "But I want you to . . . to know, to understand."

"Understand what? That everything that has gone down between us has been a lie?"

"No!" he said. "No, no, God, no. This has been more . . . more *real* than anything in my life for—"

"For what?" she sneered. "For years? For *decades?*"

He let out a long, shuddering sigh. He couldn't even protest that she was being unfair. The fact that she was even still *talking* to him was more, he knew, than he had a right to. Still, he tried to defend himself, although, as soon as the words were out, he realized how ill-advised they were. "Look," he said, "you're the one who turned things physical."

"Because I thought you were somebody you *aren't*. You lied to me."

He thought about protesting that he hadn't, not technically, or at least not often. "And, anyway," she continued, "who started things is so beside the point it's not even in the same solar system. You're an *octogenarian,* for God's sake. You're old enough to be my grandfather."

He'd expected those last few words, but they didn't hurt any less for that. "Sarah underwent the same treatment," he said, blurting it out. "But it didn't work for her. She's still physically eighty-seven, and I'm . . . *this*."

Lenore said nothing, but her mouth was slightly downturned and her eyebrows were drawn together.

"Cody McGavin paid for it," continued Don. "He wanted Sarah to be around when the next reply comes in from Sigma Draconis. I—I was just along for the ride, but . . ."

"But now you're Sarah's *caregiver*."

"Please," he said. "I didn't ask for any of this."

"No, no, of course not. It all just sort of happened—a multi-billion-dollar medical procedure."

He shook his head. "I should have known you wouldn't understand."

"If you want understanding, go to a support group. There must be one for people like you."

"Oh, yeah. Sure. They're meeting right now, in Vienna. I can't afford to go there. I am—I worked it out—I am four orders of magnitude poorer than the next poorest person who has undergone this process. For every single dollar I've got, they've each got ten thousand dollars. *That's* not being in the same solar system, Lenore."

"Don't snap at me. I haven't done anything wrong here."

He took a deep breath. "You're right. I'm sorry. It's just that I don't know what to do, and . . . and I don't want to lose you. I really do care about you; I haven't been able to stop thinking about you. And I don't know what I'm doing, but I do know this: the only times of late I've been happy—the *only* times—are when I'm with you."

"There must be somebody else who—"

"There's no one. My friends—what few I have who are still alive—they don't understand. And my kids—"

"Oh, crap. I hadn't thought about that. You've got kids!"

In for a penny, in for a pound. "And grandkids. But my son is fifty-five and my daughter is about to turn fifty. I can't expect them to understand a parent half their age."

"This is crazy," she said.

"We can work it out."

"Are you nuts? You're *married*. You're sixty years older than me. You've got kids. You've got grandkids. And—God, you must be retired, right? You don't even have a job."

"I've got a pension."

"A pension! Jesus."

"This doesn't have to change anything," he said.

"Are you out of your fucking mind?"

"Lenore, please—"

"Get your clothes," she snapped.

"Pardon?"

"Get your clothes, and get the hell out!"

··· Chapter 31 ···

IT HAD BEEN months since Don had seen his grandchildren. He missed them, but he'd been avoiding contact, having no idea how to explain what had happened to him. But, finally, there was no choice. Today, Thursday, September 10, was Emily's fiftieth birthday, and just as attendance for everyone else had been mandatory at Don and Sarah's anniversary party, so his attendance was non-negotiable as his daughter reached the half-century mark.

The party was being held at Emily's house in Scarborough, about an hour away, but an easy journey on the 407. They had Gunter drive them. Don was happy about that. He would have felt silly being driven about by a woman who looked like his grandmother; he still hadn't gotten his license renewed. He'd be required to attend the mandatory driver-safety lectures with a group of other people who were over eighty, and, although the examiner had the power to waive the actual in-car test, Don would still need to endure the gawks from the licensing staff and, even worse, from the old people who *looked* old, many of whom would doubtless resent that he'd managed to forestall the fate that the rest of them would face in the next few years.

When they pulled into the driveway of the house—a large home that almost completely filled its lot—Don hopped out of the rear and ran around to help Sarah get out of the front passenger's seat. And then, with him cradling her elbow to guide her up the driveway, they went to the front door, leaving Gunter in the car, placidly looking out at the tiny strip of lawn. Carl and company were already here, but he'd parked his car on the street, leaving the driveway, and the shorter walk, for his parents.

Although the kids' biometrics were programmed into Don and Sarah's house, the reverse had never been the case, and so Don rang the doorbell. Emily appeared at once, looking out at them with apprehension on her face, and she hustled them indoors, glancing furtively back, as if concerned that her neighbors had seen the spectacle of her ancient mother arriving on the arm of some strange young man.

He tried to put that out of his mind, and managed the heartiest tone he could. "Happy birthday, Em!"

Sarah hugged Emily, and, as she did every year, she said, with a smile, "I remember precisely where I was when you were born."

"Hi," said Emily. Don sort of expected "Mom and Dad" to be appended to the greeting; the upward lilt to Emily's "hi" seemed to demand it. But she couldn't say the former without having to also give voice to the latter—and he hadn't heard either of his children refer to him as Dad since the rollback.

This house, like Don and Sarah's own, had stairs leading up from an entryway. Emily took her mother's cane and helped her climb them, and Don followed.

"Grandma!" shouted Cassie, who was wearing a pink floral-print dress and had her wispy blond hair tied into pigtails with pink ribbons. She came rushing over, and Sarah bent down as much as she could to hug her. When she released Cassie, the little girl then looked at Don without a trace of recognition on her face.

Carl bent down and picked his daughter up, balancing her in a crooked set of arms, the way one might to let a child examine a painting in a museum. "Cassie," said Carl, "this is your grandfather."

Don saw Cassie's little brow furrow. She had an arm around

Carl's neck, and she pulled herself closer to him. "Grandpa Marcynuk?" she said, sounding very unsure.

Don felt his heart sink. Gus Marcynuk was Cassie's mother's father; he lived in Winnipeg, and hadn't been in Toronto for years.

"No, honey," said Carl. "This is Grandpa Halifax."

Cassie scrunched her face up even more tightly and looked at her daddy as if to gauge his expression and see if he was playing some trick. But his face was serious. "No, it's not," Cassie said, shaking her head so that the pigtails bounced. "Grandpa Halifax is *old*."

Don tried to smile as much as he could. "Honest, cupcake, it's really me."

She tilted her head. Although his voice had changed somewhat, she should still recognize it. "What happened to your wrinkles?"

"They're gone."

Cassie rolled her blue eyes in a way that said he was stating the obvious. He went on. "There's a process," he said, but then he halted. "Process," "procedure," "technique," "treatment"—all the words he'd use in describing this to an adult would be lost on a four-year-old. "I went to see a doctor," Don said, "and he made me young again."

Cassie's eyes were wide. "Can they do that?"

He lifted his shoulders a bit. "Yup."

Cassie looked at Sarah and then back at Don. "What about Grandma? Is she going to get young, too?"

Don opened his mouth to reply, but Sarah beat him to it. "No, dear."

"Why not? Do you like being all wrinkly?"

"Cassie!" exclaimed Carl.

But Sarah didn't take offense. "I've earned every one of them," she said. Sarah obviously saw the puzzled expression on Cassie's face, so she went on. "No, dear, I don't. But the process that worked on your grandfather didn't work for me."

Don watched Cassie nod; perhaps he'd underestimated what little kids could grasp. "That's sad," Cassie said.

Sarah nodded back at her, conceding that.

Cassie turned her attention to her father. "Grandpa looks younger than you do," she said. Carl winced. "When I get old, will they be able to make me young again?"

Don could see that his son was about to respond in the negative; he'd moved his head to the left, ready to shake it. But that wasn't the correct answer. "Yes," said Don. "They will." The process was bound to be cheap and common by the time his granddaughter needed it, and that thought pleased Don.

Carl looked as though he was reaching his limit for holding Cassie. He bent down, setting her on the ground. But then Don crouched low, and turned his back to her. Looking over his shoulder he said, "Want a piggyback ride?"

Cassie scrambled onto his back, and he straightened up. He swooped around the living room, Cassie hugging his neck from behind, and her giggles were music to his ears, and, at least for a few minutes, he was truly happy that he'd had this done to him.

"HEY, LENNIE, WHY so glum?"

Lenore was filling salt and pepper shakers. She looked up to see Gabby regarding her, hands on hips. "Hmm?"

"You've been down in the dumps all night. What's up?"

This was the one evening a week that both Lenore and Gabby worked the same shift at the Duke of York.

"I broke up with Don a few days ago."

"How come?" asked Gabby.

Lenore pondered how best to answer this. "For starters, he's married."

"The fucker."

"Yeah. But, you know, there are, um, extenuating circumstances."

"Is he separated?"

"No. No, he still lives with her, but . . ."

"But his old lady doesn't understand him, right?"

Lenore felt her mouth twitch. "Something like that."

"Girl, I've heard it a million times before. You're better off without him."

"Yeah, but . . ."

"But what?"

"I miss him."

"Why? Was he good in the sack?"

"As a matter of fact, yes. But it's not just . . ."

"What?"

"He's *gentle*."

"I like it a little rough myself," Gabby said, smiling lasciviously.

"No, no. I mean in life. He's gentle. He's kind, considerate."

"Except to his wife."

Lenore winced. But she recalled when Don had been here before, how he'd defended Professor Halifax when Makoto had attacked her. "No, in his way, he's good to her, too, I think. And she's really sweet."

"You *know* his wife?"

She nodded. "A bit."

"Earth to Lenore! Wake up, girl!"

"I know, I know. But I just can't stop thinking about him."

"Let me get this straight. You dumped Makoto because he was a messy eater—"

"A girl has to have standards."

"—but you want to go back to a *married* guy?"

"No," said Lenore. "I want to go back to him *despite* the fact that he's married."

"I'm not working on any damn master's degree," said Gabby.

"Maybe that kind of hair-splitting means something in your circles, but . . ."

"He's unlike any guy I've ever met."

"Why? Has he got three nipples?"

"Seriously, Gabs, I miss him so much."

"Really?"

"Yeah."

Gabby was quiet for a moment. "Well, then, there's only one thing to do."

"What's that?"

She started transferring the filled shakers onto a serving tray. "Follow your heart."

AT DINNER, SARAH ended up sitting next to her grandson Percy, who had turned thirteen over the summer. "So," she said, "how is grade eight?"

"It's okay," he said.

"Just okay?"

"They give us a lot of homework. I've got tons to do by Monday."

Sarah remembered being in grade eight, and getting her first calculator. Such things had only just started to appear on the market, and everybody was debating whether they should be allowed in the classroom. After all, with a machine that could do figuring for them, kids might never learn to really understand math, the critics said. A host of scenarios ranging from the unlikely to the downright silly had been suggested, including the notion that if civilization fell, we'd endure a protracted dark age once the supply of batteries had been exhausted, since the magic boxes that did math would no longer function. Sarah had often wondered if the early appearance of solar-powered calculators had been due to some anonymous Japanese engineer's desire to put that canard to rest.

And she'd remembered the later debates about allowing data-coms into classrooms. Although that had affected all levels of instruction, it had gone down while she'd been teaching at U of T. Was there any point in asking students to memorize, for instance, that Sigma Draconis II was, according to data from the first Dracon message, a rocky world about 1.5 times as big as Earth, with an orbital radius of ninety-odd million kilometers and a year equal to 199 Earth days, when there was no conceivable working environment in which they couldn't access that information in an instant?

"What sort of homework?" Sarah asked, genuinely curious.

"I've got some for my bioethics class," Percy said. Sarah was impressed: bioethics in grade eight; you certainly could move a lot faster if you didn't waste so much time on mere memorization.

"And what do you have to do?"

"Look up some stuff on the web, and do a report about what I think about it."

"On any particular topic?"

"We get to choose," Percy said. "But I haven't picked mine yet."

Sarah looked over at Don. She thought about suggesting Percy do something on the ethics of rollbacks, but Don was already too sensitive about that.

"I was thinking of maybe something about abortion," Percy continued.

She was momentarily shocked. The boy was just thirteen, for God's sake, but—

But abortion, birth control, and family planning were all things kids needed to know about. Percy's birthday was in July, meaning he wouldn't turn fourteen until after he'd finished this grade, but most of his classmates would have their birthdays during the academic year, and fourteen was plenty old enough to get pregnant, or make someone pregnant.

"What do you think about abortion, Grandma?" Percy asked.

Sarah shifted in her seat. She could feel the eyes of Angela, Percy's mother, on her, as well as those of her own daughter, Emily. "I believe every child that's born has the right to be wanted," she said.

Percy considered this. "But what about if a guy and a girl decide they want to have a kid, but then, before it's born, the pregnant girl changes her mind. What then?"

There was definitely some of her in her grandson; she'd wrestled a lot with the very issue he'd raised. Indeed, now that she thought about it, that was one of the points the aliens at Sig Drac had been interested in. Question forty-six had asked whether the partner actually carrying the child had the right to terminate a pregnancy that was initially mutually desired. Sarah remembered struggling with her own answer to that question when filling out the survey herself, all those years ago.

She took a sip from the glass of water in front of her. "I go back and forth on that one, dear," she said. "But, today, I think my answer would be that the mother gets the final say."

Percy considered this for a time, then: "You're pretty skytop, Grandma, to talk to me about all this."

"Why, thanks," Sarah said. "I think."

Chapter 32

DON SAT ON the couch early the next morning, browsing email on his datacom. There were two messages from acquaintances asking for the same thing Randy Trenholm had wanted, an email from his brother forwarding a cartoon he thought Don would like, and—

Beep!

A new message had just arrived. The sender's address was—

My God...

The address was ldarby@utoronto.ca.

He opened the message, and his eyes flew all over it in mad saccades, trying to absorb it as a gestalt. And then, his pulse racing, he re-read it carefully, from top to bottom:

```
Hey, Don--

Guess you thought you'd never hear from me again,
and I guess I don't expect you to answer cuz I
know I wasn't that understanding the last time we
were together, but, dammitall, I miss you. Can't
believe I'm sending this--Gabby thought I was
looped at first--but I was hoping you'd like to
get together and talk a bit. Maybe play some
Scrabble or . . . Anyway, lemme know.
L.
--

Be kind, because everyone you meet is fighting a
hard battle --Plato
```

Don looked up. Gunter had a perfect sense of balance and could easily carry Sarah, seated in one of the wooden kitchen chairs that had now been conscripted for that purpose, up and down the staircase; they were descending now. "'Morning, dear," Sarah said, the usual quaver in her voice.

"Hi," he said.

Gunter put the chair down, and helped Sarah to her feet. "Any interesting email?" she asked.

Don quickly turned off the datacom. "No," he said. "None at all."

DON AND LENORE'S first day back together had gone well, right up until the evening.

They were just finishing a meal of take-out Chinese food in her basement apartment on Euclid, after an afternoon of walking around downtown, looking in shops. "Anyway," Lenore said, continuing an account of what she'd been up to since Don had last seen her, "the university ripped me off. They say I didn't pay my tuition on time, but I did. I made the electronic transfer just before midnight on the due date. But they charged me a day's worth of interest."

Don never ate fortune cookies, but he still liked cracking them open. His said, "Prospects for change are favorable." "How much?" Don said, referring to the interest.

"Eight dollars," she replied. "I'm going to go by the registrar's office tomorrow and complain."

Don motioned for her to show him her fortune. It said, "An endeavor will be successful." He nodded, acknowledging that he'd read it. "You could do that," he said, going back to their conversation, "but you'll end up spending half your day dealing with it."

She sounded frustrated with him. "But they shouldn't be able to *do* that."

"It's not worth it over eight bucks," said Don. He got up from his chair and started clearing the table. "You've got to learn to pick your battles. Take it from me. I know. When I was your age, I—"

"Don't say that."

He turned and looked at her. "What?"

She crossed her arms in front of her chest. "Don't say shit like, 'When I was your age.' I don't need to hear that."

"I'm just trying to save you from going through—"

"From going through what? Going through life? Spare me from having my own experiences, from learning for myself? I *want* to learn for myself."

"Yes, but—"

"But what? I don't want a *father,* Don. I want a boyfriend. I want a peer, an equal."

He felt his heart sink. "I can't just erase my past."

"No, of course not," she said, noisily wadding up the paper bag the take-out had come in. "They don't make erasers that big."

"Come on, Sarah, I—"

Don froze, realizing his mistake at once. He felt himself turning red. Lenore nodded, as if a vast conspiracy had been confirmed. "You just called me Sarah."

"Oh, God, I'm sorry. I didn't—"

"She's always there, isn't she? Hanging between us. And she always will be. Even when she's—"

Lenore stopped herself, perhaps realizing that she was about to go too far. But Don picked up on the thought. "Yes, she will be, even after . . . even after she's gone. That's a reality we'll have to face." He paused. "Anyway, I can't help the fact that I've been alive longer than—"

"Than ninety-nine percent of all the people in the world," said Lenore, which stopped him cold for a moment while he thought about whether that was true. He felt his stomach clench as he realized it must be.

"But you can't ask me to *deny* that reality, or what I've learned," he said. "You can't ask me to forget my past."

"I'm not asking that. I'm just asking that you—"

"What? Keep it to myself?"

"No, no. But just don't, you know, always bring it up. It's hard for me. I mean, God, what was the world like when you were born? No home computers, no nanotech, no robots, no television, no—"

"We had television," Don said. *Just not in color.*

"Fine. Fine. But, God, you lived through—through the Iraq War. There was a Soviet Union when you were alive. You saw people walk on the moon. You saw Apartheid end, in South Africa and in the US. You lived through the Month of Terror. You were alive when the first extraterrestrial signal was detected." She shook her head. "Your life is my history book."

He was about to say, "Then you should listen to me when I tell you what I've learned." But he stopped himself before the words got free. "It's not my fault that I'm old," he said.

"I know that!" she snapped. And then, the same words again, but more softly: "I know that. But, well, do you have to rub it in my face?"

Don was leaning against the sink now. "I don't mean to. But you think stuff like a few bucks in interest is a disaster, and—"

"It's not a *disaster*," Lenore said, sounding exasperated. "But it does make my life hard, and—" She must have seen him move his head a bit. "What?" she demanded.

"Nothing."

"No, tell me."

"You don't know *hard*," he said. "Burying a parent, that's hard. Having a spouse go through cancer is hard. Getting screwed out of a promotion you deserve because of office politics is hard. Suddenly having to spend $20,000 you don't have on a new roof is hard."

"Actually," she said, rather stiffly, "I *do* know what some of those things are like. My mother died in a car crash when I was eighteen."

Don felt his jaw dropping. He'd avoided asking her about her parents, doubtless because he felt way too *in loco parentis* when he was with her.

"I never knew my dad," she continued, "so it fell to me to look after my brother Cole. He was thirteen then. That's why I work now, you know. I've got enough graduate support to cover my current expenses, but I'm still trying to dig out from the debt I ran up taking care of Cole and me."

"I'm, um . . ."

"You're sorry. Everybody is."

"Was . . . wasn't there any life insurance?"

"My mom couldn't afford that."

"Oh. Um, how did you manage?"

She lifted her shoulders. "Let's just say there's a reason I have a soft spot in my heart for food banks."

He was embarrassed and contrite, and didn't know what to say. Still, it explained why she seemed so much more mature to him than her contemporaries did. When he had been her age, he was still living cozily with his parents, but Lenore had been out in the world for seven years, and had spent part of that time raising a teenager.

"Where's Cole now?" he said.

"Back in Vancouver. He moved in with his girlfriend just before I came out here to do my master's."

"Ah."

"I *do* let most things go," she said. "You know that. But when it comes to someone taking my money—when you've had so little, you . . ." She shrugged slightly.

Don looked at her. "I—I haven't been conscious of being condescending because of my age," he said slowly, "but now that you've alerted me to it, I'll try to be more . . ." He trailed off, he knew that when he was under emotional stress his vocabulary tended to the highfalutin. But he couldn't think of a better term just then, and so he said it: "Vigilant."

"Thanks," she said, nodding slightly.

"I don't say I'll always get it right. But I really will be trying."

"You certainly will be," she said, with the sort of long-suffering smile he was more used to seeing from Sarah. Don found himself smiling back at her, and he opened his arms, inviting her to stand up and step into them. She did so, and he squeezed her tight.

--- Chapter 33 ---

SARAH'S BROKEN LEG was still bothering her, but Gunter was a godsend, gladly bringing her fresh cups of decaf while she sat at the desk in the room that used to be Carl's. She was still working with the stack of papers Don had brought from the university—a hardcopy of the reply that had been sent to Sigma Draconis from Arecibo, and the source material it was based on: the one thousand sets of survey answers that had been chosen at random from those collected on the website. The decryption key must be somewhere buried in there, Sarah felt sure.

It had been decades since Sarah had looked at these documents and she only vaguely remembered them. But Gunter had merely to glance at each page to be able to index it, and so when Sarah said, for instance, "I remember a pair of answers that struck me as contradictory—somebody who said 'yes' to the question about terminating no-longer-productive old people, and 'yes' to the question about *not* terminating people who were an economic burden," the robot had replied, "That's in survey number 785."

Still, she found herself often angry and sometimes even crying in frustration. She couldn't think as clearly as she used to. Perhaps that wasn't obvious in her day-to-day life of cooking and dealing with grandkids, but it was painfully clear when she tried to puzzle things out, tried to do math in her head, tried to concentrate, to *think*. And she grew fatigued so easily; she found herself often needing to lie down, which just prolonged the work even more.

Of course, many people had already gone back to look at the message sent from Arecibo to see if it contained the decryption key. And, she realized, if those keen young minds hadn't found it, she likely didn't have a prayer.

Many had suggested that the key might be one particular set of answers, from one of the thousand surveys: a unique sequence of eighty-four responses, one for each question, something like "yes," "no," "much greater than," "I prefer option three," "equal to," "no," "yes," "less than," and so on. There were over 20,000,000,000,000,000,000,000,000,000,000,000,000 possible combinations, Sarah knew. Those who didn't have access to the full Arecibo transmission might be trying sequences at random, but even with the world's fastest computers it would take decades to test them all. Others, of course, did have the full reply that had been sent, and had doubtless already tried using each of the thousand answer strings in turn, but had failed to unlock the message. Sarah continued to pour over the original surveys, looking for something—anything—that might stand out. But, damn it all, nothing did. She hated being old, hated what it was doing to her mind. *Old professors never die,* the joke went. *They just lose their faculties.* It was so funny, as her friends at public school used to say, that she forgot to laugh.

She tried another sequence, but again the message "Decryption failed" flashed on her monitor. She didn't slam her hand down on the desktop in anger—she didn't have the strength for that—but Gunter must have read something in her body language anyway. "You seem frustrated," he said.

She swiveled her chair and looked at the Mozo, and a thought occurred to her. Gunter was an example of a nonhuman intelligence; maybe he'd have a better idea of what the aliens were looking for. "If it were you, Gunter, what would you have chosen as a decryption key?"

"I am not disposed to secrecy," he said.

"No, I suppose not."

"Have you asked Don?" the Mozo said, his tone even.

She felt her eyebrows going up as she looked at the robot. "Why do you say that?"

Gunter's mouth line twitched, as if he'd started to say something then thought better of it. After a moment, though, he looked away and said, "No special reason."

Sarah thought about letting it go, but . . .

But, damn it all, Don had *his* confidant. "You don't think I know, do you?"

"Know what?" asked Gunter.

"Puh-lease," she said. "I can translate messages from the stars. I can certainly pick up signals closer to home."

You could never tell if a robot was meeting your gaze. "Ah," said Gunter.

"Do you know who it is?" she asked.

The Mozo shook his blue head, then: "Do you?"

"No. And I don't want to."

"If I may be so bold, how do you feel about this?"

Sarah looked out the window—which showed some sky and the red bricks of the house next door. "It would not have been my first choice, but . . ."

The Mozo was silent, infinitely patient. At last, Sarah went on. "I know he has . . ." She vacillated between saying "wants" and "needs," and finally settled on the latter. "And I can't become a— a *gymnast*. I can't turn back the clock." She realized she'd said the part about the clock as if citing an archetypal impossibility like "I can't make the sun stand still." But for Don, the hands—good God, when had she last seen a clock with hands?—had indeed been turned way, way back. She shook her head. "I can't keep up with him, not anymore." She was quiet for a time, then looked at the robot. "How do *you* feel about this?"

"Emotions are not my forte."

"I suppose."

"Still, I prefer things to be . . . simple."

Sarah nodded. "Another admirable trait you have."

"As we have been speaking, I have been accessing the web for information on such things. I freely confess to not understanding it all, but . . . are you not angry?"

"Oh, yes. But not, so much, at Don."

"I do not understand."

"I'm angry at—at the *circumstances*."

"You mean that the rollback did not work for you?"

Sarah looked away again. After a moment, she spoke, softly but clearly. "I wasn't angry that it didn't work for me," she said. "I was angry that it *did* work for Don." She turned back to face the Mozo. "Awful, isn't it, that I should be upset that the person I love most in all the world is going to get another seventy years or more of life?" She shook her head, amazed at what she'd found herself capable of. "But, you know, it was because I knew what was bound to happen. I knew he would leave me."

Gunter tilted his spherical head. "But he hasn't."

"No. And, well, I don't think he's going to."

The robot considered this, then: "I concur."

Sarah lifted her shoulders slightly. "And that's why I have to forgive him," she said, her voice soft and faraway. "Because, you see, I know, in my heart of hearts, if the situation had been reversed, I would have left him."

"HOW DO YOU feel?" asked Petra Jones, the Rejuvenex doctor, who had come by the house for Don's latest checkup. Sarah never sat in on these anymore; it was too much for her to bear.

Don knew he suffered from a misplaced stubborn pride. When his mother had been dying, slowly, painfully, all those years ago, he'd toughed it out. When Sarah was fighting her battle with cancer, he'd kept his chin up, hiding his pain and fear as best he could from her and his children. He was his father's son, he knew; to ask for help was to show weakness. But he needed help now.

"I—I don't know," he said softly.

He was sitting on one end of the couch; Petra, clad in an expensive-looking burnt-orange pantsuit, was at the other. "Is something wrong?" she asked, leaning forward, the beads in her dreadlocks making soft clicking sounds.

Don tilted his head. He could just make out Sarah and Gunter talking, upstairs in the study. "I, um, I haven't really been feeling like myself," he said.

"In what way?" Petra said, the words lilting a bit thanks to her slight Georgia accent.

He took a deep breath. "I've been doing . . . uncharacteristic things—things I never thought I would do."

"Like what?"

He looked away. "I, um . . ."

Petra nodded. "Your libido is high?"

Don looked at her, said nothing.

She nodded again. "That's common. A man's testosterone levels drop as he ages, but a rollback restores them. That can affect behavior."

Tell me about it, thought Don. "But I don't remember it being like this the first time around. Of course, back then . . ." He trailed off.

"What?"

"I was much bigger when I really was twenty-five."

Petra blinked. "Taller?"

"Fatter. I probably weighed forty pounds more than I do now."

"Ah, well, yes, that could be a factor, too, in the severity of the hormonal imbalance. But we can make some adjustments. Have you noticed anything else?"

"Well, I'm not just feeling"—there was probably a better, more polite word, but he couldn't think of it just then—"horny. I'm feeling *romantic.*"

"Again, hormones," said Petra. "It's common as the body adjusts to a rollback. Any other problems?"

"No," he said. It had been hard enough alluding to what had happened with Lenore; to give voice to *this* would—

"No depression?" Petra said. "No suicidal thoughts?"

He couldn't meet her eyes. "Well, I . . ."

"Serotonin levels," Petra said. "They can go out of whack, too, what with all the changes to your biochemistry that happen during a rollback."

"It's not just chemical," Don said. "Bad things have actually happened. I—I've been trying to get a job, for instance, but no one wants me."

Petra lifted a hand slightly. "Just because your depression might be situational doesn't mean it shouldn't be treated. Have you ever been prescribed an antidepressant before?"

Don shook his head.

She got up and opened her leather bag. "All right. Let's take some blood samples; we'll see exactly where your levels of various hormones are right now. I'm sure we can fix everything up."

Chapter 34

DON WAS AT home, lying in bed next to Sarah, when he was awoken from a dream. He and Sarah were standing on opposite sides of a vast canyon, and the gap between them kept widening, geologic forces working in real time, and—

—and the phone was ringing. He fumbled for the handset, and Sarah found the switch for the lamp on her nightstand.

"Hello?" said Don.

"Don, is . . . is that you?"

He frowned. Nobody quite recognized his voice these days. "Yes."

"Oh, Don, it's Pam." His sister-in-law; Bill's wife. She sounded hoarse, stressed.

"Pam, are you okay?" Next to him, Sarah struggled to sit up, concerned.

"It's Bill. He's—oh, God, Don, Bill is dead."

Don felt his heart jump. "Christ . . ."

"What is it?" asked Sarah. "What's wrong?"

He turned to her, and repeated the words, his own voice full of shock now: "Bill is dead."

Sarah brought a hand to her mouth. Don spoke into the phone. "What happened?"

"I don't know. His heart, I guess. He—he . . ." Pam trailed off.

"Are you at home? Are you okay?"

"Yes, I'm at home. I just got back from the hospital. He was pronounced DOA."

"What about Alex?" Bill's fifty-five-year-old son.

"He's on his way."

"God, Pam, I'm so sorry."

"I don't know what I'm going to do without him," said Pam.

"Let me get dressed and get over there," he said. Bill and Pam normally wintered in Florida, but hadn't yet headed south. "Alex and I, we can take care of all the details."

"My poor Bill," Pam said.

"I'll be there soon," he said.

"Thanks, Don. Bye."

"Bye." He tried to put the handset on his nightstand, but it tumbled to the floor.

Sarah reached over and touched his arm. God, he couldn't remember the last time he'd seen his brother. And then it hit him—

Not since *before*. He normally only saw Bill a couple of times a year, but they did usually go to a Jays game each summer, although Don had begged off this year. This damned laying low, this foolish embarrassment about seeing people he knew, had cost him his last chance to see his brother.

He left the bedroom, walked to the bathroom, and started getting ready to go. Sarah slowly followed him in. He was about to say she didn't have to come, that he could get Gunter to drive him. But he wanted her with him; he needed her.

"I'm going to miss him," Sarah said, standing next to him by the sink.

He glanced briefly at the mirror above the basin, showing his own youthful reflection, and her aged one. "Me, too," he said, very softly.

"SARAH," SAID PAM, as they stood at the door to Bill's condominium apartment, "thank you for coming." Don's sister-in-law was a thin woman in her late seventies, short, with high cheekbones. She looked at Don and scowled. She probably recognized the distinctive Halifax features, including the large nose and high forehead, but not the specific face. "I'm sorry . . . ?"

"Pam, it's me. It's Don."

"Oh, right. The rollback. I—I didn't imagine . . ." She stopped. "You look good."

"Thanks. Look, how are you holding up?"

Pam was clearly frazzled, but she said, "I'm okay."

"Where's Alex?"

"In the den. We're trying to find Bill's lawyer's name."

Sarah said, "I'll go help Alex." And she made her way further into the apartment.

Don looked at Pam. "Poor Bill," he said, having nothing better to offer.

"There's so much to do," said Pam, sounding overwhelmed. "A notice on the *Star*'s website. Organizing the . . . the funeral."

"It'll all get taken care of," said Don. "Don't worry." He gestured toward the living room, and led Pam further into her own home. "Do you need a drink?"

"I've already got one going." She lowered herself into an amorphous fluorescent-green chair with a tubular metal frame; his brother's taste in furniture had always been more avant-garde than his own. Don found another, matching chair.

Pam's drink—amber colored, with ice—was on a table by her chair. She took a sip. "God, look at you."

Don felt uncomfortable, and he shifted his gaze to look out the fifth-floor window, taller, more-expensive condo towers filling most of the view. "I didn't ask for it," he said.

"I know. I know. But my Bill—if he'd had a rollback, why . . ."

He'd still be alive, Don thought. *Yes, I know.*

"You were . . . you were . . ." Pam was shaking her head back and forth. She stopped speaking with her thought uncompleted.

"What?" asked Don.

She looked away. The living-room walls were lined with

bookcases; Pam and Bill even had bookshelves built-in above the door lintels. "Nothing."

"No, tell me," he said.

She turned back to him, and the anger and betrayal were apparent on her face. "You're older than Bill," she said.

"By fifteen months, yes."

"But now you're going to be around for decades!"

He nodded. "Yes?"

"You were the older brother," she said, as if resenting that it had to be spelled out. "You were supposed to go first."

ALL SAINTS' KINGSWAY Anglican Church had been the church of Don's childhood, remembered now more for the Boy Scout meetings he'd attended there than for anything the minister had said. Don hadn't been in the building for—well, the phrase that came to his mind, no doubt because of his current surroundings, was "for God knows how long," although he didn't in fact believe in a God who kept track of such minutiae.

The coffin was closed, which was just as well. People had always said that Don and Bill looked a lot alike, but Don had no desire to have the comparison—and the contrast—highlighted. Indeed, since Bill had never had a weight problem, Don looked more like Bill had at twenty-five than he himself had at that age. He was the only one in the room who had known Bill back then, and—

No. No, wait! Over there, talking to Pam, could that be—?

It was. Mike Braeden. God, Don hadn't seen him since high school. But there was no mistaking that broad, round face, with the close-together eyes and the one continuous eyebrow; even wrinkled and sagging, it was still obviously him.

Mike had been in Bill's year, but Don had known him, too. One of only four boys on a block mostly populated by girls, Mike—Mikey, as he'd been known back then, or Mick, as he'd styled himself briefly during his early teens—had been a mainstay of street-hockey games, and had belonged to the same Scout troop that had met here.

"That's Mike Braeden," Don said to Sarah, pointing. "An old friend."

She smiled indulgently. "Go over and say hello."

He scuttled sideways between two rows of pews. When he got to Mike, Don found he was doing what one does at funerals, sharing a little remembrance of the dearly departed with the next of kin. "Old Bill, he loved his maple syrup," Mike was saying, and Pam nodded vigorously, as if they'd reached agreement on a nanotech-test-ban treaty. "And none of that fake stuff for him, if you please," Mike continued. "It had to be the real thing, and—"

And he stopped, frozen, as motionless as Bill himself doubtless was in his silk-lined box. "My . . . God," Mike managed after a few moments. "My God. Sorry, son, you took my breath away. You're the spitting image of Bill." He narrowed his beady eyes and drew his one eyebrow, now thundercloud gray, into a knot. "Who . . . who are you?"

"Mikey," Don said, "it's me. Don Halifax."

"No, it—" But then he stopped again. "My God, it—you *do* look like Donny, but . . ."

"I've had a rollback," Don said.

"How could you—"

"Someone else paid for it."

"God," said Mike. "That's amazing. You—you look fabulous."

"Thanks. And thanks for coming. It would have meant a lot to Bill to have you here."

Mike was still staring at him, and Don was feeling very uncomfortable about it. "Little Donny Halifax," Mike said. "Incredible."

"Mikey, please. I just wanted to say hi."

The other man nodded. "Sorry. It's just that I've never met anyone who's had a rollback."

"Until recently," said Don, "neither had I. But I don't want to talk about that. You were saying something about Bill's fondness for maple syrup . . . ?"

Mike considered for a moment, clearly warring with himself over whether to ask more questions about what had happened to Don, or to accept the invitation to change the subject. He nodded once, his decision made. "Remember when the old Scout troop used to go up north of Highway Seven each winter and tap some trees? Bill was in heaven!" Mike's face showed that he realized he'd probably chosen not quite the right metaphor under the current circumstances, but that simply gave him an incentive to quickly push on, and soon the topic of Don's rollback was left far behind.

Pam was listening intently, but Don found his eyes scanning the gathering crowd for other familiar faces. Bill had always been more popular than Don—more outgoing, and better at sports. He wondered how many people would come to his own funeral, and—

And, as he looked around the room, his heart sank. None of these people, that was for sure. Not his wife, not his kids, not any of his childhood friends. They'd all be dead long, long before he would. Oh, his grandchildren might yet outlive him; but they weren't here right now, nor, he saw, were their parents. Presumably Carl and Angela were off somewhere else in the church, perhaps busily straightening collars and smoothing dresses on youngsters who had rarely, if ever, had to wear such things before.

In a few minutes, he would present the eulogy, and he'd reach back into his brother's past for anecdotes and revelatory incidents, things that would show what a great guy Bill had been. But at his own eventual funeral, there would be no one who could speak to his childhood or his first adulthood, no one to say anything about the initial eighty or ninety years of his life. Every single thing he'd done to date would be forgotten.

He excused himself from Pam and Mike, who had moved on

from Bill's love of maple syrup to extolling his general prudence. "Whenever we were playing street hockey and a car was coming, it was always Bill who first shouted, 'Car!'" Mike said. "I'll always remember him doing that. 'Car! Car!' Why, he . . ."

Don walked down the aisle, to the front of the church. The hardwood floor was dappled with color, thanks to the stained-glass windows. Sarah was now sitting in the second row, at the far right, looking weary and alone, her cane hanging from the rack that held the hymn books on the back of the pew in front of her.

Don came over and crouched next to her in the aisle. "How are you doing?" he asked.

Sarah smiled. "All right. Tired." She narrowed her eyes, concerned. "How about you?"

"Holding together," he said.

"It's nice so many people came."

He scanned the crowd again, part of him wishing it were fewer. He hated speaking in front of groups. An old Jerry Seinfeld bit flitted through his brain: the number-one fear of most people is public speaking; the number-two fear is death—meaning, at a funeral, you should feel sorrier for the person giving the eulogy than for the guy in the coffin.

The minister—a short black man of about forty-five, with hair starting to both gray and recede—entered, and soon enough the service was under way. Don tried to relax as he waited to be called upon. Sarah, next to him, held his hand.

The minister had a surprisingly deep voice given his short stature, and he led the assembled group through a few prayers. Don bowed his head during these, but kept his eyes open and stared at the narrow strips of hardwood flooring between his pew and the one in front.

". . . and so," the minister said, all too soon, "we'll now hear a few words from Bill's younger brother, Don."

Oh, Christ, thought Don. But the mistake had been a natural

one, and, as he walked to the front of the church, climbing three
stairs to get onto the raised platform, he decided not to correct it.

He gripped the sides of the pulpit and looked out at the people
who had come to bid farewell to his brother: family, including
Bill's own son Alex and the grown children of Susan, Don and
Bill's sister who had died back in 2033; a few old friends; some of
Bill's coworkers from the United Way; and many people who
were strangers to Don but doubtless meant something to Bill.

"My brother," he said, trotting out the first of the platitudes
he'd jotted down on his datacom, which he'd now fished from
his suit pocket, "was a good man. A good father, a good husband,
and—"

And he stopped cold, not because of his current failings in the
category he'd just enumerated, but because of who had just entered at the back of the room, and was now taking a seat in the
last row of pews. It had been thirty years since he'd seen his ex-
sister-in-law Doreen, but there she was, dressed in black, having
come to quietly say good-bye to the man she'd divorced all those
years ago. In death, it seemed, all was forgiven.

He looked down at his notes, found his place, and stumbled
on. "Bill Halifax worked hard at his job, and even harder at being
a father and a citizen. It's not often—"

He faltered again, because he saw what the next words he'd
written were, and realized he'd either have to skip them, or else
force the minister's error into the light. *Screw it,* he thought. *I
never got to say this when Bill was alive. I'll be damned if I don't say
it now.* "It's not often," he said, "that an older brother looks up to
a younger brother, but I did, all the time."

There were murmurs, and he could see the perplexed faces.
He found himself veering from his prepared comments.

"That's right," he said, gripping the pulpit even harder, needing its support. "I'm Bill's older brother. I was lucky enough to
have a rollback." More murmurs, shared glances. "It was . . . it

wasn't something I sought out, or even something I wanted, but . . ."

He stopped that train of thought. "Anyway, I knew Bill his whole life, longer than anyone else"—he paused, then decided to finish his sentence with, "in this room," although "in the world" would have been equally true; everyone else who'd known Bill since birth was long gone, and Mike Braeden hadn't moved onto Windermere until Bill was five.

"Bill didn't make many mistakes," Don said. "Oh, there were some, including"—and here he tipped his head at Doreen, who seemed to nod in acknowledgment, understanding that he meant things Bill had done in their marriage, not the fact of the marriage itself—"some doozies that he doubtless regretted right up until the end. But, by and large, he got it *right*. Of course, it didn't hurt that he was sharp as a whip." He realized he'd mangled the metaphor as soon as he'd said it, but pressed on. "Indeed, some were surprised that he chose to work in the charitable sector, instead of in business, where he could have made a lot more money." He refrained from glancing now at Pam, refrained from conveying the point that Bill never could have afforded what Don himself had been given. "He could have gone into law, could have been a corporate big shot. But he wanted to make a *difference;* he wanted to do good. And he did. My brother *did*."

Don looked out at the crowd again, a sea of black clothes. One or two people were softly crying. His eyes lingered on his children, and his grandchildren—whose children's children he would likely live to see.

"No actuary would say that Bill was shortchanged in quantity, but it's the quality of his life that really stands out." He paused, wondering how personal he should get, but, hell, this was *all* personal, and he wanted Sarah, and his children, and maybe even God to hear it. "It looks like I might get damn near"—he faltered, realizing he'd just sworn during a service, then went on—"double the number of years my brother did."

He looked at the coffin, its polished wood gleaming.

"But," Don continued, "if out of all of that, I can do half as much good, and deserve to be loved half as much as Bill was, then maybe I'll have earned this . . . this . . ." He fell silent, seeking the right word, and, at last, continued: ". . . this *gift* that I've been given."

--- Chapter 35 ---

DON AND SARAH went to bed early the night after the funeral, both exhausted. She fell asleep at once, and Don rolled onto his side, looking at her.

He had no doubt the antidepressants Petra had given him were working. He was having a better time dealing with life's little irritations, and, on a larger level, the idea of killing himself now seemed totally alien—the remembered joke about public speaking aside, not for one second had he wished today to trade places with his brother.

The hormone adjustments were working, too; he was no longer hornier than a hoot owl. Oh, he was still frisky, but at least he felt he had some measure of control now.

But although his lust for Lenore might have abated somewhat, his love had not. *That* had never been just raging hormones; of that he was sure.

Nonetheless, he had an obligation to Sarah that predated Lenore's birth by decades; he knew that. Sarah needed him, and although he didn't need her—not in the sense of requiring her assistance with day-to-day living—he *did* still love her very much. Until recently, the quiet, gentle relationship they'd grown into had been enough, and surely it could *still* be enough, for whatever time they had left together.

And, besides, the current situation was unfair to Lenore. There was no way that he could be the lover she deserved, her full-time companion, her life partner.

To break up with Lenore, he knew, would feel like amputation—like cutting off a part of himself. But it *was* the right thing to do, although—

Although a typical young man losing a young woman might console himself by thinking that there are plenty of other fish in the sea, that someone equally or even more wonderful was bound to come along soon. But Don had lived an entire life already, and in all of it, he'd only met two women who had captivated him, one in 1986 and the other in 2048. The chances of meeting a third, even in the many decades he had left, seemed exceedingly slim.

But that was beside the point.

He knew what he had to do.

And he would do it tomorrow, even though . . .

No, that didn't matter. No excuses.

He would do it tomorrow.

THE CALENDAR WAITS for no man, and, as it happened, today, Thursday, October fifteenth, was Don's birthday. He hadn't told Lenore that it was coming up; he hadn't wanted her spending any of what little money she had on a present for him, and now, of course, given what he was planning to do today, he was doubly glad that he'd kept it to himself.

And besides, was an eighty-eighth birthday significant, if your body had been rejuvenated? When you're a kid, birthdays are a big deal. By middle age, they're given much less importance, with parties only for those that begin new decades, and maybe some moments of quiet reflection when one's personal clock clicks over to a number ending in a five. But after a certain age, it changes again. Every birthday is to be celebrated, every birthday is an accomplishment . . . because every birthday might be one's last—except when you've had a rollback. Was his eighty-eighth to be fussed about or ignored?

And it wasn't as if this automatically meant that his biological age was now twenty-six instead of twenty-five. The twenty-five figure had been a guesstimate, he knew. The rollback was a suite of biological adjustments, not a time machine with digital readouts. Still, he did find himself thinking he was now physically twenty-six, and that was all to the good. Twenty-five had seemed obscenely young; there was something ridiculously insouciant about that age. But twenty-six, why, that was pushing thirty, and starting to get respectable. And even if it were only a guesstimate, he *was* getting older, just as everyone else did, one day at a time, and those days did need to be bundled together into groups, didn't they?

Today being his birthday was an unfortunate coincidence, he knew, for he'd be reminded of the end of his relationship with Lenore on each of the many birthdays he still had ahead of him.

He arrived at the Duke of York around noon, and ran into Gabby. "Hi, Don," she said, smiling. "Thanks for joining us at the food bank last weekend."

"No problem," he said. "My pleasure."

"Lennie's already here. She's in the snug."

Don nodded and headed off to the little room. Lenore had been reading on her datacom, but she looked up as he approached, and immediately got to her feet, stretching up to kiss him. "Happy birthday, sweetheart!" she declared.

"How—how did you know?"

She smiled mischievously—but, of course, almost all information was online somewhere these days. As soon as they sat down, Lenore produced a floppy package wrapped in metallic-blue paper. "Happy birthday," she said again.

Don looked at the package. "You shouldn't have!"

"What sort of girlfriend would I be if I missed your birthday? Go ahead, open it."

He did so. Inside was an off-white T-shirt. It had the familiar red barred-circle symbol for "No" with the word QWERTY written as six Scrabble tiles superimposed on it.

Don's jaw dropped. He'd told her the first time they played

Scrabble that he disapproved of *qwerty* being in the *Official Scrabble Players Dictionary*. In his experience, it was always spelled with all caps, and capitalized words weren't legal in Scrabble. All dictionaries he'd ever consulted agreed with him about the spelling, save one: a note in *Webster's Third New International Dictionary, Unabridged,* said the term was "often not capitalized." But that same far-too-liberal dictionary said "toronto" was acceptable with a lowercase T when used as an adjective, and the *OSPD* hadn't included *that,* thank God. Since countless tournament-level games had been won using *qwerty,* nobody wanted to hear that it was bogus. As with Don's "Gunter" campaign, he'd won few converts.

"Thank you!" he said. "This is *fabulous.*"

Lenore was grinning. "I'm glad you like it."

"I do. I love it!"

"And I love you," she said, giving voice to the words for the first time, as she reached across the table and took his hand.

THE LEAVES ON the trees along Euclid Avenue had turned color, a mixture of orange and yellow and brown. The year was old; winter would be upon them soon. Don and Lenore walked along, holding hands. She was chatting animatedly, as usual, but he was too preoccupied to say much, for he knew he was heading back to her place for the very last time.

Dead leaves mixed with litter were blown by an afternoon breeze along the cracked asphalt. They passed houses with boarded-up windows, and a wino camped out by a sewer grate, before they reached her place. They walked around to the side of the ramshackle house and headed down to the basement apartment. When they got in, and their jackets were removed, Lenore set about making coffee, and Don looked around. There really wasn't much that was personal to Lenore here; he knew the shabby furniture had come with the place. What few belongings she had would probably fit in a couple of suitcases. He shook his head in wonder, remembering when his own life had been so manageable, so uncluttered.

"Here," said Lenore, handing him a steaming cup. "This should help warm you up."

"Thanks."

She perched on the armrest of the couch. "And I know something else that might warm you up, Birthday Boy," she said, eyes twinkling.

But he shook his head. "Um, how 'bout we play Scrabble instead?"

"Seriously?" asked Lenore.

He nodded.

She looked at him like he was from another planet. But then she smiled and shrugged. "Sure, if you like."

They lay down on the worn carpeting, and she used her datacom to project a holographic Scrabble board between them. She drew an *E* to Don's *J*, so went first.

Sometimes when playing Scrabble, a player will realize he has some of the letters needed to form a good word, and will set those aside at one end of his rack, hoping to acquire the others in later turns. Early in the game, Don ended up with a *Y* and a *K,* worth four and five points respectively. He passed over several opportunities to use them, but ultimately did manage to get most of what he needed, although the serious player in him hated wasting an *S.* He placed his tiles running to the left from a *P* that Lenore had put down earlier:

$$\boxed{S}\boxed{K}\boxed{Y} \quad \boxed{O}$$

"The blank is a *T,*" Don said, in response to her appropriately blank expression. "Skytop."

She wrinkled her nose. "Um, I don't think that's really in the dictionary."

He nodded. "I know. I just wanted to, you know, just wanted

to . . ." He stopped, tried again. "For the rest of my life, every time I hear that word, I'm going to think of you." He paused. "More than anything Rejuvenex's doctors did, more than any part of the rollback, it was you who made me feel young again, feel alive."

She smiled that radiant smile of hers. "I do love you," she said, "with all my heart."

He replied, echoing as much of her sentiment as he could. "And I love you, too, Lenore." He looked at her beautiful face, her freckles, her green eyes, her orange hair, committing them to memory. "And," he added, absolutely sure it was true, "I always will."

She smiled again.

"But," he continued, "I—I'm so sorry, darling, but—" He swallowed, and forced himself to meet her gaze. "But this is the last time we can see each other."

Lenore's eyes went wide. "What?"

"I'm sorry."

"Why?"

Don looked at the threadbare carpeting. "I'm about as grown-up as it's possible for a human to be, and it's time I started acting that way."

"But, Don . . ."

"I've got an obligation to Sarah. She needs me."

Lenore began crying softly. "I need you, too."

"I know," Don said, very softly. "But I have to do this."

Her voice cracked. "Oh, Don, please don't."

"I can't give you what you need, what you deserve. I've . . . I've got a prior commitment."

"But we're so good together . . ."

"Yes, we are. I know that—and that's why this hurts so very much. I wish there were another way. But there isn't." He swallowed hard. "The stars are aligned against us."

DON MADE HIS way slowly, sadly back to the subway, bumping into pedestrians, including one robot, on Bloor Street's sidewalk, and getting honked at as he stepped into traffic without checking the light.

He wasn't up to changing trains—something he'd have to do if he took the shortest route—and so he decided to go south. He'd go down one side of the great U and then almost all the way up the other side.

He waited for the train to arrive. When it did, there was a mad scrum as passengers jostled to get on while others were still trying to get off. Don remembered how it used to be when he was young: people wanting to get on stood to either side of the subway doors, and waited patiently until all those who wished to get off had done so. Somewhere along the line, that little civility—like so many of those that had once allowed Toronto to actually deserve its nickname of "Toronto the Good"—had fallen by the wayside, despite all the PA announcements urging orderly behavior.

The train was crowded, but he managed to get a seat. And, as the train started up, he thought nothing about that. He was used to people offering him a seat; some few crumbs of goodness still existed, he supposed. But it came to him that although he was indeed eighty-eight, as of today, there were people who *looked* that old who really needed to sit down. He got up and motioned for an elderly woman wearing a sari to take his seat, and she rewarded him with a very grateful smile.

As it happened, he was in the first car. At Union, lots of people got off the subway, and Don maneuvered close to the front window, next to the driver's cubicle, with its robot within. Some stretches of the tunnel were cylindrical, and they were illuminated by rings of light at intervals. The effect reminded him of an old TV series, *The Time Tunnel,* a show he'd enjoyed in the same way he'd enjoyed *Lost in Space,* for the nifty art direction, while cringing at the stupid stories.

After all, you can't go back in time.

You can't undo what's done.

You can't change the past.

You can only, to the best of your abilities, try to meet the future head-on.

The train rumbled on, through the darkness, taking him home.

DON CAME INTO the entryway and paused, looking down at the tiles, at where Sarah had once lain, fallen, waiting for him to return. He took the six stairs one at a time, trudging up into the living room.

Sarah was standing by the mantel, looking either at the holos of their grandchildren or at her trophy from Arecibo; with her back to him, it was impossible to tell which. She turned around, smiled, and started walking toward him. Don's arms opened automatically, and she stepped into them. He hugged her lightly, afraid of breaking her bones. Her arms against his back felt like sapling branches pushed by a gentle breeze. "Happy birthday again," she said.

He glanced past her, at the foot-high digital display on the wall monitor, and saw it change from 5:59 to 6:00. When they let go of each other, she started a slow walk toward the kitchen. Rather than hurry ahead, Don fell in behind her, taking one step for every two of hers.

"You sit down," Don said, when they'd finally made it into the kitchen. Although he knew he shouldn't, he found Sarah's slow, methodical movements frustrating to watch. And, besides, he ate three times as much food as she did these days; he *should* do the work. "Gunter," he said—loudly, but certainly not yelling; it wasn't necessary to yell. The Mozo appeared almost at once. "You and I are going to make dinner," he said to the robot.

Sarah slowly lowered herself onto one of the three wooden chairs that encircled the little kitchen table. As Don and Gunter moved about the cramped space, getting down a pot and a frying pan and finding ingredients in the fridge, he felt her eyes upon him.

"What's wrong?" she asked at last.

He hadn't said anything, and he'd taken pains not to bang cookware or utensils together. But Sarah had known him for so long now, and even if the veneer on his body had changed his body language doubtlessly hadn't. Whether it had been the way he'd been hanging his head, or simply the fact that he wasn't speaking except to give Gunter the occasional perfunctory instruction that tipped her off, he couldn't say. But he couldn't hide his moods from her. Still, he tried to deny it, futile though he knew that would be. "Nothing."

"Did something go wrong downtown today?" she asked.

"No. I'm just tired, that's all." He said it while bent over a chopping board, but stole a sideways glance at her, to gauge her reaction.

"Is there anything I can do?" she asked, her brow knitted in concern.

"No," said Don, and he allowed himself one more, final lie— just this one last time. "I'll be fine."

Chapter 36

SARAH WOKE WITH a start. Her heart was pounding probably more vigorously than was healthy at her age. She looked over at the digital clock. It was 3:02 a.m. Next to her lay Don, his breathing making a gentle sound with each exhale.

The idea that had roused her was so exciting she thought about waking him, but, no, she wouldn't do that. After all, it *was* a long shot, and he'd been having so much trouble sleeping lately.

Her side of the bed was the one near the window. A million years ago, when they'd chosen who would sleep where, Don had said she should have that side so she could look out at the stars anytime she wished. It was an ordeal getting out of bed. Her joints were stiff, and her back hurt, and her leg was still healing. But she managed it, pushing off her nightstand, forcing herself to her feet as much through an effort of will as through bodily strength.

She took small, shuffling steps toward the door, paused and steadied herself for a moment by holding on to the jamb, then continued out into the corridor and made her way to the study.

The computer's screen was blank, but it came to life the moment she touched the scroller, bringing up a suitably dim image for viewing in the darkened room.

Within moments, Gunter was there. He'd been downstairs, Sarah imagined, but he'd doubtless heard her stir. "Are you all right?" he asked. He had lowered the volume of his voice so much that Sarah could only just make it out.

She nodded. "I'm fine," she whispered. "But there's something I've got to check out."

Sarah loved stories—even apocryphal ones—about *ah hah!* moments: Archimedes jumping out of his bath and running naked down the streets of Athens shouting "Eureka!," Newton watching an apple fall (although she preferred the even-less-likely version about him being hit on the head by a falling apple), August Kekule waking up with the solution to the structure of the benzene molecule after dreaming of a snake biting its own tail.

In her whole career, Sarah had only ever had one such epiphany: that time, long ago, while playing Scrabble in this very house, when she'd realized how to arrange the text of the first message from Sigma Draconis.

But now, perhaps, she was having another.

Her grandson Percy had asked her about her views on abortion, and she'd told him that she'd gone back and forth on some of the tricky points.

And she had, her whole life.

But what she'd remembered just now was another night, like this one, when she'd woken at 3:00 a.m. That night had been Sunday, February 28, 2010, the day before the response to the initial Dracon message was to be sent from Arecibo. She and Don were in their VSQ cabin at the Arecibo Observatory, the fronds slapping against its wooden walls making a constant background hushing sound.

She'd decided she wasn't happy with her answer to question forty-six. She'd said "yes," the mother's wishes should always trump the father's during a mutually desired pregnancy, but then she'd found herself leaning toward "no." And so Sarah had gotten out of the narrow bed. She fired up her notebook, which contained the master version of the data that would be transmitted the next day, changed her answer to that one question, and recompiled the response file. Her notebook would be interfaced to the big dish tomorrow, and this revised version would be the one actually sent.

It didn't matter much, she'd thought at the time, in the grand scheme of things, what one person out of a thousand said in response to any one question, but Carl Sagan's words had echoed in her head. "Who speaks for the Earth? We do." *I do.* And Sarah had wanted to give the Dracons the truest, most honest answer she could.

By that point, copies of the supposedly finalized reply had already been burned to CD-ROM, and the backup hardcopy printout Don had recently retrieved from U of T had already been made. Sarah had forgotten all about that night in Puerto Rico, some thirty-eight years in the past, until moments ago.

"Is there anything I can do to help?" Gunter asked.

"Just keep me company," Sarah said.

"Of course."

While Gunter looked over her shoulder, she began to softly dictate instructions to the computer, telling it to bring up a copy of her old set of responses to the Dracon questionnaire.

"Okay," she said to the computer. "Go to my answer to question forty-six."

The highlight on the screen moved.

"Now, change that answer to 'no,'" she said.

The display updated appropriately.

"Now, let's recompile all my answers. First . . ." and she went on, giving instructions that were dutifully executed.

"Your pulse is elevated," said Gunter. "Are you okay?"

Sarah smiled. "It's called excitement. I'll be fine." She addressed the computer again, fighting to keep her voice steady: "Copy the compiled string into the clipboard. Bring up the reply we received from the Dracons . . . Okay, load the decryption algorithm they provided." She paused to take a deep, calming breath. "All right, now paste in the clipboard contents, and run the algorithm."

The screen instantly changed, and—

Eureka!

There it was: long sequences spelled out in the vocabulary established in the first message. Sarah hadn't looked at Dracon ideograms in decades, but she recognized a few at once. That block was the symbol for "equals," that upside-down T meant "good." But, like any language, if you don't use it, you lose it, and she couldn't read the rest.

No matter. There were several programs available that could transliterate Dracon symbols, and Sarah told her computer to feed the displayed text into one of those. At once, the screen was filled with a rendering of the alien message in the English notation she had devised all those years ago.

Sarah used the scroller to quickly page through screen after screen of decrypted text; the message was massive. Gunter, of course, could read the screens as fast as they were displayed, and he surprised Sarah at one point by very softly saying, "Wow." After a bit, Sarah jumped back to the beginning, adrenaline surging. Most of the introductory text was displayed as black, but some words and symbols were color-coded, indicating a degree of confidence in the translation—the meanings of some Dracon terms were generally agreed upon; others were still contentious. But the gist was obvious, even if a few subtleties were perhaps being lost, and, as she took it all in, she shook her head slowly in amazement and delight.

Chapter 37

DON WOKE UP a little before 6:00 a.m., some noise or other having disturbed him. He rolled over and saw that Sarah wasn't there, which was unusual this early in the morning. He rolled the other way, looking into the little *en suite,* but she wasn't there, either. Concerned, he got out of bed, headed out into the corridor, and—

And there she was, and Gunter, too, in the study.

"Sweetheart!" Don said, entering the room. "What are you doing up so early?"

"She has been up for two hours and forty-seven minutes," Gunter said helpfully.

"Doing what?" Don asked

Sarah looked at him, and he could see the wonder on her face. "I did it," she said. "I figured out the decryption key."

Don hurried across the room. He wanted to pull her up out of the chair, hug her, swing her around—but he couldn't do any of those things. Instead, he bent down and kissed her gently on the top of her head. "That's fabulous! How'd you do it?"

"The decryption key was my set of answers," she said.

"But I thought you'd tried that."

She told him about the last-minute change she'd made in Arecibo. While she did so, Gunter knelt next to her, and began scrolling rapidly through pages on the screen.

"Ah," Don said. "But wait—wait! If it's your answers that unlocked it, that means the message is for you personally."

Sarah nodded her head very slowly, as if she herself couldn't believe it. "That's right."

"Wow. You really do have a pen pal!"

"So it would seem," she said softly.

"So, what does the message say?"

"It's a—a blueprint, I guess you could call it."

"You mean for a spaceship? Like in *Contact*?"

"No. Not for a spaceship." She looked briefly at Gunter, then back at Don. "For a Dracon."

"What?"

"The bulk of the message is the Dracon genome, and related biochemical information."

He frowned. "Well, um, I guess that'll be fascinating to study."

"We're not supposed to study it," Sarah said. "Or at least, that's not *all* we're supposed to do."

"What then?"

"We're supposed to"—she paused, presumably seeking a word—"to *actualize* it."

"Sorry?"

"The message," she said, "also includes instructions for making an artificial womb and an incubator."

Don felt his eyebrows going up. "You mean they want us to *grow* one of them?"

"That's right."

"Here? On Earth?"

She nodded. "You've said it yourself. The only thing SETI is good for is the transmission of information. Well, DNA is nothing but that—information! And they've sent us all the info we need to make one of them."

"To make a Dracon baby?"

"Initially. But it'll grow up to be a Dracon adult."

There was only one chair in the room. Don moved so he could perch on the desk, and Sarah swiveled to face him. "But . . . but it won't be able to breathe our atmosphere. It won't be able to eat our food."

Sarah motioned at the screen, although Don could no longer see what was on it. "They give the composition of the air it will require: needed gases and their acceptable percentages, a list of gases that are poisonous, the tolerable range of air pressure, and so on. You're right that it won't be able to breathe our air directly; we've got too much CO_2 in our atmosphere, for one thing. But with a filter mask, it should be fine. And they've given us the chemical formulas for the various foodstuffs it will need. I'm afraid Atkins didn't catch on beyond Earth; it's mostly carbohydrates."

"What about—I don't know, what about gravity?"

"Sigma Draconis II has a surface gravity about one and a third times our own. It should have no trouble with ours."

Don looked at Gunter, appealing to the robot's rationality. "This is crazy. This is nuts."

But Gunter's glass eyes were implacable, and Sarah simply said, "Why?"

"Who would send a baby to another planet?"

"They're not sending a baby. Nothing is traveling."

"All right, fine. But what's the point, then?"

"Did you ever read—oh, what was his name, now?"

Don frowned. "Yes?"

"Damn it," said Sarah, softly. She turned to face Gunter. "Who wrote 'What Is It Like to Be a Bat?'"

The Mozo, still looking at pages of text, said at once, "Thomas Nagel."

Sarah nodded. "Nagel, exactly! Have you ever read him, Don?"

He shook his head.

"That paper dates back to the 1970s, and—"

"October 1974," supplied Gunter.

"—it's one of the most famous in all of philosophy. Just like the title says, it asks, 'What's it like to be a bat?' And the answer is, fundamentally, we'll never know. We can't even begin to guess what it's like to have echolocation, to perceive the world in a totally different way. Well, only a flesh-and-blood Dracon, with Dracon senses, can report to the home world what it's really like, from a Dracon's point of view, here on Earth."

"So they want us to make a Dracon who'll grow up to do that?"

She shrugged a bit. "For thousands of years, people on Earth have been born to be kings. Why shouldn't someone be born to be an ambassador?"

"But think of the existence it would have here, all alone."

"It doesn't have to be. If we can make one, we can make several. Of course, they'll be genetically identical, like twins, and—"

"Actually, Sarah," said Gunter, standing back up now, "I've been reading further into the document. It's true that they only sent one master genome, but they've appended a tiny subset of modifications that can be substituted into the master sequence to make a second individual. Apparently, the DNA code provided was taken from two pair-bonded Dracons. Any living expressions of that DNA would be clones of those individuals."

"'If you were the only girl in the world, and I was the only boy . . .'" said Don. "At least they'll each know who to ask to the prom." He paused. "But, I mean, how do we even know that they've sent the genome for an actual, intelligent Dracon? It could be the genome for some, y'know, vicious monster, or for a plague germ."

"Of course, we'd create it in a biologically secure facility," said Sarah. "Besides, what would be the point of sending such a thing?"

"The message says the individuals whose genomes have been provided are alive on Sigma Draconis II," said Gunter. "Or, at least they were when this message was sent. They hope to converse with their clones here, albeit with a 37.6-year round-trip message time."

"So the source Dracons back home are like the parents?" asked Don. Through the window opposite him, he could see that the sun was coming up.

"In a way," said Sarah. "And they're looking for foster parents here."

"Ah, yes. The questionnaire!"

"Right," she said. "If you were going to have someone raise your children, you'd want to know something about them first. And, I guess, of all the answers they received, they liked mine best; they want me to raise the children."

"My . . . God," said Don. "I mean . . . my God."

Sarah shrugged a little. "I guess that's why they cared about things like the rights of the parent who wasn't actually carrying the child."

"And the abortion questions—were they to make sure we wouldn't get cold feet and terminate the fetuses?"

"Maybe. That would certainly be one interpretation. But remember, they liked my answers, and although I was willing to concede rights to the parent who wasn't carrying the child, the rest of my answers must have made it pretty darn clear that I'm pro-choice."

"Why would that make them happy?"

"Maybe they wanted to see if we've transcended Darwin."

"Huh?"

"You know, if we've gotten past being driven by selfish genes. I mean, in a way, being pro-choice *is* anti-Darwinian, because it tends to reduce your reproductive success, assuming you terminate normal fetuses that you could have raised, without unreasonable cost, to adulthood. Doing that would be one psychological marker for no longer being bound by Darwinian notions, for having broken free of mindless genetic programming, for ceasing to be a lifeform driven by genes that want nothing but to reproduce themselves."

"I get it," said Don, watching now as the window autopolarized in response to the rising sun. "If all you care about are your own genes then, by definition, you don't care about aliens."

"Right," said Sarah. "Notice they asked for a thousand survey replies. That means they knew we wouldn't have just one set of views. Remember, you used to say that alien races either would become hive minds or totalitarian, because, after a certain level of technological sophistication is reached, they simply couldn't survive any longer if they allowed the kind of discontent that gives rise to terrorism. But there must be some third alternative—something better than being Borg or having thought police. The aliens on Sigma Draconis apparently knew they would be dealing with complex, contradictory individuals. And they looked at the thousand responses and decided that they didn't want anything to do with human beings in general—they only wanted to communicate with one oddball." She paused. "I guess I'm not surprised, since most of the sets of survey answers *did* suggest ethnocentrism, exclusive concern about one's own genetic material, and so on."

"But knowing you, yours didn't suggest those things. And that's what makes you the one they want to be the foster mother, right?"

"Which surprises the heck out of me," Sarah said.

But Don shook his head. "It shouldn't, you know. I told you this ages ago. You're special. And you are. SETI, by its very nature, transcends species boundaries. Remember that conference you attended in Paris, all those years ago? What was it called?"

"I don't . . ."

Gunter spoke up. " 'Encoding Altruism: The Art and Science of Interstellar Message Composition.' " Don looked at the Mozo, who did a mechanical shrug. "I've read Sarah's CV, of course."

"'Encoding altruism,'" repeated Don. "Exactly. That's the fundamental basis of SETI. And, well, you were the only SETI researcher whose answers were sent to Sigma Draconis. Is it any wonder that the recipients, who, by definition, are also in the SETI business, found your responses to be the closest to what they were looking for?"

"I suppose. But . . ."

"Yes?"

"My child-rearing days are way behind me. Not that that's unusual, I suppose, in a cosmic sense."

Don frowned. "Huh?"

"Well, Cody McGavin was probably right. The Dracons, and just about every other race that survives technological adolescence, almost certainly is very long lived, if not out-and-out immortal. And unless you're endlessly expansionist, moving out to conquer new worlds constantly, you'd soon run out of room if you kept breeding *and* lived forever. The Dracons have probably all but given up reproducing."

"I guess that makes sense."

Sarah's eyebrows went up. "In fact, *that* might be the third alternative!"

"Huh?"

"Evolution is a blind process," said Sarah. "It has no goal in mind, but that doesn't mean it doesn't have a logical outcome. It selects for aggression, for physical force, for being protective of one's blood relations—for all the things that ultimately contribute to technological races destroying themselves. So maybe the Fermi paradox isn't a paradox at all. Maybe it's the natural result of evolution. Evolution eventually gives rise to technology, which has a survival value *up to a point*—but once technologies of mass destruction are readily available, the psychology that the Darwinian engine forces on lifeforms almost inevitably leads to their downfall."

"But if you stop breeding—"

"Exactly! If you voluntarily opt out of evolution, if you cease to struggle to get more copies of your own DNA out there, you probably give up a lot of aggression."

"I guess that does beat becoming a hive mind or totalitarian," said Don. "But—but, wait! They're reproducing now, in a way, by sending their DNA here."

"But only two individuals."

"Maybe they breed like rabbits, though. Maybe it's a way of launching an invasion."

"That's not a concern," Gunter said. "The two individuals are both of the same sex."

"But you said the source Dracons were pair-bonded . . ." Don stopped himself. "Right, of course. How provincial of me. Well, well, well . . ." He looked at Sarah. "So what are you going to do?"

"I—I don't know. I mean, it's not like the artificial womb and incubator are things you and I could cobble together out in the garage."

Don frowned. "But if you tell the world, governments will try to control the process, and—forgive me, but they'll probably try to squeeze you out."

"Exactly," said Sarah. "The Dracons surely understand that upbringing is a combination of nature and nurture. They wanted a specific sort of person to be responsible for the . . . the Draclings. Besides, if the genome gets out, who's to say that others wouldn't create Dracons just to dissect them, or put them in zoos?"

"But once the child is born, anyone could steal its DNA, no? Just by picking up some of its cells."

"They might be able to get that, but not the plans for the incubator or all the other things. Without actual access to the full message, it would be very hard to create a Dracon." She paused, considering. "No, we have to keep this secret. The Dracons entrusted the information to me, and I've got an obligation to protect it."

Don rubbed the sleep from his eyes. "Maybe—but there'll be those who'll say you should release all the information. They'll say your principal obligation is to your own kind."

But Sarah shook her head. "No," she said. "It isn't. That's the whole point."

--- Chapter 38 ---

"IT'S IMPORTANT," SARAH said a few hours later, "that you commit to memory the decryption key—not the whole thing, of course, but how to recover it."

Don nodded. They were sitting in their kitchen, eating a late breakfast. He was now dressed in a T-shirt and jeans; she was wearing a robe and slippers.

"My survey was number 312 out of the thousand sent," she said, "and I changed my answer to one of the questions at the very last minute. It was question forty-six, and the answer I actually sent was 'no.' Got that?"

"Three-twelve, forty-six, and no. Can I write that down somewhere?"

"As long as you don't put any explanatory text with it, sure."

"So number forty-six was the magic question? The one the Dracons cared about the most?"

"What? No, no. It just happened to be the one I changed my answer to. The key consists of all eighty-four of my answers exactly as I actually transmitted them. Any time you need the key you can reproduce it by looking up the archival copies of what was supposedly sent to Sigma Draconis, and making that one change."

"Got it."

"Now, make sure you keep it secret!"

He looked across the table at his wife, who seemed visibly older, and not just because she'd gotten very little sleep. Over the last few weeks, she had aged noticeably. "I, ah, don't think we can keep it secret from *everybody,*" he said. "I really think you need to tell Cody McGavin."

Sarah was hugging a cup of coffee with both hands. "Why?"

"Because he's one of the richest people on the planet. And a project like this is going to take deep pockets. Synthesizing the DNA, building the womb, building the incubator, synthesizing the food, and, I'm sure, lots of other things. You need somebody like him to come on board."

Sarah was quiet.

"You have to tell *someone*," Don said. "You'll . . ."

He trailed off, but she nodded. "I'll die soon. I know." She paused, considering, and Don knew enough to just let her do that. After a time she said, "Yeah, you're right. Let's call him."

Don crossed the room, got the cordless handset, and told it who he wanted to speak to. After a few rings, a crisp, efficient voice came on. "McGavin Robotics. Office of the president."

"Hello, Ms. Hashimoto," Don said. "It's Donald Halifax."

Her voice became slightly cold. They had, after all, butted heads repeatedly during his many attempts to reach McGavin back in the spring. "Yes, Mr. Halifax?"

"Don't worry. I'm not calling about the rollback. And, in fact, it's not me who's calling at all. I just dialed the phone for my wife, Sarah. She'd like to speak to Mr. McGavin about the Dracon message."

"Ah," said Ms. Hashimoto. "That would be fine. Please hold. I'll put you through."

Don covered the mouthpiece and spoke to Sarah. "She's putting the call through." Sarah motioned for him to give her the phone, but he held up a hand, palm out. After a moment, the familiar Bostonian accent came on. "Cody McGavin speaking."

"Mr. McGavin," said Don, with great relish, "please hold for Dr. Sarah Halifax." He then counted silently to ten before handing the handset to Sarah, who was grinning from ear to ear.

"Hello, Mr. McGavin," Sarah said.

Don moved close enough so that he could hear both sides of the conversation. It wasn't hard, given that the handset had automatically pumped up its volume when Sarah had taken it. "Sarah, how are you?" McGavin said.

"I'm fine. And I've got big news. I've decrypted the Dracon message."

Don could practically hear McGavin jumping up and down. "Wonderful! What does it say?"

"I—I don't want to say over the phone."

"Oh, come on, Sarah—"

"No, no. You never know who's eavesdropping."

"God, all right. We'll fly you down here again, and—"

"Um, could you come here? I'm not really feeling up to flying these days."

Don could hear McGavin blowing out air. "It's our annual stockholders' meeting in two days. There's no way I can come up until after that's over."

"All right," said Sarah. "How about Friday, then?"

"Well, I *could*. But can't you just email me the decryption key, so I can look at the message here?"

"No. I'm not prepared to divulge it."

"What?"

"The message was intended for me alone," Sarah said.

There was a long pause. Don could only imagine the incredulous look that must be on McGavin's face.

"Sarah, is, um, is Don still there? Maybe I could have a word with him . . ."

"I'm not senile, Mr. McGavin. What I'm saying is absolutely true. If you want to know what the message says, you're going to have to come here."

"Oh, all right, but—"

"And don't tell anyone that I've found the decryption key. You have to promise to keep this secret, at least until you get here."

"All right. Let me get the details of where you are . . ."

After she got off the phone, Don looked around. "Gunter does such a good job of keeping the place clean, I guess there's not much we have to do to get ready for McGavin's visit."

"There is one thing," Sarah said. "I want you to take the Dracon survey."

Don was surprised. "Why?"

She didn't quite meet his eyes. "We'll be talking a lot with McGavin about it. You should be up to speed on it."

"I'll read it over."

"No, don't just do that." She sounded emphatic. "Actually fill it out."

He raised his eyebrows. "If you like."

"I do. Go get your datacom; you can download a copy from the official response website."

He nodded. It was hardly as though he had anything better to do. "All right."

Once he'd loaded the survey, he lay down on the couch and started working through the questions. It took almost two hours, but finally he called out, "Done!"

Sarah made her way slowly into the living room, and he handed her the datacom. "Now what?" he said.

She looked at the device. "Save as 'Answers Don,' " she said to it. "Run Flaxseed. Load Answers Don. Load and unlock Answers Sarah Revised—passphrase 'Aeolus 14 umbra.' Execute."

"What are you doing?" Don said, sitting up. "What's 'Flaxseed'?"

"It's a program an ethics prof designed years ago, when we were studying the million-plus sets of survey responses that were uploaded to our website. It measures the degree of agreement between respondents. See, comparing survey responses is a bit tricky. Many of the eighty-four questions have four or five possible answers, or use graduated scales, so you can't just look for exact matches—two answers that are different might only be subtly different. A person who chooses 'A' might be thinking along the same lines as someone who chose 'B,' while someone who picked 'C' clearly has a different mind-set."

"Ah," said Don. He gestured at the datacom Sarah was holding. "And?"

She glanced down at the display, then looked back up at him, a smile on her face. "I knew there was a reason I married you."

Chapter 39

"CODY McGAVIN ARRIVES tomorrow," Sarah said, "and there's something we should discuss before he gets here."

They were sitting at the dining-room table, drinking coffee. "Yes?" Don said.

"It's just that I won't be able to do what the aliens want," she said.

He made his voice soft. "I know."

Light was streaming in through the window. Don could see Gunter outside, raking leaves.

"So," she continued, "I've got to find somebody else to do it, if we're going to do it at all."

He considered this. "You could use that Flaxseed program to see who else of the original respondents had replies close to yours."

She nodded. "I did that. Of the thousand sets of responses we sent, there were only two that were really close to mine. But God knows who they belonged to."

"Didn't you keep records?"

"It was an anonymous survey. Professional pollsters told us we'd get much more honest answers that way. Besides, even if we had asked for names, we wouldn't have been able to keep them. The website was at U of T, remember, and you know what Canadian privacy laws are like."

"Ah." He took a sip of coffee.

"Of course, each participant got to chose a login name and a password, which we told them to keep secure. But even if we had the names, it might not have done any good."

"Why not?"

"As I said before, McGavin was probably right, back at his office, when he said that most advanced races would likely be very long-lived. Indeed, since the Dracons apparently have ring-shaped chromosomes, they might in fact have *always* lived a very long time, since they'd have avoided one of our principal causes of aging. Anyway, although it probably never even occurred to them that anyone they were replying to might be dead a mere thirty-eight years later, probably half of those who originally filled out the survey have passed on by now."

"I suppose that's true," he said.

"But," said Sarah, looking sideways at him, "you and I had very similar answers."

"So you said."

"So, maybe, I mean, if you wanted to . . ."

"What?"

"You could do it. You could look after the Dracon children."

Don felt his eyebrows going up. "Me?"

"Well, you and Gunter, I suppose." She smiled. "I mean, he's a Mozo; he's designed to look after the elderly, but taking care of alien children can't be much more difficult than looking after a crazy old bat like me."

Don's head was swimming. "I—I don't know what to say."

"Well, think about it," she said. "Because you're definitely my first choice."

MONTHS AGO, WHEN Sarah and Don were contemplating rolling back, Carl had said they'd have to do more babysitting— but that seemed to have fallen by the wayside when Sarah's rejuvenation had failed. But tonight Carl and Angela had dropped Percy and Cassie off at the house on Betty Ann. The ostensible reason was that the adults were going to see a hockey game, but Don suspected there was also a feeling that the children wouldn't have their grandmother much longer, and so they should spend time with her while they could.

Percy was thirteen, all loose limbs and long hair. Cassie, at four, was a whirlwind with pigtails. Because of the age difference, it was hard to entertain them both together, so Cassie and Sarah had gone upstairs with Gunter to look at whatever treasures Sarah's closets held, and Don and Percy were on the couch in the living room, half-watching the same hockey game Percy's parents had gone to on the TV above the fireplace, and making their own game of trying to spot Carl and Angela in the crowd.

"So," Don said, muting the sound during a commercial break, "how's grade eight treating you?"

Percy shifted on the couch a bit. "It's okay."

"When I was a kid, we went all the way to grade thirteen."

"Really?"

"Yup. Ontario was the only place in North America that had that."

"I'm glad we only have to go to grade twelve," said Percy.

"Yeah? Well, in grade thirteen we were old enough to write our own notes for missing class."

"That'd be cool."

"It was. But I actually had fun in grade thirteen. Lots of interesting courses. I even took Latin. It was practically the last year they taught that in public schools in Toronto."

"Latin?" said Percy incredulously.

Don nodded sagely. *"Semper ubi sub ubi."*

"What's that mean?"

"'Always wear underwear.'"

Percy grinned.

The game resumed. The Leafs were doing okay, although it was still early in the season. Don didn't really know the players anymore, but Percy did. "And," Don said, when there was a lull in the play, "our school had a little radio station, Radio Humberside. I was involved with that in grade thirteen, and that's what got me into my career."

Percy looked at him blankly; Don had retired long before he'd been born. "I used to work at CBC Radio," Don said.

"Oh, yeah. Dad listens to that in the car."

Don smiled. He'd once had a friendly argument with a guy who wrote for the Canadian edition of *Reader's Digest*. "Better," Don had said, "to produce something that people only listen to in the car than something they only read on the toilet."

"So, when did you work there?" asked Percy.

"I started in 1986 and left in 2022." Don thought about adding, "And, to save you from asking, Sally Ng was prime minister when I retired," but he didn't. Still, he remembered being Percy's age and thinking World War II was ancient history; 1986 must have sounded positively Pleistocene to Percy.

They watched the game some more. The defenseman for Honolulu got three minutes for high-sticking. "So," Don said, "any thoughts about what you're going to do—" He stopped himself from saying "when you grow up"; Percy doubtless thought he was plenty grown-up already. "—when you finish school?"

"I dunno," he said, without taking his eyes off the screen. "Maybe go to university."

"To study . . . ?"

"Well, except on weekends."

Don smiled. "No, I meant, 'To study what?' "

"Oh. Maybe ornithology."

Don was impressed. "You like birds?"

"They're all right." Another commercial break was upon them, and Don muted the sound. Percy looked at him, and then, maybe feeling that he wasn't holding up his end of the conversation, he said, "What about you?"

Don blinked. "Me?"

"Yeah. I mean, now that you're young again. What are you going to do?"

"I don't know."

"Have you thought about going back to the CBC?"

"Actually, yeah."

"And?"

Don shrugged. "They don't want me. I've been out of the game too long."

"That sucks," Percy said, with a perplexed face, as if unused to the notion that life could be unfair to adults as well.

"Yeah," said Don, "it does."

"So what are you going to do?"

"I don't know."

Percy considered for a time, then: "It should be something— you know—something *important*. I looked up how much a rollback costs. If you're lucky enough to get one of those, you should do something with it, right?"

Don tilted his head, regarding Percy. "You take after your grandmother."

The boy frowned, clearly not sure if he liked that notion.

"I mean," said Don, turning the sound back on as the action started up again, "you're very insightful."

AFTER CARL AND Angela had picked up their kids, Don decided to go for a walk. He needed to clear his head, to think. There was a convenience store three blocks away; he would head over there to get some cashews. They were his favorite indulgence—reasonably low in carbs, but still decadent.

It was a cold, crisp night, and some houses had jack-o'-lanterns out in anticipation of Halloween; appropriately, the trees, denuded of leaves, looked like twisted skeletons writhing toward a clear, dark sky. In the distance, a dog was barking.

His walk took him along the descriptively but prosaically named Diagonal Road, which deposited him near the grounds of

Willowdale Middle School. On a whim, he wandered into the school's large back field, where he used to occasionally go to watch Carl play football all those years ago. He got as far away as he could from the streetlamps—not that it made much difference—and pulled out his datacom. "Help me find Sigma Draconis," he said to it, holding up the small hinged tablet with the display facing toward him, the way he oriented it when using it as a camera.

"Turn around," the datacom said, in its pleasant male voice. "Tilt me higher . . . higher. Good. Now move me to the left. More. More. No, too far. Back up. Yes. Sigma Draconis is in the center of the display."

"That bright one near the top?"

"No, that is Delta Draconis, also known as Nodus Secundus. And the bright one farther down is Epsilon Draconis, or Tyl. Sigma Draconis is too dim for you to see." Crosshairs appeared on the display, centered on a blank part of the sky. "But that's where it is."

Don lowered the datacom and looked directly at the same emptiness, focusing his thoughts on that star, so close by cosmic standards but still unfathomably distant on a human scale.

Somehow, despite the fact that the Dracons had been part of the background of his life for four decades now, they'd never quite seemed real. Oh, he *knew* they were there—right there, right now, along his current line of sight. Indeed, perhaps at this very moment, there were Dracons looking this way, regarding Sol—which would be almost as dim in their night sky as Sigma Draconis was in Earth's—and thinking about the strange beings that must be here. Of course, Sarah would say that the concept of a simultaneous "right now" was meaningless in a relativistic universe; even if Don could have spotted Sigma Draconis, the light he'd have seen would have left there 18.8 years ago. That discontinuity added to the unreal quality the aliens had always had for him.

But if they went ahead with what the Dracons were asking for, the aliens would go from mere abstractions to being here, in the flesh. Granted, the ones born on Earth would know nothing firsthand of their home world, but they would nonetheless be tied to it.

He closed up his datacom, slipped it into his jacket pocket, and began walking again. Maybe because he'd been thinking about prime ministers earlier, it occurred to him that Pierre Trudeau had held that office when he himself had been in middle school. There were many famous Trudeau moments, he knew: the "just watch me" response when asked how far he'd go to put down the terrorists in the October Crisis of 1970; giving the finger from his railcar to detractors in British Columbia; decriminalizing homosexuality and telling the country that "the state has no place in the bedrooms of the nation." But one that had always haunted Don was the famous walk in the snow, when Trudeau had wandered off, alone, to contemplate, weighing his own future against that of his nation. The great man had decided to quit politics that night, to step down as PM.

Trudeau had been twenty-four years younger than Don was now, but he'd been worn out, exhausted. Don, though, had lots of energy and more years ahead than he could really envision; those future years were also an abstraction, like the aliens around Sigma Draconis. Oh, one by one, the years would become concrete, but for now, they, too, didn't quite seem real.

He made his way out of the field, moving from behind the vast dark form of the school, and continued his walk. Someone was coming toward him, and Don felt a little surge of adrenaline—an old man's fear about how a late-night encounter might go. But, as the other person got closer, Don saw that it was a bald-headed middle-aged fellow, who looked quite apprehensive; to him, it was the sight of a twenty-something man that was frightening. Sarah was right; everything was relative.

She would do it in a heartbeat, he knew, if she could: she'd commit to help create, and raise, the Dracon children. And he also knew that he himself wouldn't have all this extra time ahead if it weren't for her. So maybe he owed this to his wife, and to Mc-Gavin, too, who, after all, had actually made it possible.

He continued along, and soon was approaching the convenience store. It was a 7-Eleven, one of countless such stores, all part of a vast chain. Don was old enough to remember when they really had been open only from 7:00 a.m. to 11:00 p.m., instead of twenty-four hours a day. Doubtless, if they had it to do over, the chain's management would have picked a less-restrictive name. But if a giant company couldn't have foreseen what the future held, or that the time they had to deal with would hugely expand, how could he? But, even so, they had changed; they'd adapted. And, he thought, as he went through the sliding glass doors, coming out of the darkness into the light, maybe he could, too.

Chapter 40

WHEN DON GOT back home, Sarah was in the *en suite* bathroom, getting ready for bed. He joined her in there, coming up behind her as she stood at the sink, and oh-so-gently embracing her from behind.

"Hi," she said.

"All right," he replied. "I'll do it."

"Do what?"

"Look after the Dracon children."

Don's grip was loose enough that Sarah managed to gingerly rotate to face him. "Really?"

"Why not?"

"You can't do it just out of a sense of obligation, you know. Are you sure you want to do this?"

"How can I be sure about anything? I'm going to live to be maybe a hundred and sixty. That's *terra incognita* for the whole human race. I know as much about what that's going to be like as—as I know about what it's like to be a bat. But I've got to do *something,* and, as your grandson said to me this evening, it should be something important."

"Percy said that?"

Don nodded, and Sarah made an impressed face.

"Still," she said, "you have to really want this. Every child has the right to be wanted."

"I know. And I do want to do it."

"Yeah?"

He smiled. "Sure. Besides, at least I won't have to worry about these kids ending up with my nose."

DON SUSPECTED THEIR neighbors couldn't be surprised any further by the happenings at his house, but he wondered if any of them took note of the very-expensive-looking rental car pulling into the driveway. If they did, perhaps they zoomed in on Cody McGavin as he got out, and did a face-scanning search to identify him, doubtless the richest man ever to set foot on Betty Ann Drive.

Don opened the front door and watched through the screen as McGavin walked toward him, the mesh dividing him into pixels. "Hello, Don," McGavin said, in his Boston accent. "Great to see you."

"Hello," Don replied, swinging the screen door open. "Won't you come in?" He took McGavin's heavy winter coat and watched him remove his fancy shoes, then ushered him up the stairs to the living room.

Sarah was seated on the couch. Don saw a look flit over Mc-Gavin's face, as if he were startled by how much she'd aged since he'd last seen her. "Hi, Sarah," he said.

"Hello, Mr. McGavin."

Gunter entered from the kitchen. "Ah," McGavin said, "I see you got the Mozo we sent over."

Sarah nodded. "We call him Gunter."

McGavin's eyebrows went up. "After the robot on *Lost in Space?*"

Don was startled. "That's right."

"Gunter," said Sarah, her voice quavering as usual, "I'd like you to meet Cody McGavin. He runs the company that made you."

Don sat down next to Sarah and watched with interest: the creation meeting the creator. "Hello, Mr. McGavin," Gunter said, extending a blue mechanical hand. "It's a true pleasure to meet you."

"And you," said McGavin, shaking the hand. "I hope you've been working hard at helping Dr. Halifax."

"He's been a godsend," said Sarah. "Haven't you, Gunter?"

"I've tried," the Mozo said to McGavin. "I was with her when she made the breakthrough. I'm very proud."

"That's my boy!" said McGavin. He turned to the Halifaxes. "Wonderful machines, aren't they?"

"Oh, yes," said Sarah. "Please, have a seat."

McGavin moved over to the La-Z-Boy. "Nice place you've got here," he said, as he settled in.

Don thought about that. McGavin was known for his philanthropy. Don had seen pictures of him visiting hovels in the third world, and it humbled him to think that this place was closer in cost to one of those than it was to McGavin's famed mansion in Cambridge. The walls here had scuffs, the plaster was chipped, the carpet was worn and stained. The couch, with its hulking lines, had perhaps been stylish late in the last century, but looked hopelessly dated now, and its wine-colored upholstery was wearing thin in a lot of places.

"All right," Sarah said at last, echoing what McGavin had said to them all those months ago, "let's talk turkey. As I said on the phone, I've succeeded in decrypting the Dracon message. Once I tell you what it says, I'm hoping you'll agree with me that we should not make the reply public."

McGavin leaned forward, a hand on his receding chin. "I'm listening. What's it say?"

"The aliens have sent us the Dracon genome—"

"Really?"

"Yes, and instructions on how to produce an artificial womb to bring a couple of Dracon children to term here on Earth, as well as plans for an incubator."

"Jesus," said McGavin softly.

"Wonderful, isn't it?" said Sarah.

"It's . . . amazing. Will they be able to live here?"

"Yes, I think so."

"Wow."

"But there's a snag," said Sarah. "The aliens want me to be, essentially, the foster parent. But I'm too old."

"Well," McGavin began, "I'm sure an appropriate lab could be set up—"

"No," said Sarah, firmly. "No labs, no institutions. These are *people,* not specimens. It'll happen in a home. As I said, I can't do it myself, but I *do* get to choose who does it in my place."

McGavin's voice was gentle, and he looked sideways at Sarah as he spoke. "I'm not quite sure that's your prerogative."

"Oh, yes it is. Because, you see, the message with the genome was addressed to me."

"You said that before. But I still don't know what you mean."

"The decryption key. It's . . . personal to me. And I'm not going to tell you what it is."

"It's not your sequence of survey answers, or any subset of that sequence," said McGavin. "We already tried that. What else could the aliens possibly know about you?"

"With all due respect, I decline to answer."

McGavin drew his eyebrows together but said nothing.

"Now," continued Sarah, "as I say, I can't personally do this. But I can pass on the genome to whomever I wish—by handing over the decryption key."

"I might be willing . . ." began McGavin.

"Actually," said Sarah, "I see you more in the rich-uncle role. Someone has to bankroll the building of the artificial womb, the synthesizing of the DNA, and so on."

McGavin shifted in the chair.

"Besides, you have a full-time job," said Don. "Hell, you've got multiple full-time jobs: president of your company, running your charitable foundation, all the public speaking you do . . ."

The rich man nodded. "True. But if not me, then who?"

Don cleared his throat. "Me."

"You? But weren't you a—what was it?—a DJ, or something?"

"I was a recording-engineer/producer," Don said. "But that was my *first* career. It's time I started to embark on my second."

"With all due respect," McGavin said, "surely there should be a search committee."

"*I'm* the search committee," Sarah said. "And I've made my choice."

"Seriously, Sarah, there should be a formal selection procedure," McGavin said.

"There already has been: the Dracon questionnaire. Using that, they chose me, and I choose Don. But we need your help."

McGavin did not look happy. "I'm a businessperson," he said, spreading his arms. "What's in it for me?"

Don glanced at Sarah, and he saw her wrinkles contort. McGavin's comment made clear that his survey responses couldn't possibly be close to Sarah's—or to Don's. But she had an answer ready for him. "You'll reap any biotech benefits that come from this—not just from studying alien DNA, but from the designs for the womb and the incubator, the formulas for the alien foodstuffs, and so on."

McGavin frowned. "I'm used to fully controlling those operations I'm involved with," he said. "Will you sell me the decryption key? You can name your price . . ."

But Sarah shook her head. "We've already determined that the one thing I might want your money can't buy."

McGavin was quiet for a time, considering this, then: "You're talking about a lot of technology. I mean, sure, DNA synthesis is easy; there are commercial labs that can spit out any sequences we order up. But fabricating the artificial womb, and so forth—that may take a while."

"That's all right," Don said. "I need time to prepare, anyway."

"How?" said McGavin. "How would you prepare for something like this?"

Don shrugged. At this stage, he knew, he was just guessing. "I suppose I'll look at those models we do have: cross-fostering of chimpanzee babies into human homes, feral children, and so on. None of that is exactly comparable, but it'll give me a place to start. And . . ."

"Yes?"

"Well, I made this list years ago: twenty things I want to do before I die. One of them was visit the Dalai Lama. Not that that's likely, but I figure I should prepare . . ." He paused, surprised to hear himself using such an unfamiliar word. ". . . *spiritually* for something like this."

"Well, that's easy enough to arrange," said McGavin.

"You . . . you know the Dalai Lama?"

McGavin smiled. "You've heard that old saw about six degrees of separation? The moment you met me, your score went to two degrees for just about every famous person. We'll set it up."

"Wow. Um, thanks. I just, you know, want to do a good job at . . ."

"At raising aliens," McGavin said, shaking his head, as if the idea were still sinking in.

Don tried to make it sound less portentous. "Think of it as Dr. Spock meets Mr. Spock."

McGavin looked at him blankly; he'd doubtless heard of the Vulcan, but the pediatrician's heyday had been well before his time.

"So," said Sarah, "will you help us?"

McGavin didn't look happy. "I really wish you'd let me control this; no offense, but I've got a lot more experience managing major undertakings."

"Sorry," said Sarah. "It's got to be this way. Are you with us?"

McGavin frowned, considering. "All right," he said, looking at Sarah, then back at Don. "I'm in."

Chapter 41

A FEW DAYS later, Don went up to the study, looking for Sarah, but she wasn't there. He continued down the corridor and peeked into the dark bedroom, and dimly made her out, lying on the bed.

"Sarah . . ." he said softly. It was a tough judgment call: too quiet and she wouldn't hear him regardless of whether she was awake, and too loud and he'd awaken her if she was sleeping.

Sometimes, though, you *do* get the right balance. "Hi, sweetheart," she said. But her voice was weak, low.

He moved quickly to the side of the bed and crouched down. "Are you okay?"

She took a few seconds to reply, his pounding pulse counting each one off. "I'm . . . I'm not sure."

Don looked back over his shoulder. "Gunter!" he called. He could hear the Mozo's footsteps coming up the stairs with metronome precision. He turned back to Sarah. "What's wrong?"

"I feel . . . dizzy," she said. "Weak . . ."

Don swung to look at Gunter's solicitous blue face, which was now looming over him. "How is she?"

"Her temperature is 38.1," said Gunter, "and her pulse is 84 and somewhat erratic."

Don took her thin hand in his. "My God . . ." he said. "We should get you to the hospital."

"No," said Sarah. "No, it's not necessary."

"Yes, it is," said Don.

Her voice grew a little firmer. "What do you say, Gunter?"

"You're not in immediate danger," the robot said. "But you would be wise to see your physician tomorrow."

She nodded, almost imperceptibly.

"Is there anything I can do for you right now?" Don asked.

"No," said Sarah. She paused, and he was about to say something else, when she added, "But . . ."

"Yes?"

"Sit with me a bit, dear."

"Of course." But before he could do anything, Gunter was off like a shot. Moments later, he returned carrying the wheeled stenographer's chair Sarah used at her workstation in the study. The Mozo placed it next to the bed, and Don sat on it.

"Thank you," said Sarah, to the robot.

The Mozo nodded, his mouth looking like a flatlining EKG.

IN THE MORNING, Sarah sat on the couch in the living room, writing on her datacom with a stylus, drafting her reply to the aliens; Cody McGavin had promised to arrange for it to be sent.

So the Dracons would know her message was from their intended recipient, she would ultimately encrypt it using the same key that had decrypted the Dracons' message to her. For now, she was using the English-like notation system she'd developed; later, she'd have a computer program translate the message into Dracon ideograms:

```
!! [Sender's] [Lifespan] << [Recipient's] [Lifespan]
[Recipient's] [Lifespan]&
[Sender's] [Lifespan] ≈ [End]
```

As she jotted down the pseudocode, a more colloquial version ran through her head: *I've figured out that my lifespan is much shorter than yours. Your life goes on and on, but mine is near its end . . .*

She would go on to tell the Dracons that although she couldn't personally do what they'd asked, she'd found a worthy successor, and that they should look forward to receiving reports from their representatives here.

She looked at the words and symbols she'd written so far; the datacom had converted her shaky handwriting into crisp, clean text.

But mine is near its end . . .

Almost ninety years of life, sixty years of marriage. Who could say it was too little? And yet . . .

And yet.

A thought came to her, from so many years ago, from her first date with Don, when they'd gone to see that *Star Trek* film—the one with the whales; he'd know which number it was. Funny how she could remember things from long ago, but had trouble with more-recent stuff; she vividly recalled how the film began, with a screen proclaiming:

> *The cast and crew of Star Trek wish to dedicate this film*
> *to the men and women of the spaceship Challenger*
> *whose courageous spirit shall live to the 23rd century*
> *and beyond. . . .*

Sarah also remembered the other Shuttle disaster, the one in 2003, when *Columbia* had disintegrated on reentry.

She'd been devastated both times, and although it was ridiculous to try to weigh one tragedy against the other, she remembered what she'd said to Don after the second one: she'd rather have been part of *Columbia*'s crew than have been aboard *Challenger*, for the people aboard *Columbia* died at the end of their mission, on the way home—on the *voyage* home. They'd lived long enough to see their lifelong dream realized. They'd gone into orbit, had floated in microgravity, and had looked back down on the wonderful, chaotic, hypnotic blue vista of the Earth. But the *Challenger* astronauts had died within minutes of lifting off, without ever making it into space.

If you have to die, better to die after achieving your goals rather than before. She had lived long enough to see aliens detected, to send a response, and to receive a reply, to engage in a dialogue, however brief. So this was now *after*. Even if there was a lot that she would have liked to have been part of yet to come, this was still after. This was after so very much.

She lifted her stylus to continue writing, and, as she did so, a teardrop fell onto the datacom's display, magnifying the text beneath.

HOW DOES ONE die in the age of miracle and wonder? Incipient strokes and heart attacks are easily detected and prevented. Cancers are simple to cure, as are Alzheimer's and pneumonia. Accidents still happen, but when you have a Mozo to look after you, those are rare.

But, still, at some point, the body *does* wear out. The heart grows weak, the nervous system falters, catabolism far outpaces anabolism. It's not as dramatic as an aneurysm, not as painful as a coronary, not as protracted as a cancer. There's just a slow fade to black.

And that's what had been happening, step by tiny step, to Sarah Halifax, until—

"I don't feel very well," she said one morning, her voice weak.

Don was at her side in an instant. She'd been sitting on the couch in the living room, Gunter having carried her in a chair downstairs about an hour earlier. The robot came over almost as quickly, scanning her vital signs with his built-in sensors.

"What is it?" Don asked.

Sarah managed a weak smile. "It's old age," she said. She paused and breathed in and out a few times. Don took her hand, and looked up at Gunter.

"I will summon Dr. Bonhoff," the robot said, his voice sounding sad. At the very end of life, house calls had come back into fashion; there was no need to tie up a hospital bed for someone who had no hope of getting better.

Don squeezed her hand gently. "Remember what we agreed," she said, her voice low but firm. "No heroic measures. No pointless prolonging of life."

"SHE'S NOT GOING to last the night," said Dr. Tanya Bonhoff, after ministering to Sarah for several hours. Bonhoff was a broad-shouldered white woman of about forty, with close-cropped blond hair. Don and she had withdrawn from the bedroom, and now were standing in the study, the computer monitor blank.

He felt his stomach clenching. Sarah had been promised another six or eight decades, but now . . .

He groped for the stenographer's chair and lowered himself unsteadily onto it.

Now, she might not have another six hours.

"I've given her painkillers, but they won't affect her lucidity," the doctor said.

"Thank you."

"I think you should phone your children," she said gently.

DON RETURNED TO the bedroom. Carl was on a business trip to San Francisco; he'd said he'd take the next possible flight, but even if he could get a red-eye, he still wouldn't be in Toronto until morning. And Emily was out of town as well, helping a friend close up his cottage for the winter; she was now racing back, although it would take her at least four hours to get here.

Sarah was lying in the bed's center, her head propped up by pillows. Don sat on the edge of the bed and held her hand, his smooth skin such a stark contrast with her wrinkled, loose skin.

"Hey," he said, softly.

She tilted her head slightly and let out a breath that hinted at being the same word in reply.

They were quiet for a time, then, softly, Sarah said, "We did all right, didn't we?"

"For sure," he replied. "Two great kids. You've been a wonderful mother." He squeezed her hand just a little harder; it looked so fragile, and bore bruises on its back from needles having been inserted there today. "And you've been a wonderful wife."

She smiled a little, but probably as much as her weakened state would allow. "And you were a won—"

He cut her off, unable to bear the words. "Sixty years" is what came out of his mouth, but that, too, he realized, was a reference to their marriage.

"When I'm . . ." Sarah paused, perhaps vacillating between saying "dead" and saying "gone," then opting for the latter: "When I'm gone, I don't want you to be too sad."

"I . . . don't think I'll be able to help it," he said softly.

She nodded almost imperceptibly. "But you've got what none of the rest of us ever had." She said it without remorse, without bitterness. "You were married for six decades, but have even more than that amount of time to get over . . . get over the loss of your spouse. Until now, no one who'd been married that long ever had that luxury."

"Decades won't be long enough," he said, his voice cracking slightly. "Centuries wouldn't be."

"I know," said Sarah, and she rotated her wrist so she could squeeze his hand, the dying woman comforting the living man. "But we were lucky to have so long together. Bill didn't have nearly that long with Pam."

Don had never believed in such nonsense, but he felt his brother's presence now, one ghost already hovering in this room, perhaps ready to conduct Sarah on her journey.

Sarah spoke again, although it was clearly an effort. "We were luckier than most."

He considered that for a moment. Maybe she was right. Despite everything, maybe she was right. What had he thought, back on the day of their sixtieth wedding anniversary, while waiting for the kids to show up? *It had been a good life*—and nothing that had happened since could erase that.

She was quiet for a time, just looking at him. At last, she shook her head slightly. "You look so much like you did when we first met, all those years ago."

He tilted his head dismissively. "I was fat then."

"But your . . ." She sought a word, found it: "Intensity. It's the same. It's all the same, and—" She winced, apparently feeling a knife-edge of pain, sharp enough to cut through the drugs Bonhoff had given her.

"Sarah!"

"I'm—" She stopped herself before giving voice to the lie that she was okay.

"I know it's been difficult for you," she said, "this last year." She paused, as if exhausted from speaking, and Don had nothing to fill the void with, so he simply waited until she had regained enough strength to continue: "I know that . . . that you couldn't possibly have wanted to be with someone so old, when you were so young."

His stomach was as tight as a prizefighter's fist. "I'm sorry," he said, almost in a whisper.

Whether she'd heard him, he couldn't say. But she managed a small smile. "Think about me from time to time. I don't—" She made a sound in her throat, but he perceived it as one of sadness, not a sign of further deterioration. "I don't want the only person thinking about me 18.8 years from now to be my pen pal on Sigma Draconis II."

"I promise," he said. "I'll be thinking about you constantly. I'll be thinking about you forever."

She made a weak smile again. "No one could do that," she

said, very softly, "but of all the people I know in the world, you're the one who could come the closest."

And, with that, her hand went limp in his.

He let go of her hand and shook her ever so gently. "Sarah!"

But there was no reply.

--- Chapter 42 ---

WHEN MORNING CAME, Don and Emily—who had arrived around midnight, and had slept in her old room while Don slept on the couch—started making the requisite phone calls to family and friends. The fifteenth or twentieth one Don made was to Cody McGavin. Ms. Hashimoto put him through at once, after he told her why he was calling.

"Hello, Don," McGavin said. "What's up?"

Don said it simply, directly: "Sarah passed away last night."

"Oh, my . . . Oh, Don, I'm sorry."

"The funeral will be in three days, here in Toronto."

"Let me—no, damn it. I have to be in Borneo. I'm so sorry."

"That's okay," Don said.

"I, um, I hate to even mention this," McGavin said, "but, ah, you *do* have the decryption key, don't you?"

"Yes," replied Don.

"Good, good. Maybe you should give me a copy. You know, for backup."

"It's safe," Don said. "Don't worry."

"It's just that—"

"Anyway," said Don. "I've got to make a lot more calls, but I thought you'd want to know."

"I do appreciate it, Don. And, again, my condolences."

WHEN THE CALL had come from McGavin Robotics, saying it was time for his Mozo's routine-maintenance service check, Don had resisted the urge to put it off. "Fine," he said. "What time will you be here?"

"Whenever you like," the male voice had said.

"Don't you have to schedule these things weeks in advance?"

The person at the other end of the line chuckled. "Not for Mr. McGavin's priority customers."

The dark-blue van had shown up punctually at 11:00 a.m., just as Don had requested. A dapper little black man of about forty-five came to the door, carrying a small aluminum equipment case. "Mr. Halifax?" he said.

"That's right."

"My name's Albert. Sorry to be a bother. We like to tune things up periodically. You understand—better to nip problems in the bud than to let a major systems failure occur."

"Sure," said Don. "Come in."

"Where is your Mozo?" Albert asked.

"Upstairs, I think." Don led him up to the living room, then said loudly, "Gunter!"

Normally, Gunter appeared in a flash—Jeeves on steroids. But this time he didn't, so Don actually yelled the name. "Gunter! Gunter!" When there was still no response, Don looked at the roboticist, feeling a bit embarrassed, as though a child of Don's was misbehaving in front of guests. "Sorry."

"Could he be out back?" Albert asked.

"Maybe. But he knew you were coming . . ."

Don ascended the big staircase, Albert following him. They looked in the study, in the bedroom, in the *en suite* bathroom, in the other bathroom, and in what had been Emily's old room. But there was no sign of Gunter. Going downstairs, they checked the kitchen and the dining room. Nothing. Then they headed to the basement, and—

"Oh, God!" said Don, sprinting to the fallen Mozo. Gunter was sprawled facedown in the middle of the floor.

The roboticist ran over, too, and kneeled. "His power's off," he said.

"We never turn him off," said Don. "Could his battery have failed?"

"After less than a year?" Albert said, as if Don had suggested an absurdity. "Not likely."

The roboticist rolled Gunter over onto his back. *"Shit,"* he said. There was a small panel open in the center of Gunter's chest. Albert took a penlight from his breast pocket and shone it within. "Damn, damn, damn . . ."

"What is it?" asked Don. "What's wrong?" He peered into the opening. "What are those controls for?"

"They're the master mnemonic registers," Albert replied. He reached below the open panel, to Gunter's recessed on/off switch, located right where a navel would have been, and he gave the switch a firm push.

"Hello," said the familiar voice, as the mouth outline twitched into life. "Do you speak English? *Hola. Habla Español? Bonjour. Parlez-vous français? Konichi-wa. Nihongo-o hanashimasu-ka?"*

"What is this?" said Don. "What's happening?"

"English," Albert said to the robot.

"Hello," said the Mozo again. "This is the first time I've been activated since leaving the factory, so I need to ask you a few questions, please. First, from whom do I take instructions?"

"What's he talking about?" said Don. " 'First time.' What's with that?"

"He's done a system restore," Albert said, shaking his head slowly back and forth.

"What?"

"He's wiped his own memory, and reset everything to its factory-default state."

"Why?"

"I don't know. I've never seen one do that before."

"Gunter . . ." said Don, looking into the two, round glassy eyes.

"Which of you is Gunter?" replied the robot.

"No," said Don. *"You're* Gunter. That's your name."

"Is that G-U-N-T-H-E-R?" asked the machine.

Don felt his stomach knotting. "He's—he's gone, isn't he?"

The man nodded.

"No way to bring him back?"

"I'm sorry, no. It's a total wipe."

"But—" And then Don got it. It had taken him longer than it had taken Gunter, but he got it. The only—the only *person* who had been with Sarah when she'd unlocked the Dracon message had been Gunter. This technician hadn't come here to give the Mozo a tune-up. He'd come to tap into Gunter's memories, to steal the decryption key for McGavin. The rich man had wanted to control everything—and with the decryption key he could, taking over the creating of the Dracon children himself and cutting Don right out of the process.

"Get out," Don said to the roboticist.

"Excuse me?"

Don was furious. "Get the hell out of my house."

"Mr. Halifax, I—"

"Do you think I don't know what you were sent here to do? Get out."

"Honestly, Mr. Halifax—"

"Now!"

Albert looked frightened; Don was physically twenty years younger than him and six inches taller. He grabbed his aluminum case and hurried up the stairs, while Don gingerly helped Gunter get back on his feet.

DON KNEW WHAT must have happened. After he'd called McGavin to tell him that Sarah had passed on, McGavin had thought back to the last time he'd seen Sarah, and, in replaying it in his mind, he must have realized that Gunter would have seen Sarah apply the decryption key, and so probably knew what it was.

Don was livid as he told his phone to call McGavin. After two rings, a voice he knew answered. "McGavin Robotics. Office of the president."

"Hello, Ms. Hashimoto. It's Donald Halifax. I'd like to speak to Mr. McGavin."

"I'm sorry, but he's not available right now."

Don spoke with controlled rage. "Please take a message. Tell him I need to hear back from him today."

"I can't commit to when Mr. McGavin might return any given call, and—"

"Just give him the message," Don said.

DON'S PHONE RANG two hours later. "Hi, Don. Ms. Hashimoto said you called—"

"If you ever try a stunt like that again, I swear I'll cut you completely out," Don said. "Jesus, we thought we could trust you!"

"I don't know what you're talking about."

"Don't play games. I know what you were trying to do with Gunter."

"I'm not—"

"Don't deny it."

"I think you should take a deep breath, Don. I know you've been through a lot—"

"You're damn right I have. They say people aren't really gone, so long as we remember them. But now one of those who remembered Sarah *perfectly* is gone."

Silence.

"Damn it, Cody! We can't do this if I can't trust you."

"That robot is *mine*," McGavin said. "He's on loan from my company—so everything in his memories is *my* property."

"There's nothing in his memories now," snapped Don.

"I—I know," said McGavin. "I'm sorry. If I'd thought for one second that he'd—" Silence for a time, then: "No robot has ever done that before."

"You could take a lesson from him," said Don, sharply. "A lesson in loyalty."

McGavin's tone grew stiff; doubtless he was almost never spoken to like this. "Well, since the Mozo was loaned to Sarah, to help her, maybe I should—"

Don felt his pulse racing. "No, please—don't take him back. I . . ."

McGavin still sounded angry. "What?"

Don shrugged a little, although there was no way McGavin could see it. "He's family."

A long pause, then an audible intake of breath. "All right," said McGavin. "If it'll make things right between us, you can keep him."

Silence.

"Are we okay, Don?"

Don was still furious. If he'd really been twenty-six, he might have continued fighting. But he wasn't; he knew when to back down. "Yeah."

"All right." McGavin's tone slowly regained its warmth. "Because we're making good initial progress on the artificial womb, but, God, it's tough. Every part has to be machined from scratch, and there are technologies involved my engineers have never seen before . . ."

DON LOOKED AROUND the living room. The mantel now had dozens of sympathy cards on it, each one dutifully printed out and folded by Gunter. Don lamented the death of paper mail, but he supposed sending streams of data that could be reconstituted by the recipient was appropriate under the circumstances.

One of the sympathy cards was propped up by the trophy the IAU had given Sarah. Another was leaning against Don and Sarah's wedding photo in a way that covered the image of Don.

He walked over to the mantel, moved that card, and looked at Sarah as she had been, and at himself, back when he'd been in his twenties the first time around.

There were flowers, too, both real and virtual. A vase of roses sat on the little table between the couch and the La-Z-Boy; a projection of pink carnations hovered above the coffee table. He remembered how much Sarah had enjoyed planting flowers in her youth, how she still gardened well into her seventies, how she'd once described the Very Large Array as looking like God's flower bed.

As he looked at the cards some more, Don became conscious of movement out of the corner of his eye. He turned and beheld the round blue face of Gunter.

"I'm sorry that your wife is gone," the robot said, and its emoticon line was turned downward at the ends in a way that might have been comical in other circumstances but just now seemed touchingly genuine.

Don regarded the machine. "Me, too," he said softly.

"I hope it was not presumptuous," said the robot, "but I have read what is written in these cards." He tilted his head at the mantel. "She sounds like a remarkable woman."

"That she was," Don said. He didn't enumerate them out loud, but the categories ran through his head: wife, mother, friend, teacher, scientist, and, earlier, daughter and sister. So many roles, and she'd filled them all well.

"If I may ask, what did people say about her at the funeral?"

"I'll show you the footage later."

Footage. The word echoed in Don's head. No one used the term anymore. It referred to an obsolete technology and a measuring system that had all but passed out of living memory.

"Thank you," said Gunter. "I wish I had known her."

Don looked at the unblinking glass eyes for a time. "I'm going to go to the cemetery tomorrow," he said. "Would—would you like to come with me?"

The Mozo nodded. "Yes. I would like that very much."

YORK CEMETERY'S NORTHERN border was marked by the back fences of the houses on Park Home Avenue, and Park Home was just one block south of Betty Ann Drive, so Don and Gunter simply walked there. Don wondered if any of his neighbors were watching them through their windows, or zooming in on them with their security cameras: the robot and the rollback, two miracles of modern science, marching along, side by side.

After a few minutes, they reached the gated entrance. When Sarah and he had bought their house, its proximity to a cemetery had depressed its value. Now it was seen as a plus, since green spaces of any type were so rare these days. And, fortunately, they'd bought the plot here early on; they'd never have been able to afford the luxury of interment today.

Don and Gunter had to walk along a path for several hundred meters to get to where Sarah was buried. Gunter was looking around with what Don could have sworn were wide eyes. Tested in a factory, and then used exclusively since his memory wipe inside a house, the robot had never seen so many trees and such wide expanses of manicured lawns.

At last they came to the spot. The hole had been filled in, and new sod covered the grave, a scar of dirt outlining it.

Don looked over at the robot, who, in turn was looking toward the headstone. "The inscription is off-center," Gunter said. Don turned to it. Sarah's name and details were confined to the right half of the oblong block of granite.

"I'll be buried here, too," said Don. "My information will be added on the other side."

Sarah's half said:

SARAH DONNA ENRIGHT HALIFAX
BELOVED WIFE AND MOTHER
29 MAY 1960 — 20 NOVEMBER 2048
SHE TALKED TO THE STARS

Don looked at the blankness onto which his own dates would someday be written. The death year would likely start with a two and a one, he supposed: nineteen-sixty to twenty-one-something. His poor, darling Sarah would likely lie here alone for the better part of a century.

He felt a tightness in his chest. He hadn't cried much at the funeral. The strain of greeting so many people, the rushing to and fro—he'd endured it all in a state of near shock, he supposed, ferried about by Emily.

But now there was no more rushing around. Now, he was alone except for Gunter, and he was exhausted, emotionally and physically.

He looked again at the headstone, the letters blurring.

Beloved wife.

Beloved mother.

The tears started coming in force, streaming down his too-smooth cheeks, and, after valiantly trying to stay standing on his own for maybe half a minute, Don collapsed against Gunter. And whether it was a behavior he'd been programmed with, or whether it was something he'd seen on TV, or whether it had just spontaneously emerged didn't really matter, but Don could feel the flat of Gunter's hand patting him gently, soothingly, in the center of his back as the robot held him.

--- Chapter 43 ---

DON REMEMBERED WONDERING whether time would pass quickly or slowly for him now that he was young again. One possibility was that years might crawl by the way they had in his actual youth, each one seeming to take forever to run its course.

But that wasn't what happened. Before Don knew it, more than a full year had slipped by: the calendar freshly read 2050, and he was twenty-seven and he was also eighty-nine.

But, even if its passage had seemed rapid, that year did change things, although he did still find himself often just staring into space, thinking about Sarah and—

And—

No. Just about Sarah; only about Sarah. He knew she was the only one who should be in his thoughts, although—

Although Lenore doubtless knew that Sarah had died. For the first few weeks after her passing, Don had assumed he'd hear something from her. In a previous age, she might have sent a consolatory telegram or a paper card, neither of which would have invited dialogue, neither of which would have required a response. But these days Lenore's only real options would have been to phone, which certainly would have engendered a conversation, or to send an email, which netiquette would have required Don to reply to.

But as first one month and then another passed, Don realized she wasn't going to be in touch—which, he supposed, might have been just as well, for what could she have said? That she was sorry that Sarah was dead? And yet, wouldn't there have been, between the lines, too horrible to acknowledge directly but impossible to dismiss from consciousness, a concomitant thought that she was sorry Sarah hadn't died sooner? Not out of any animus but simply in recognition of the fact that Sarah's existence was what had ultimately kept Lenore and Don apart?

Every few weeks, he searched the web, looking at references to Sarah. There was so much about her, and even though most of it was quite old, it made it seem, in a strange way, like she was still around.

He never googled himself anymore, though. There was, as Randy Trenholm had said, lots of discussion of the peculiar circumstances of his rollback, and he found reading it made his stomach turn. But every now and then he did put in Lenore's name, to see what would come up. She had indeed finished her master's, and, as she'd said she'd hoped to, had now moved to Christchurch, and was working there on her doctorate.

He looked at whatever his searches found: references to her on the University of Canterbury website, citations of a paper she was junior author on, her occasional postings to political newsgroups, and video of her on a panel discussion at a conference in Tokyo. He watched the clip over and over again.

He would never get over the loss of Sarah; he knew that. But he *did* have to get on with life, and soon enough that life would change totally and completely, in ways he couldn't begin to guess. McGavin said the womb should be ready in a matter of weeks now. Of course, the gestation would take a while—seven months, according to the message the Dracons had sent.

Lenore had been out of his life for almost a year and a half now. It was too much to hope that she might still be free. And, even if she were free, maybe the whole *episode* (that was the word she'd use) was something she wanted to put behind her, anyway:

the insane time during which she'd fallen for what she'd thought was a contemporary, only to discover to her shock and disgust that he was—that hated term again—an octogenarian.

And yet . . .

And yet, in the end, she seemed to have more or less come to terms with the reality of what he was, accepting his dual ages, his youthful exterior and his less-youthful interior. It would be a miracle to find someone else who could deal with that, and although this *was* the age of miracle and wonder, Don didn't believe in *that* kind of miracle.

Of course, he thought, a sensible man would contact Lenore by phone or email. A sensible man wouldn't fly halfway around the planet in the faint hope that he'd be greeted with open arms. But he wasn't a sensible man; he was a supremely silly one—both the women he'd loved had told him that.

And so . . .

AND SO, HERE he was, on a flight to New Zealand. As he took his seat on the plane, he realized he had a real advantage over the aliens on Sigma Draconis. The Dracons could only broadcast their messages into the darkness, and, unless a reply was sent back, they'd never even know if their signals had been received, and then not for years to come. He at least would see Lenore's face—and, he expected, that *was* all he'd need to see: the message it contained when she first laid eyes on him would be unguarded and honest, an unencrypted signal. And yet, what he'd give to know the answer now . . .

> *By that Heaven that bends above us—*
> *by that God we both adore—*
> *Tell this soul with sorrow laden if,*
> *within the distant Aidenn,*
> *It shall clasp a sainted maiden*
> *whom the angels named Lenore*

Don had ended up with a window seat. That was perhaps a plum position on a domestic flight, but when one wanted to get up frequently to stretch one's legs, it meant disturbing, in this case, not one but two fellow passengers, one of whom, the one with the middle seat, adjacent to Don's, was a man of at least seventy-five. Don all too vividly remembered what it was like to try to haul himself to his feet, especially in a cramped, awkward space, at such an age, and so he mostly endured being trapped, alternating between looking out at the endless vistas of cloud tops and watching a succession of programs on his seat-back monitor.

About four hours into the flight the old man next to him struck up a conversation. "God eye," he said—and, after a moment, Don's brain decoded it as "Good day" filtered through an Australian accent. "Name's Roger." He must be heading home, Don presumed; this flight would continue on to Melbourne after its stop in Auckland, where Don himself would change planes for Christchurch.

"What were you doing in Toronto?" asked Don, after they had confirmed Roger's pedigree in conversation.

"Actually, I was in Huntsville," Roger said. "You know it?"

"Sure," said Don. "Cottage country."

"Bingo. My daughter lives there. Runs a B-and-B. And she just had a baby girl, so I had to go see."

Don smiled. "Grandkids are great."

Roger looked at him quizzically, but then nodded and said, "That they are, mate."

"Have you been to Canada before?" Don asked.

"This was my fourth trip, but . . ." His face, so full of delight when he mentioned his new granddaughter, now looked sad, and Don thought he was perhaps going to say it was likely to be his last time. But what he actually said was "It was my first time going on my own. My wife passed away last year."

Don's heart skipped a beat. "I'm sorry."

"Thanks. A wonderful woman, my Kelly was."

"I'm sure. How long were you married?"

"Fifty years. Fifty years and one week, actually. It was like she'd been holding on, wanting to make that milestone."

Don said nothing.

"I miss her so much," Roger said. "I miss her every day."

Don just listened as Roger talked about his wife, and the fine times they'd had together, and he resisted the almost overwhelming urge to say, "I know," or "Same here," or "That's just the way it was with Sarah and me."

Finally, though, Roger looked at him with an embarrassed expression. "Sorry," he said. "I guess I've been rambling. You'll have to forgive an old geezer."

"Not at all," said Don.

Roger smiled. He had a roundish head and very little hair, and the rough skin of a man who'd enjoyed being out in the sun much of his life. "You're a fine young bloke, listening to me go on like that."

Don found he had to suppress a grin. "Thanks."

"So, mate, what's your story? Why are you going to Oz?"

"Actually, I'm not. I'm heading to New Zealand."

"North Island or South?"

"South."

"Well, they're both lovely. Lots of sheep, though."

This time Don didn't suppress his grin. Still, he couldn't say he'd been there almost sixty years ago, and he didn't know enough contemporary details to speak convincingly of a more-recent trip, so he simply said, "So I hear."

"What's bringing you to Kiwi-land? Business or pleasure?"

"Honestly? I'm chasing after a girl."

To his surprise, Roger slapped him on the knee. "Good on you, mate! Good on you!"

"Maybe," said Don. "Maybe not. We broke up over a year ago. She went to Christchurch to study. But I've missed her more than I can say."

"She knows you're coming, though, right?"

Don shook his head and steeled himself for being told he was being foolish.

Roger lifted his eyebrows. "Can you stand a spot of advice from an old man?"

"Best kind I know," Don said.

Roger tilted his head; he'd presumably expected an attempt to deflect his input. But then he nodded sagely. "You're doing the right thing. The only regrets I have are over the mad, impetuous things I *didn't* do."

Don smiled. "You are a very wise man."

Roger chuckled. "Live long enough and you'll be one, too."

Chapter 44

AFTER CHANGING PLANES, Don finally made it to the airport in Christchurch around 5:00 a.m. local time. He hated having to pay for a night's hotel when he wasn't checking in until almost dawn, but the alternative would be trying to rendezvous with Lenore in a disheveled, wild-eyed, sleep-deprived state, and he felt enough like a crazy person doing this already.

He'd booked the cheapest hotel he could find online, and took a taxi over to it. His room was small by North American standards but it had a little balcony. After he'd washed up a bit, he stepped out onto it. Even though it was summer here, he could see his own breath in the crisp early-morning air.

Almost all the lights were off in the surrounding buildings. He went back into his room for a moment and killed the lights there, then returned to the balcony and let his tired eyes adjust to the dimness.

You can't be married to an astronomer for sixty years without learning some constellations, but Don saw almost nothing familiar in this moonless sky, although there were two stars brighter than all the others. Alpha Centauri and Beta Centauri—just about all he could remember from his brief trip here all those years ago, except . . .

He scanned about, and—yes, there they were, impossibly large: the Clouds of Magellan, two smudges against the darkness. He stood there for a time, shivering, looking at them.

By and by, the sun started to come up, the horizon growing pink, and—

And suddenly there was a cacophony of bird songs: trills and tweets unlike any he ever heard back in Canada. An unfamiliar sky, bizarre background sounds: he might as well be on an alien world.

He went back inside, set an alarm for five hours hence, lay down, and closed his eyes, wondering what the new day would hold.

WHEN DON GOT up, he used his datacom to check his email. There was the usual daily progress report from Cody McGavin: all was going well with fabricating the womb. The alien DNA sequences had now been synthesized, too, done in bits and pieces at four separate commercial labs, then reassembled through a version of the whole-genome shotgun technique that had been used half a century earlier to make the first map of the *Homo sapiens* genome. Soon, McGavin said, everything would be ready to start growing the embryos.

DON HAD THOUGHT about trying to intercept Lenore as she was leaving from or arriving at her flat; it had been easy enough to find out where she lived. But some might view what he was doing as the ultimate act of stalking; she might be quite disconcerted if he showed up unannounced there. Besides, for all he knew, she was living with someone, and he didn't want a confrontation with a jealous boyfriend.

And so he decided to go see her at the university. It took nothing but a few questions asked of his datacom to reveal the astronomy grad-student colloquium schedule. Before leaving the hotel, he got a little money from the cash machine in the lobby; Don remembered all the predictions of a cashless society, but that, too, had failed to pan out, mostly because of concerns over privacy.

Although he received crisp new bills, a much younger version of King William appeared on them than Don was used to from the banknotes back home; it was as though His Royal Highness had had a little rollback of his own down here.

The robot-driven taxi let him off at the entrance to the campus, by a big sign:

NAU MAI, HAERE MAI KI TE
WHARE WĀNANGA O WAITAHA

Strange words, alien text. But a Rosetta stone was provided as a matching sign on the opposite side of the roadway:

WELCOME TO THE UNIVERSITY OF CANTERBURY

A river ran through the campus, and he walked along one of its banks toward the building a passerby told him housed the astronomy department, a new-looking red-brick affair half-sunk into a hillside. Once he got inside, he started looking for the right room, although he had trouble figuring out the sequence of room numbers.

He stumbled upon the astronomy-department office and stuck his head in the door. There was a Maori man of about thirty at a desk, his face covered by intricate tattoos. "Hi," said Don. "Can you please tell me where room 42-214B is?"

"Looking for Lenore Darby?" asked the man.

Moths danced a ballet in Don's stomach. "Um, yes."

The man smiled. "Thought so. You've got a Canadian accent. Anyway, go down the hall, turn right at the next corridor, and it'll be on your left."

Don had twenty minutes until the colloquium would be over. He thanked the man then made a pit stop in a washroom, and checked for anything in his teeth, fixed his hair, and straightened his clothes. And then he headed to the classroom. The door was closed, but it had a little window and he chanced a peek through it.

His heart jumped. There was Lenore, standing at the front of the room; apparently it was her turn to present to the colloquium. As if to underscore that time had passed and many things might be different, he noted that she'd cut her red hair much shorter than he was used to seeing it. And she looked older, although she was still in that range of years during which that meant more grown-up, not more decrepit.

The room was a small lecture theater, with a steep bank of chairs facing a central stage. There was a podium, but Lenore wasn't hiding behind it. Instead she stood confidently, in full view, in the middle of the stage. Perhaps a dozen other people were in the room. All he could see of them were the backs of their heads. Some had gray hair; presumably they were faculty members. Lenore was using a laser pointer to indicate things within a complex graphic on the room's front wall screen. He couldn't make out what she was saying, but the squeak was unmistakable.

Don sat on the floor beside the door, waiting for the session to end. He felt a surge of adrenaline when the door swung open— but it was only some guy wearing an All Blacks T-shirt stepping out to use the washroom.

Finally other classrooms along the same hallway started opening, but the door to Lenore's room remained maddeningly shut. Don got up off the floor and dusted off the seat of his pants. He was just about to look through the window when the door swung open again. He stepped to one side, the way people used to with subway doors in Toronto.

When there was a lull, he looked into the room again. Lenore was down at the front, her back to him, talking with the final remaining person, a slim young man. Don watched until, at last, the man nodded and started walking up the stairs. Lenore, meanwhile, was doing something at the podium.

Don took a deep breath, hoping it would calm him, and he went through the door. He got only four steps down before Lenore looked up, and—

—and her eyes went wide, almost fully circular, and her mouth dropped open, forming another circle, and he continued down, feeling shakier than he'd ever felt even before the rollback.

She clearly couldn't believe what she was seeing, and she looked as though she was trying to convince herself that this was someone who just happened to bear a strong resemblance to Don. It had been a long time since she'd seen him, after all, and—

"Don?" she said at last.

He smiled, but could feel the corners of his mouth quivering. "Hello, Lenore."

"Don!" She practically shouted the name, and a giant grin grew across her face.

He found himself running down the remaining stairs, and she was coming up them, taking two in each stride, and suddenly they were in each other's arms. He so desperately wanted to kiss her—but just because he was being greeted like an old friend didn't mean she'd welcome that.

After all too brief a time, he felt her pulling away. She looked at him, her eyes flicking back and forth, staring first at his left eye, then his right. "What *are* you doing here?"

"I—I hope you don't mind."

"Mind?" she said.

"I didn't know whether you'd be happy to see me."

"Of course I'm happy! Are you taking a vacation down here?"

He shook his head. "I came just to see you."

She looked thunderstruck. "My . . . God. You should have called."

"I know. I'm sorry."

"No, no. Don't be sorry, but . . ." She paused. "All this way just to see me?"

He nodded.

"My God," she said again. But then she tilted her chin down a bit. "I was so sorry to hear about Sarah. When was that? Four or five months ago?"

"Over a year," said Don, simply.

"I'm so sorry," she said. "I—I'm just so sorry."

"Me, too."

"And now," she said, a shift in her tone indicating that the enormity of the situation had struck her, "you're here."

"Yes." He didn't know how to ask his next question politely, or how to segue to it elegantly, so he just blurted it out. "Are you seeing anyone?"

She looked at him a moment longer, and it was clear that she understood the import of the question, and also understood that she'd been offered an out: she could simply respond in the affirmative and not have to deal further with him. "No," she said, firmly if squeakily. "No one."

He felt air rushing out of him, and he pulled her close again. "Thank God," he said. He hesitated for a second, then gently tilted her face up, and kissed her—and, to his delight, she kissed him back.

Suddenly there was a loud sound, and another, and another. He turned his head and looked up, and—

And there, standing at the top of the stairs, were a handful of students, waiting to come into the room, and one of them had started to applaud, a big grin on his face. The others joined him, and Don felt an even bigger grin splitting his own features, and he looked at Lenore, whose skin had turned bright red.

"If you'll excuse us," Don said, and he took Lenore's hand, and the two of them began walking up the stairs, and the students started coming down, passing them, and one of them slapped Don on the shoulder as he went by.

LENORE AND DON headed out into the warm midday air, which was a wonderful contrast to the Canadian winter he'd left behind. There was so much he wanted to tell her, and yet he found it impossible to begin. At last, though, he said, "I like your hair that way."

"Thanks," said Lenore, still holding his hand. They were walking along the banks of the little river, which Lenore said was called the Avon; it made a pleasing background sound. On the opposite side of it were campus buildings and a car park. The pathway was paved, and there were trees of types Don couldn't name on its margin. Lenore nodded occasionally to passing students or faculty members.

"So, what are you doing now?" she asked. A couple of birds with black bodies, long curving bills, and orange cheek patches hopped out of their way. "Have—have you found a job?" She said it gently, knowing that the issue was a delicate one.

Don stopped walking, and Lenore stopped, too. He let go of her hand and looked into her eyes. "I want to tell you something," he said, "but I need you to promise to keep it a secret."

"Of course," she said.

He nodded. He trusted her completely. "Sarah decrypted the message."

Lenore's eyes narrowed. "That can't be," she said. "I'd have heard . . ."

"It was a *private* message."

She looked at him, brow knitted.

"I'm serious," he said. "It was private, for the person whose survey answers the Dracons found most to their liking."

"And that was Sarah?"

"That was my Sarah, yes."

"So what did the message say?"

Two students were running toward them, obviously late for class. Don waited until they passed. "They sent their genome, and the instructions for all the supporting hardware needed to create two Dracon children."

"My . . . God. Are you serious?"

"Absolutely. Cody McGavin is involved in the project. And so am I. I'm going to be the . . ." He paused, even now still somewhat amazed at the notion. ". . . the foster father. But I'll need help raising the Dracon children."

She looked at him blankly.

"And, well, I want you back in my life. I want you in the children's lives."

"Me?"

"Yes, you."

She looked stunned. "I, um, I mean, you and me—that's one thing, and I . . ."

Don's heart was pounding. "Yes?"

She smiled that radiant smile of hers. "And I *have* missed you so. But . . . but this stuff about raising—my God, the very idea!—about raising Dracon children. I—I'm hardly qualified for that."

"No one is. But you're a SETI researcher; that's as good a background as any to start with."

"But I'm years away from finishing my Ph.D."

"Have you picked a thesis topic?" he said. " 'Cause I've got a doozy . . ."

She looked stunned, but then she frowned. "But I'm down here, in New Zealand. Presumably you're planning to do this in North America."

"Don't worry about that. When we go public with this—and we will, just as soon as the children are born—every university on the planet will want a piece of it. I'm sure arrangements can easily be made with the administration here so that your degree won't be jeopardized."

"I don't know what to say. I mean, this is—it's almost too much to take in."

"Tell me about it," said Don.

"Dracon children," she said again, shaking her head. "It would be an amazing experience, but there are tenured profs who—"

"This isn't about credentials; it's about *character*. The aliens didn't ask the survey respondents to rank themselves socioeconomically or to indicate how much education they had. They asked about their morals, their ethics."

"But I never took the survey," she said.

"No, but I did. And I'm a pretty darn good judge of character myself. So what do you say?"

"I'm—overwhelmed."

"And intrigued?"

"God, yes. But talk about bringing baggage into a relationship! You've got kids, grandkids—and you're going to have . . . um . . ."

"Sarah called them 'Draclings.'"

"*Awww!* So cute! Still, kids, grandkids, and Draclings . . ."

"And the robot—don't forget I've got a robot."

She shook her head, but was smiling as she did so. "What a family!"

He smiled back at her. "Hey, this is the Fifties. Get with the times."

She nodded. "Oh, I'm sure it'll be great. But it's not—you know—not *complete*. The family, I mean. I'll want to have a child or two of my own."

"Oooh! More presents on Father's Day!"

"*If* you're the father . . ." She looked at him. "Is that . . . is that something you're interested in doing?"

"I think so, yes. If the right woman comes along . . ."

She whapped him on the arm.

"Seriously," he said, "I'd be thrilled. Besides, the Draclings will need playmates."

She smiled, but then her eyes went wide. "But our kids will be—my God, they'll be younger than your grandkids . . ." She shook her head. "I don't think I'll ever get used to all this."

Don took her hand. "Of course you will, darling. Just give it time."

"COME ON, EVERYONE! Let's go!"

Don had pulled the big van up to the edge of the large concrete plaza in front of the docks. Hundreds of tourists were
milling about, either waiting to get on one of the high-speed fer-
ries, or, like Don's family, having just gotten off one. The plaza
was ringed by vendors selling T-shirts, hot dogs, and more.
Lenore was standing near the barrier that prevented Don from
bringing the van any closer. "You heard your father!" she called.
"We want to get there while the sun's still up."

Don couldn't blame them for dawdling. This spot, at the foot
of Hurontario Street, was the only place they'd been where they
could get a good view of the entire fairgrounds, sprawling across
two artificial islands out in Lake Ontario. The American pavilion
was a gigantic diamond—quite literally—and the Chinese pavilion honored both its nation's culture and Earth's most famous
nonhuman citizens by being built in the shape of a rampant
dragon whose body curved and twisted to match the one depicted
by the constellation of Draco. Rising between them was the glis-
tening carbon-nanotube Spire of Hope, which had brought back
to Toronto the title of being home to the world's tallest building.

Don was used to his sons' three-legged walk, but the tourists
who had been discreetly watching them now gawked openly at
the surprisingly graceful spectacle of them in motion. His
daughter, though, was standing still. Fifteen-year-old Gillian,
who had her mother's freckles but her father's sandy brown hair,

was one place from the head of the line for a cotton-candy vendor. She looked at her dad with an anxious expression, wondering if she'd have to bail before securing her treat.

"It's okay," Don called out. "But hurry!"

He and Lenore had done their best raising Gillian, and Don had been pleased to find how relaxing it had been to be a parent the second time around; with the quiet confidence of experience, he'd had a much better handle on what were genuine crises and which things would pass of their own accord.

The boys, who, at two and a half meters tall and two hundred kilos apiece, had no trouble making their way through the crowd, had also turned out all right. They'd been raised alongside Gillian in a house Cody McGavin had paid for—in Winnipeg, as it happened, since prudence suggested that it be somewhere near a level-four biohazard containment lab, and the one there was the only one in North America designed to handle livestock and other large lifeforms. Hundreds of experts watched the goings-on in the house through webcams, and provided what advice they could. But Don and Lenore were the boys' parents, and ultimately, as all parents did, they went with their best instincts.

Don touched the control that opened the rear passenger compartment. The van—the Dracmobile, as the press had dubbed it—had a high enough roof to accommodate the boys, neither of whom could sit; their two front legs and thick hind leg weren't built for that. Once they were in, Don sealed the compartment, and let the carbon-dioxide scrubbers get to work. By the time Gillian had arrived, gingerly carrying her giant ball of pink cotton candy, the green light on the dashboard had gone on, and the boys had removed their filter masks.

Don had never thought he'd own such a big van, but, then again, the days of worrying about gas mileage were long since gone. It had taken a while, but he'd finally gotten tired of intoning, as Robin had in the 1960s *Batman* series, "Atomic batteries to power! Turbines to speed!" whenever he climbed in. Lenore got into the front passenger seat, and Gillian and Gunter—the Gees, as they were collectively referred to in the Halifax-Darby household—piled into the second row of seats.

"When does the ceremony start tonight?" Don asked.

"Nine o'clock," Gunter supplied.

"Perfect," he said, pulling away from the curb. "Plenty of time." He could have let the Mozo do the driving, but, gosh darn it, driving your whole family around in the big old family vehicle was one of the joys of fatherhood.

"So," said Lenore, looking back over her shoulder, "everybody having a good time so far?"

"Oh, yeah!" said Amphion, and his crests rippled enthusiastically. "Terrific!" The boys had no trouble making the sounds for English; they had a much wider vocal range than humans did. But despite the best possible language instruction, they seemed constitutionally incapable of using the passive voice. Some opined that this was the seat of Dracon morality: the inability to conceive of an action having occurred without a responsible party.

"I thought the utility-fog demo was amazing," added Zethus. A contest had been held to name the Draclings when they were born; the winning entry had been Amphion and Zethus, after the twin sons of Zeus who had been raised on Earth by foster parents.

Don nodded. The nanotech fog had been incredible to watch, but for him the most exciting thing had been the flying cars—a technology he'd finally lived long enough to see.

Canada had turned two hundred this past summer, and it was celebrating this centennial the same way it had the last one: by hosting a world's fair. Don remembered visiting the first one as a child with his parents, and being amazed by giant lasers, touch-tone phones, monorails, and a massive geodesic sphere filled with American space capsules. That fair, like this one, had been called Expo 67, with only a two-digit year; just two-thirds of a century into the new millennium and the lessons old Peter de Jager had tried to teach the world were totally forgotten. But, also like the original, this fair was at least in part a showcase for the latest and greatest technology, some of which had been derived from the artificial womb and incubator plans the Dracons had beamed to Earth.

Don pulled the van into traffic. A few other drivers honked politely and waved; Amphion and Zethus were famous, the hulking green Dracmobile was unmistakable—and the Manitoba vanity plate that said STARKIDS didn't hurt.

Don had been six years old when Canada had turned one hundred in 1967. Back then, the government had contacted people who were born the same year the nation was, and arranged for school visits by those who were well enough. Even after all this time, Don vividly remembered meeting his very first centenarian then, an impossibly ancient man confined to a wheelchair.

But now a hundred more years had passed, and Don himself was a centenarian; in fact, he was a hundred and six, and soon would turn a hundred and seven. People younger than him—men and women born in 1967—were touring schools now, among them Pamela Anderson. She'd been the first baby born in her hometown in British Columbia on the actual day of Canada's hundredth birthday, and her own rollback, performed just a few years ago when the price had fallen enough that mere TV stars could afford it, had left her as lovely as when she'd first graced the pages of *Playboy*.

Don no longer looked that young; physically, he was now forty-four or so. His hair was mostly gone again, but that was fine with him. He was feeling better this time around than when he'd gone through his forties originally; it had been six decades since he'd had his one and only heart attack.

Lenore also was in her mid-forties—but doubtless not middle-aged. The cost of rolling back would continue to drop; seven million people had already undergone the procedure. By the time she needed it, they'd be able to pay for a rollback for her, and—the thought was staggering, but doubtless true—they'd be able to afford a *second* rollback for Don.

As they drove along, Amphion and Gillian were bickering, while Zethus was just looking out the window at the crowded streets of Toronto. Despite being named for twins, the Draclings had grown up to be distinct individuals. Amphion had blue-black skin and two small fluted crests running down the back of his head, while Zethus had teal and silver skin and three crests. Each boy was distinct in character, too. Amphion was adventurous and outgoing, and incapable of letting even the smallest irony go unremarked upon, while Zethus was cautious and shy with strangers but enjoyed word games almost as much as his father did.

Don looked at them in his rearview mirror. "Amphion," he said, "stop teasing your sister."

Amphion swiveled two of his four eyes to look at Don. "She started it!" Each Dracon eye had a unique visual range: two saw to varying degrees into the ultraviolet, the third saw into the infrared, and the fourth saw into both but not in color; the combination of eyes the boys chose to bring to bear on an object not only affected what it looked like to them but also how they felt about it. They also possessed a sense that had no terrestrial analog, enabling them to detect heavy objects even when they were out of view.

Amphion and Zethus each had five limbs: three legs and two arms. If their embryonic development was a reliable echoing of their evolutionary history, the two front legs had evolved from what had been pelvic fins in an earlier aquatic form, and the thicker rear leg was derived from what had been a tail fin. The arms, meanwhile, had developed not from pectoral fins, as in humans, but rather from the complex array of bones that had supported two ancestral gills.

Dracons had only three fingers on each of their two hands, but they nonetheless came honestly by the base-ten counting system used in their radio messages. The boys each had ten feeding tendrils around their mouth slits—two pairs of them above and a row of six below; Zethus was using his tendrils just now to maneuver a hunk of cotton candy that Gillian had passed through a small airlock to him. Because their four eyes were recessed in bony sockets, Dracons couldn't actually see their own tendrils, so whatever help they were in math involved some mental picture of their deployment, rather than actually counting them.

The original Expo 67 had been subtitled, in phrasing that seemed horribly sexist only a few years later, "Man and His World." This Expo 67 had no subtitle that Don was aware of, but "Humanity and Its Worlds" might have been appropriate: people had finally returned to the moon, and a small international colony had been established on Mars.

And, of course, there were other worlds, too, although they didn't belong to humanity. As the timing would have it, it was now 18.8 years since Sarah Halifax had sent her final message to the stars, acknowledging receipt of the Dracon genome and explaining that her designated successor would help create Dracons here. That meant that Sarah's pen pal on Sigma Draconis II was just now getting word that what he'd asked for was going to be done. There was, everyone assumed, a celebration of that news going on right now on that alien world; it seemed fitting to have a matching celebration here, and it would be held tonight. One could transmit signals to Sigma Draconis at any time of the day from Canada, but it seemed appropriate to beam a message into space when the stars were actually visible, although the lights from Toronto would drown out the dim sun of the boys' ancestral home.

At the ceremony, a statue of Sarah—as she'd looked in 2009, when the first message was received—would be unveiled. After Expo 67 ended, it would be moved to its permanent home out front of the McLennan Physical Laboratories. Following the unveiling, greetings would be broadcast to Sigma Draconis not just by Amphion and Zethus—who had been sending weekly reports there for ten years now, although none of them would have been received yet—but also by dignitaries from the dozens of countries that had pavilions at the fair.

Traffic was moderate, and after an hour, the Dracmobile was getting close to their destination. Don had come back to Toronto often over the years to visit his grandchildren, and—more recently, heartbreakingly—to attend the funeral of his son Carl, who had died at the obscenely young age of seventy-two. He took this pilgrimage on each trip, but Gillian and the boys had never been this far north in the city.

As they drove along Park Home Avenue, Don was saddened to see that the library he so fondly remembered was gone. Most libraries were, of course. Don was a bit of a Luddite, and still had a pocket datacom, but Lenore and Gillian had web-accessing brainlink implants.

He drove the van into the cemetery—another anachronism—and parked it as close to Sarah's grave as he could. The boys put their filter masks back on and they all walked the rest of the distance, kicking through fallen leaves as they did so.

Don had brought a virtual bouquet with a cold-fusion battery; the hologram of red roses would last almost forever. His kids, normally boisterous, understood he needed a quiet moment, and gave it to him. Sometimes when he came here, he found himself overwhelmed by memories: scenes from when he and Sarah were dating, events from early in their marriage, moments with Carl and Emily as children, the brouhaha when Sarah had decoded the first message. But this time all that came to mind was the celebration, almost twenty years past, of their sixtieth wedding anniversary. He'd gone down on one knee then—as he had just now to place the flowers. He still missed Sarah, every single day of his life.

He stood up and just stared for a time at the headstone, and then he read Sarah's inscription. He turned and contemplated the blank space next to it. His own planned epitaph—"He was never left holding a Q"—wasn't quite as nice as hers, but it would do.

After a few moments, he glanced at Lenore, wondering how she felt knowing he'd end up here, rather than next to her. Lenore, whose freckles had faded over the years, and now had fine lines on her face, must have read his mind, for she patted his arm and said, "It's okay, hon. Nobody from my generation gets buried, anyway. You paid for it; you might as well use it . . . eventually."

Eventually. In the twenty-second century, or maybe the twenty-third, or . . .

The age of miracle and wonder. He shook his head, and turned to face his children. Sarah, he supposed, was nothing special to Gillian: just his father's first wife, a woman who had died years before she'd been born and none of whose DNA she shared—not that such trivial concerns would have mattered to Sarah. Still, society didn't have a name for such a relationship.

There was no special name for what Sarah was to the boys, either, but they would not exist without her. Amphion was staring thoughtfully at the four names on the headstone—"Sarah Donna Enright Halifax"—and must have been contemplating the same thing, for he said, "What should I call her?"

Don considered this. "Mom" wasn't appropriate—Lenore was their mother. "Professor Halifax" was too formal. "Mrs. Halifax" was still available; Lenore, like most women of her generation, had kept her birth name. "Sarah" conveyed an intimacy, but wasn't quite right, either. He shrugged. "I don't—"

"Aunt Sarah," said Lenore, who had always called her "Professor Halifax" in life. "I think you should refer to her as 'Aunt Sarah.'"

Dracons couldn't nod, so Amphion did the slight bow that he'd adopted to convey the same thing. "Thank you for bringing us to see Aunt Sarah," he said; one of his eyes was looking at Don, while the other three faced the headstone.

"She would have loved to have met you," Don said, and he smiled in turn at each of his three children.

"I wish I could have known her," said Zethus.

Gunter tilted his head and said, very softly, "As do I."

"She was a wonderful woman," Don said.

Gillian turned to face Lenore. "You must have known her, too, Mom—you were in the same field. What was she like?"

Lenore looked at Don, then back at their daughter. She sought an appropriate word, and, after a moment, smiling at her husband, she said, "Skytop."

--- Acknowledgments ---

I'VE HAD MANY writing students over the years, but none was more talented than my dear friend **Robyn Herrington**, to whom this book is dedicated. I first met Robyn at Calgary's science-fiction convention Con-Version in 1996 and published one of her poems in the 1997 anthology *Tesseracts 6,* which my wife Carolyn and I coedited. Robyn workshopped with me at the Banff Centre in 2000 and 2001, and you can find stories by her in, among other places, three of Mike Resnick's DAW anthologies: *Return of the Dinosaurs, Women Writing Science Fiction as Men,* and *New Voices in Science Fiction.* Robyn passed away in May 2004, after a long battle with cancer; at her request, I read the eulogy she herself had written at her funeral in Calgary. The one-sentence high-concept behind part of this novel was Robyn's, and I thank her, and her husband, **Bruce Herrington,** for letting me pick it up and run with it.

Many thanks to those kind souls who read and commented on an entire draft of this book in manuscript: **Asbed G. Bedrossian, Ted Bleaney, Reinhardt Christiansen, David Livingstone Clink, Marcel Gagné, Richard Gotlib, Peter Halasz, Andrew Zimmerman Jones, Al Katerinsky, Herb Kauderer, Joe Mahoney, Terry McGarry, Howard Miller, Kirstin Morrell, Ariel Reich, Sally Tomasevic, Hayden Trenholm, Andrew Weiner, Elizabeth Westbrook-Trenholm,** and my brother **Alan B. Sawyer.**

In addition, I thank the friends and colleagues who let me bounce ideas off them or otherwise provided input, including **Paul Bartel, Charissa Bartlett, Dan Evens, Chris Ellis, Terence M. Green, W. Thomas Leroux, Charles Levy,** and **Irwin Tan.**

Special thanks to **Dr. Jerome H. Barkow,** Department of Sociology and Social Anthropology, Dalhousie University (who gave the keynote address at the symposium "Encoding Altruism: The Art and Science of Interstellar Message Composition," referred to in this novel); **Dr. David DeGraff,** Chair, Department of Astronomy and Physics, Alfred University; and **Greg Armstrong,** Senior Research Technician, Robotics Institute, Carnegie Mellon University.

Huge thanks to my lovely wife, **Carolyn Clink,** and my agent, **Ralph Vicinanza,** and his associates **Christopher Lotts, Vince Gerardis,** and **Eli Kirschner.**

Many thanks, too, to my editor **David G. Hartwell** and his associate **Denis Wong;** to **Tom Doherty, Linda Quinton, Irene Gallo, Dot Lin,** and everyone else at Tor Books; to **Harold** and **Sylvia Fenn, Janis Ackroyd, David Cuthbertson, Marnie Ferguson, Steve St. Amant, Heidi Winter,** and everyone else at H. B. Fenn and Company, Tor's Canadian distributor; and to **Dr. Stanley Schmidt** and **Trevor Quachri** of *Analog Science Fiction and Fact.*

Thanks also to **Danita Maslankowski,** who organized the Fall 2005 "Write-Off" retreat weekend for Calgary's Imaginative Fiction Writers Association, at which much work on this manuscript was accomplished, and to my father, **John A. Sawyer,** who loaned me his vacation home on Canandaigua Lake in Upstate New York, where I squirreled myself away while finishing this book.

Please note that Scrabble Brand Crossword Game is a registered trademark of Hasbro, Inc., in the United States and Canada. Outside of the United States and Canada, the Scrabble trademark is owned by J. W. Spear & Sons PLC, a subsidiary of Mattel, Inc.

Finally, thanks to the 1,200 members of my online discussion group, who always provide wonderful support and feedback. Feel free to join us at:

www.groups.yahoo.com/group/robertjsawyer

Robert J. Sawyer is one of only seven writers in history to win all three of the world's top awards for best science fiction novel of the year: the Hugo (which he won for *Hominids*), the Nebula (which he won for *The Terminal Experiment*), and the John W. Campbell Memorial Award (which he won for *Mindscan*); the other winners of all three are David Brin, Arthur C. Clarke, Joe Haldeman, Frederik Pohl, Kim Stanley Robinson, and Connie Willis.

In total, Rob has won thirty-eight national and international awards for his fiction, including nine Canadian Science Fiction and Fantasy Awards ("Auroras") and the Toronto Public Library Celebrates Reading Award, one of Canada's most significant literary honors. He's also won *Analog* magazine's *Analytical Laboratory* Award, the *Science Fiction Chronicle* Reader Award, and the Crime Writers of Canada's Arthur Ellis Award, all for best short story of the year, as well as the Collectors Award for Most Collectable Author of the Year, as selected by the clientele of Barry R. Levin Science Fiction & Fantasy Literature, the world's leading SF rare-book dealer.

Rob has won the world's largest cash prize for SF writing, Spain's 6,000-euro *Premio UPC de Ciencia Ficción,* an unprecedented three times, and he's also won a trio of Japanese *Seiun* awards for best foreign novel of the year. In addition, he's received an honorary doctorate from Laurentian University and the Alumni Award of Distinction from Ryerson University.

Rob's books are top-ten national mainstream bestsellers in Canada and have hit number one on the bestsellers' list published by *Locus,* the American trade journal of the SF field. His nonfiction has appeared in *Archaeology, Maclean's,* and *Sky & Telescope,* and he edits the acclaimed "Robert J. Sawyer Books" SF imprint for Canada's Red Deer Press. He's also a frequent TV guest, with over two hundred appearances to his credit, and has been keynote speaker at many science, technology, and business conferences.

Born in Ottawa in 1960, Rob now lives in Mississauga, a city just west of Toronto, with poet Carolyn Clink, his wife of twenty-two years.

For more information about Rob, and access to his blog, visit his World Wide Web site, which contains more than one million words of material, including a readers' group guide for this novel. You'll find it at **sfwriter.com.**